INDECENT VENTURES

BELLES OF BROAD STREET BOOK 2

AK LANDOW

DEDICATION

To my beautiful friend, Jade Dollston, for whom Jade McGinley was named:
You are the sunshine on a stormy day, you bring laughter on a dull day, and, at times, are my reason to keep writing. You may be my book-world bestie, but I know you are my genuine real-world friend.

"She needed a hero, so that's what she became." -
Anonymous

Knight & Lawrence
FAMILY TREE

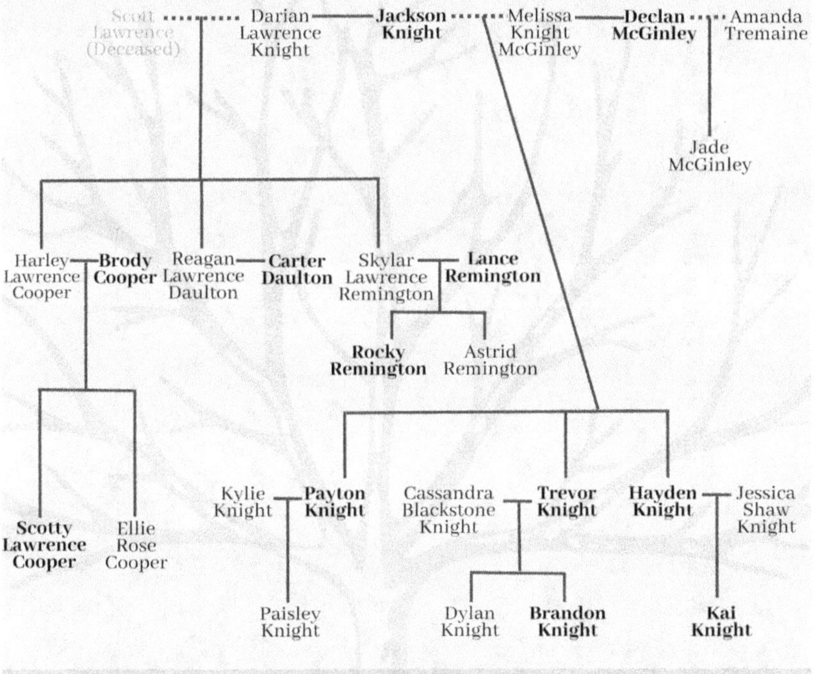

AK Landow

AK LANDOW AUTHOR

PROLOGUE

FOUR YEARS AGO

REAGAN'S TWENTY-EIGHTH BIRTHDAY PARTY

COLLIN

"You better be on your way."

"Carter, I told you I'd come. I'll make a brief appearance."

"What do you mean by brief? It's my wife's birthday party. You're my closest friend. It better be more than brief. Since when do you pass up the chance to party?"

I blow out a breath. "I just left a construction site outside of town. I need to run home to shower, and then I'll be there. I promise."

I hear him whisper, "Holy shit."

"What's wrong?"

"Reagan just walked out of our bedroom dressed for tonight. Fuck, my wife is hot."

I can't disagree with him on that. Reagan Lawrence is the hottest, most perfect woman ever created. I guess she's Reagan Daulton now. They recently got married.

I hear a slightly muffled, "Sorry, babe, we're going to be late. Lift up your dress."

I swallow at what that must look like. My cock starts to harden.

"Carter, I think Reagan told me she wants a threesome for her birthday."

"No, she didn't, asshole. Nice try."

I can't help but let out a laugh.

"We used to share women all the time. You're going soft."

"Not my wife. I'm not sharing her. Ever. She's all mine. No other man's hands will ever touch her body again. You'll understand that feeling one day."

Unlikely.

"Can't blame a guy for trying."

I hear her in the background. "We don't have time for sex, but how about I suck your..." The line goes dead.

Of course she would offer to suck his dick. On her birthday. She's perfect.

My cell phone rings again. There's no way it's Carter calling back. We're best friends, but a blow job is a blow job. I get that. I look at my screen and see that it's my brother, Cormac. I accept the call. "What's up, Mac?"

"How did the Paulson job go today?"

"It was fine. Another boring, cookie-cutter home

is well under way. We're ahead of schedule. Stop babysitting me. I know what I'm doing. It's not that hard to build the same house over and over again."

I work with my brothers at Fitz and Sons Construction. My father, Nolan, started the company, and Mac, Shane, Braden, and I all work there. Mac is the oldest and has taken a quarterback-type role in our operations. Self-appointed. Being the family goofball means that none of them think I can do my job properly, and none of them take my ideas seriously.

"Sometimes you need it. I'm glad it's going well though. How are the plans coming for Carter's house?"

Carter and Reagan are building a giant mansion in a Philadelphia suburb. No expense spared. They hired us to build it. I'm thankful to my best friend for this job. It's one of the biggest in our company's history. Every contractor wanted the job and submitted bids. Carter and Reagan didn't even consider them. They hired us immediately and Carter insisted on incorporating all my crazy, unusual ideas. He's the best friend you can imagine. I'm the dickhead that has a thing for his wife.

"I'm just waiting on the final permits and a few materials bids. We should be good to break ground in the next few weeks."

"Look at you being a grown-up, Collin. Following through on something for once."

"Screw you. I'm thirty-four. I *am* a grown-up."

"In age, not maturity."

"I'm giving you the finger." I'm literally giving the finger to my phone right now.

"Exactly. Back at you. What are you up to tonight? Ash and I are hanging at home with the kids. You're welcome to come over."

"As enticing as a Saturday night with you, your wife, and kids sounds, I have other plans."

"What's her name? Or is it names?"

"It's not a date. It's Reagan's birthday party."

"Have you told Carter that you're in love with his wife?"

"Fuck you. I'm not in love with her."

"Sure."

"I'm not." God, I hope I'm not. I'd be an asshole friend if I was. "I just want a woman exactly like her."

"Hot?"

"It's not just that she's hot," which she is.

"Great body?"

"Yeah, yeah. That too. But it's everything. Her personality, her brashness, her lack of filter, her intelligence, her confidence. I dig all of that. It's so unique to find those things in a singular woman."

"Well, keep the stallion in the corral. Carter's project is huge money for us. Don't fuck it up."

"It has nothing to do with the money. Carter is my best friend. He's like a brother to me. I like him better than I like all of you. I would never want to jeopardize that. I hate myself for being attracted to his wife. I'll get over my crush. It's not like I would ever act on it."

"Good. Behave tonight."

I can't help but smile. "Never. There's no fun in being well-behaved."

We hang up and I head home to shower and get dressed. I'm in a black suit and a blue button-down shirt that matches my eyes. No tie. I'm sure every other man will be in a tie. It's just not my style.

I brush the top of my hair back. The sides are short and don't need to be brushed. The top is a little longer. My face is clean shaven. I look damn good. Eat your heart out, ladies.

I arrive at the hotel. It's in an older, famous Philadelphia hotel. I look up at the giant chandelier in the lobby. I wonder what kind of crane they needed to get that sucker in here. I don't envy that crew.

I make my way to the ballroom. The party is in full swing. Carter must have dropped a bundle on this. Several bars, crazy décor, a band, lighting, and an endless supply of upscale food. There must be over three-hundred people here. Everyone loves Reagan. What's not to love? Ugh. Stop, Collin.

Carter and Reagan see me and immediately make their way over. Reagan looks gorgeous. She's tall, probably about five feet, eight inches. Closer to six feet when in heels. She's got wavy, natural blonde hair, the most expressive blue eyes, huge breasts, and a flawless curvy figure. She's all woman. A perfect woman. She's wearing a blue, strapless dress that hugs her figure and makes my heart race.

I'm six feet, three inches, but Carter probably has an inch or so on me, and a good amount of muscle. I'm muscular, but he's a giant. Admittedly, they're a good-looking couple.

He smiles and gives me a big hug. "Finally. I was afraid you weren't coming."

I lean over and kiss Reagan's cheek. "I wouldn't miss a party for the future Mrs. Fitz."

Carter narrows his eyes at me, but I simply grin. I

turn to Reagan. "You look beautiful. Happy birthday."

"You're making my husband jealous." She licks her lips. "Keep doing it. I like when he goes all alpha possessive on me."

Carter grabs her hip and pulls her close. He lifts an eyebrow. "Is that so?"

She leans her entire body into him, runs her hand up his chest, and gives him a nod. The sexual tension between them is making it hard to breathe. It's always high. I would kill to watch them go at it. Actually, I would kill to be a part of it.

I let out a quick whistle to break their trance. They both turn to me. Reagan asks, "Have you seen my sister? I haven't seen her in a while."

"Which one?" Reagan has two sisters. Harley is older and Skylar is younger. They both look like models too. The whole damn family does.

"Skylar. I might need to call her. I want her with us when I speak in a little while. I hope she's off getting some ass. She could use it."

I can't help but laugh. I love the way Reagan speaks. She's like one of the guys.

Carter grabs her hand. "I'll help you find her." He turns to me. "We'll have a drink later?"

"You bet."

"Are you okay alone?"

"I'm not a child. I can manage myself. There are tons of hotties here to occupy my time." I give him a wink. "I'm going to grab a drink at the bar, maybe a woman too. I'll see you guys later."

They walk off and I can't help but watch her ass as

they go. Such a perfect...damn it, Collin. Stop. She's off limits.

I turn and head toward one of the bars. I'm stopped by one or two people that I know, but I keep the conversations short.

I approach the bartender and order a double whiskey. I lean on the bar with one elbow as I take in the party. People are having a good time. They're dancing, drinking, eating, and laughing. I guess I should expect that from anyone that knows Reagan.

I can't help but smile for my friend Carter. He deserves this life. He got a shitty draw growing up. He may have grown up with money, excessive money, but I wouldn't have traded places with him for all the money in the world. His dad is a pretentious, abusive asshole, his mom is zoned out most of the time, and he lost his only sibling when he was a little kid. His house was stuffy, cold, and miserable. The only family member he was close to was his grandfather, and he died in a plane crash when we were in junior high.

Carter loved hanging at my house. The whole house could have fit in his foyer, but he loved my happy, hectic home, full of my crazy, loud family.

Now he has Reagan's crazy ass, big, close family. They spend a ton of time with them. He's never been happier, and I'm thrilled for him. Yes, I have a crush on Reagan, but it's because she's so great and Carter is a lucky man. I know I'm a bit of a playboy, but I think I want the same thing one day. If only Reagan had a twin sister. Her older sister is married, and her younger sister, though just as hot, doesn't have Reagan's dynamic, filter-less demeanor. Oh, and she also can't stand me. She makes that abundantly clear every time we're together.

I hear a woman's voice next to me. "I'll have a vodka tonic." She pinches my ass. "And one of him."

I turn around. She looks me up and down. "Ooh, this evening just got a lot more interesting."

I give her an obvious once-over. She's very tall. Well over six feet in heels. She's a leggy blonde, with familiar blue eyes. A little skinny for my tastes, but she's gorgeous. She looks like she's in her mid-twenties, putting her about ten years younger than me.

She smiles when my eyes eventually meet hers. It's full of mischief. "Do you like what you see?"

I nod. "I imagine most men do."

She crosses her arms. "I'm not interested in their opinions. I'm interested in yours."

I shake my head. "Sweetheart, I'm the Big Bad Wolf. You want no part of me."

She runs her hand down her red, form-fitting long dress. "As the story goes, Little Red Riding Hood couldn't manage to stay away from the Big Bad Wolf."

Ooh. I like her playfulness.

I run my finger up her arm. "What does Little Red Riding Hood have in mind for this evening?"

She runs her tongue over her plump, red-painted bottom lip. "To see just how big and bad your wolf is."

I can't help but let out a laugh. "Why don't we start with your name, beautiful."

"I'm Jade. What's your name?"

"Collin. How do you know Reagan?"

She hesitates for a brief moment, but then answers, "I work for her."

"Oh, then you work for Carter too. I'm his best friend."

Her eyes light up. "Interesting." She takes a few sips of the drink I hadn't noticed the bartender leave in front of her. I guess I've been staring at her. She's an undeniably stunning woman. She could model. Maybe she does.

Carter and Reagan run Daulton and Lawrence Holdings, one of the biggest companies in the world. Reagan is the CEO and Carter is the president. They're Philadelphia's biggest power couple.

"What is it that you do, Collin?"

"I run a construction business with my family."

She tilts her head to the side. "So, if you were to take your shirt off, would I see muscles from all your *hard* work?"

"I'm in management, but I do like to get my hands dirty now and then."

She grabs my big hand and runs hers over all the callouses. "Maybe they should get dirty tonight."

"Is that what you want?"

She nods.

I intertwine my fingers through hers. She curls her delicate, soft fingers through mine.

"I like how rough your hands are, Collin."

I pull her to follow me. "Do you like it rough?"

"I do."

We enter the hallway. I open one door and quietly peek my head inside before quickly pulling it out and closing the door before Jade sees anything.

"Umm, that was occupied." That was Reagan's

stepfather, Jackson, drilling her mother. Damn, her mom's body is as hot as hers. That fucking family. They got all the hot genes on the planet.

I try the next door, but it's locked, and I hear moaning. Jade giggles. "It sounds like we're not the only ones with this idea."

I nod in agreement. "Seems like it."

I get to the next door, and it opens. Unfortunately, it's a supply closet. There are several high shelving units with supplies lining them. I turn to leave. She pinches her eyebrows together. "What's wrong?"

"I'm not taking you in there. It's a fucking supply closet."

"Collin, we don't have much time. This is fine."

She turns the light on and pulls me into the closet, closing and locking the door behind us. She pulls my shirt to her and immediately brings her lips to mine. She bites my lip. Hard. Damn, she's really aggressive. I love it.

I pull her dress up so I can lift her, and she wraps her mile-long legs around me. Turning, I push her against the door. I grab her exposed ass with both hands and slide my tongue into her mouth. She tastes like vodka and mint.

I move my tongue around until it meets hers. As soon as it does, she pushes it into my mouth. Our kiss turns hard and deep, lips pressing and tongues battling for supremacy. I grind my hardened cock into her center, and she lets out a moan. She digs her nails into my neck. She whispers into my mouth. "Fuck me, Collin. Now."

"How do you want it?"

"I told you. Rough."

"Of course it's going to be rough. I meant which hole."

Her eyes widen, which tells me all I need to know. The front.

She attempts to play it cool. "Whichever one you want."

I run my thumb and pointer finger up her neck, applying a little pressure. I need to test my boundaries. The more pressure I apply, the more her eyes flutter.

I whisper in her ear, "Do you like my hand around your neck?"

She tightens her legs around me and manages a, "Umm hmm."

"Use words. I like words."

She breathes, "Yes, I like it."

I reach my other hand down and slip her panties to the side so I can run my fingers through her drenched core. "Seems as if you *do* like it."

I sink two fingers deep into her and she lets out a loud moan. "You're very needy, Jade. You seem to want it very badly."

She whimpers, "Yes."

"Yes? Use more words."

"I want it. I want you."

I pull my fingers out of her. I use them to rub around her kiss-swollen lips. I can tell a lot about a woman from her reaction to tasting herself.

She traces her lips with her tongue. "Hmm. Good."

I smile as I place her on her feet. I look around and grab an extension cord that's on the shelf. "Give me your wrists."

She visibly swallows, telling me she has a small amount of fear, but then does as I asked. I wrap the cord around her wrists, leaving some room at the end. I move her so her front is facing one of the shelves, using the remaining part of the cord to tether her to the shelf stand with her hands above her head.

I pull her dress over her ass to her waist. She's wearing a red thong. I rub her. "You have a perfect ass, Jade."

"Is...is that where you're going to take me?"

I can tell she's new to it. "Not with my cock. No lube."

I see her shoulders relax. I turn her face, so our eyes meet. "If there's anything you're not into, speak up."

She leans her head toward mine and licks along the seam of my lips. She pulls her head back up. "I'm up for anything. We just can't be gone for long."

"Did grandma give Little Red Riding Hood a curfew?"

She smiles. "Something like that. Get moving, Collin."

I pull her thong down her legs. I bunch them in my fist and shove them in her mouth. "As much as I want your words, trust me, you're going to need that for what I'm about to do to your body."

She nods as she turns her head and faces forward.

I unbuckle my belt, unzip my pants, and pull out my cock. I grab a condom from my wallet and sheath myself.

I spread her legs wider and run my fingers through her pussy again. "Are you ready? It feels like it to me."

She mumbles, "Umm hmm."

I bring my tip to her entrance and slowly slide into her. She's so tight. I have to wiggle my way in.

She gasps as she tilts her head back. She mumbles some version of, "Oh, fuck."

I grab her hair and turn her head so our eyes meet again. "Am I the biggest you've ever had?"

She nods.

"Fuck yeah, I am."

I let go of her hair and begin my movements inside her. I wrap my arm around her front and pound into her with forceful thrusts as deep as I can go. Over and over. Harder and harder.

She's moaning and writhing. I'm glad I stuffed her panties in her mouth, otherwise it would be too loud in here.

She sticks her ass out allowing me to push deeper into her. "That's right, Jade. You like it deep, don't you? You feel incredible."

She manages to pant out, "Yes, yes." I see her arms pulling on her restraints, desperate for more.

I wrap one of my big hands around her neck and squeeze. Her moans get louder. This girl likes all the things I like.

I look down at her perfect ass. I wish I could take that, but I know she's not up for it. Maybe a little finger play, though.

I spit into the crack of her ass and use my thumb to rub my saliva around her puckered hole. I feel her stiffen a bit.

I lean over to her ear. "Just my finger, not my cock."

She nods.

I haven't let up my pace, but I slide my thumb in her back entrance. She's tight. As suspected, no one has been here before. The thought of being the first nearly sends me over the edge, but I hold off. She needs to come first.

As I slide my thumb in, I can feel a shot of moisture in her pussy and then she squeezes my cock. She's about to come.

She yells out, albeit garbled because of the panties in her mouth. "Ah, Collin."

Her pussy trembles as she comes on a loud scream. As soon as she does, I let go too with an unusually loud grunt for me.

Fuck, that was good. After taking a few moments to catch my breath, I pull out and make quick work of the condom. I tuck myself back in and refasten my pants and belt.

Her hands are still bound, but I'm able to turn her around. We're both still breathing loudly. Her arms are above her head and her red dress is around her waist. She's bare and exposed to me. Those long legs on full display in her red *fuck me* heels. Her face is flushed with a post-orgasmic glow. I don't think I've ever seen anything hotter.

I hold my hand in front of her mouth and she spits out her panties. I bring them to my nose and inhale deeply.

"Hmm. You smell good. I wish I got to taste you. Maybe another time."

She stares at me with all the confidence and bravado in the world. "It's still on my lips, if you need a little taste."

I grab her face and give her a hard, wet kiss,

licking all around her lips. I pull my head away and lick my own lips. "You're right. It's delicious."

"Can you untie me now?"

I shake my head. "In a minute."

I bend down and hold out her panties. She lifts her feet, one at a time, so I can slip them back on. I pull them up and then pull down her dress, smoothing it out for her.

She looks at me in bewilderment. She's not used to any aftercare. She must have only been with assholes.

I stand and untie her. As soon as I do, she rubs her wrists.

"Was it too tight?"

She shakes her head. "No, I liked it."

I bend again and grab her purse, which she must have dropped when we walked in. She opens it, pulls out her lipstick, and reapplies it.

She removes a tissue from her purse and cleans my face. She winks. "I don't want the other ladies to think you're taken."

"Maybe I want to be taken for the night. Why don't we head back to my place for another round? No one will miss us."

She smiles. It's not the mischievous smile I saw earlier. It's sweet. She's happy that I want another round.

As quickly as it came, it leaves. "I'm not sure I can. Let's get back out there. I know Reagan is giving a speech. I shouldn't miss it."

"Okay."

I take her hand in mine and we make our way back to the ballroom. As soon as we enter, she drops my hand like a hot potato.

I'm about to ask her about it when I hear Reagan on the microphone. "I don't want to stop the fun for long, but I want to say a quick hello. Thank you to everyone for coming tonight to help us celebrate. This was supposed to be a wedding reception, but Carter insisted on it being a birthday party for me instead." She looks at him with more love and need than I've ever seen in my life. "Let's just call it both and skip to the part where you kiss the bride."

She pulls him to her and kisses the living hell out of him. It's over-the-top and totally inappropriate. Perfect for the two of them. I can't help but smile and then let out a big whistle.

People join in and yell out. People even clap for the live porn show we're watching.

When it eventually ends, Reagan just gives a big, *I don't give a fuck what you all think*, smile. "Wow. I can't wait for the honeymoon."

We all laugh.

"While we're celebrating, I want to mention that it was my cousin Jade's birthday last week. Where are you, gorgeous?"

Jade, still next to me, raises her hand. Cousin? I thought Jade said she works for Reagan.

Reagan then waves Jade up to the front of the room and Jade walks up to her.

She pulls Jade close to her. "Happy birthday, beautiful. She's eighteen now, gentleman, so take a number. The line is going to be long."

I turn to the stranger next to me. "Did she just say *eighteen*?"

He nods. "It's hard to believe. Kids look older and older these days."

Kids. My throat starts to close. I'm covered in sweat. She's eighteen. Holy fuck. I just had sex with an eighteen-year-old. An eighteen-year-old who was seventeen last week.

I can't breathe. I start coughing uncontrollably. I feel like there's cotton lodged in my throat.

I run toward the bar. I croak out, "Water. Hurry." Maybe a fucking defibrillator.

I wipe my sweat-filled face with a napkin while I wait. He brings the water quickly and I down the whole glass in one go.

The band starts playing again. Some people go toward the dance floor, but others begin making their way back to the bar.

I look around for cops. No, she's an adult. Barely, but she's an adult.

I rub my face. Oh god. No one can know about this. Ever. It's Reagan's cousin. Carter will kill me. He'll hate me. Reagan will hate me too.

I need to get the fuck out of here before anyone finds out. I practically leave a trail of smoke behind me as I hightail it out of there.

CHAPTER ONE

PRESENT ~ FOUR YEARS LATER

JADE

I punch the code in the front door of Aunt Darian and Jackson's house and walk in. I look around at this spectacular house. I've been here a million times in the past four years since finding out I have an aunt and cousins, but I never get used to how incredibly nice it is here. This house oozes wealth, but also warmth and love. That's exactly what this family is. Warm and loving.

I hear voices coming from the backyard. I look through the nearly all-glass back of the house and see my big, crazy, awesome family out by the pool.

I still find it hard to believe that I have a big family. I spent the first seven years of my life with my mother as my only family. She's an only child, so I had no cousins, aunts, or uncles. My father wasn't in the picture at all. He was an addict and my mother told him he wasn't allowed around me until he got clean.

They were never married. They had a brief affair. Both were addicts at the time. My mother got clean the moment she learned she was pregnant with me. He didn't care enough to do the same.

When I was seven years old, my father came back and claimed to be sober. My mother was excited and accepting of him being in my life. I was skeptical. I didn't trust him. I basically tortured him for years. I wouldn't call him *Dad* for nearly ten years, instead calling him by his first name, Declan.

But, in fairness to him, he was patient and put in the time. He took every minute my mother allowed him to have and tried to break down my walls. Eventually, that happened, and we're close now.

Just before my senior year in high school, my mother got married to a man that lives and works in New York City. She kept her house here but spent most of her time in New York. Not wanting to leave Philly, I ended up spending my senior year of high school splitting time between my mom and dad. It was the one and only time in my life that I lived with him.

I asked him for years to meet his extended family. He had a falling out with his brother when he was in his twenties and hadn't seen any of them in twenty-five years. His brother had since passed, but I really wanted to meet my cousins. He kept putting me off.

About four-and-a-half years ago, he started dating my now stepmom, Melissa. She's the best thing that ever happened to him. Well, besides me, of course.

When they got serious, she wanted to introduce him to her whole family, including her ex-husband, Jackson

Knight, who she remains close friends with because they have three adult sons together.

In a twist right out of a great novel, it turned out that Melissa's ex-husband, Jackson, was married to my dad's widowed sister-in-law, Darian. Yep, his brother's former wife. What are the chances?

After the shock wore off, they eventually introduced me to my whole family. I went from just having a mom and dad, to having a giant family. Not only did I gain my Aunt Darian, three female first cousins, their husbands, and kids, I gained Melissa's three sons, their wives, and their kids. Now we can't go to a restaurant for a family meal without renting out an entire room. It's a good thing they're insanely wealthy and can usually make that happen.

My cousin, Reagan, and her hot-as-sin husband, Carter, run a Fortune 500 company. The day they met me, they offered me an internship in the design department during my senior year of high school, and I turned it into a career. I was able to work while in college and graduate a year early. At only twenty-two, I'm the second in charge of the design department of one of the biggest companies in the world.

I'll be forever grateful to Reagan and Carter for my dream career. I make a ton of money doing what I love every single day. Reagan always says that she may have given me the opportunity, but my hard work, dedication, and vision got me to the position I hold now. I'm proud of what I've accomplished.

I walk out back and am greeted with a huge, warm welcome, as always. My oldest cousin, Harley, hugs me. Her husband Brody, who's a full-fledged California hottie, hugs me as well. They have two gorgeous kids, Scotty and Ellie, who are playing in the pool. They're nearly seven and six respectively.

My Aunt Darian greets me next. She and Harley look so much alike, with darker hair, green eyes, and killer bodies. Ellie looks just like them.

Reagan and Carter are the next to say hello. I have two or three inches on Reagan, but we otherwise look very much alike, both resembling our fathers, who were brothers. I'm often mistaken for her around Philly. She's fairly well known, and I sometimes use it to my advantage to gain VIP entry into restaurants and clubs.

Admittedly, I've had a several-years-long crush on her husband, Carter. He's a giant muscle of a man, with brown hair, hazel eyes, and a sexy beard. He's the most perfect-looking man I've ever seen.

Frankly, I've never hidden my crush. I don't give a crap what people think about me, I never have. Growing up without a father leaves you with thick skin.

I also love getting my dad riled up about my crush. It drives him nuts, so I never miss the opportunity to mention it. Melissa always laughs and shakes her head in amusement.

Carter is thirty-nine, significantly older than my twenty-two years. But I like older men. I always have. I've never dated men my own age. My father simply chooses not to accept it.

Reagan and Carter don't have any kids yet. There's so much gossip about it at the office. Everyone is wondering why they haven't started a family. I think Reagan has been focused on her career. She's thirty-two, not fifty-two. She'll have them when she's ready. I always feel the need to protect her when the gossip mill starts churning.

My cousin, Skylar, who's thirty years old, waves from the pool. Her husband, Lance, is wrapped around her, as usual. She leans back into him.

I look at them. "Where are the kids?"

They've only been married a little over three years, but they already have two kids. Their son Rocky is two, and their daughter Astrid is about eight months old. It's no surprise, given their parents, that they're the most adorable kids I've ever seen.

Skylar also works at Daulton and Lawrence Holdings. She's the Vice President of Strategy and Operations and is awesome at her job. She secures us every big project within the United States. I'm the lucky one who gets to help her with all the virtual modeling. I get to dream up city-defining buildings on a daily basis, and then watch those dreams come to fruition.

They recently completed construction on the first project I ever worked on with Skylar, when I was only a senior in high school. It gave me a taste of this job and I was immediately addicted. Every single day on my way to work, I see the giant Bancroft building, the biggest in Philadelphia, and look at it with pride, knowing that my handiwork played a huge part in the design. I love my job.

Skylar answers, "They're inside napping. They should be up in about an hour. We're enjoying the calm before the storm."

I'm then greeted by Melissa's three sons and their wives. Payton and Kylie, who have a seven-year-old daughter, Paisley. Hayden and Jess, who have a three-year-old son, Kai. And Trevor and Cassandra, who have four-year-old twins, Brandon and Dylan. Cassandra is much older than Trevor. She's Aunt Darian's longtime best friend and fell for Trevor after Aunt Darian met Jackson. Apparently, it was quite scandalous at the time, but that was before they were in my life, so I've only known Trevor and Cassandra together, and they're the funniest couple I've ever met in my life. I adore them. No one in this family has much of a filter, but Cassandra and Trevor are on a different level.

Reagan looks at Skylar and Lance, with his hands and lips all over her perfect, bikini-clad body. "Lance, get your hands off my sister. This is why you keep knocking her up."

Both Skylar and Lance's eyes widen. Everyone looks at each other in confusion.

A huge smile spreads across Aunt Darian's face. "Skylar, do you have something to share with all of us? Are you pregnant again?"

She scrunches her face and looks up at Lance. He nods at her before softly kissing her lips.

She turns back. "I'm only about ten weeks along, but yes, I'm pregnant again." She and Lance both have huge smiles.

Aunt Darian squeals in excitement. Reagan just shakes her head. "You are one fertile woman, Skylar. At least you know birth control was a worthwhile investment for all those years."

Reagan looks up at Carter and he winks at her. She turns back to us and jokes, "Well, thanks for stealing our thunder, Sky."

Darian's head jerks toward Reagan. "Are you..."

Reagan and Carter both smile. "We are."

Darian's squeals get even louder as she runs to hug Reagan.

"Why are we screaming?" I see Dad and Melissa walk out to the pool area. Dad is in a bathing suit and T-shirt. Admittedly, he has the looks and physique of a man fifteen years his junior. Melissa, as always, is the epitome of class, in a designer bathing suit and cover-up. She's a tall, highly attractive, blonde-haired, blue-eyed woman. She looks more like she could be my mother than my actual mother, who's a petite brunette.

I answer, "Skylar and Reagan both have buns in the oven."

Both of their eyes light up. Dad lets out a laugh. "Darian, you're going to have to buy a bigger dining room table...again."

Darian giggles. "It's my greatest pleasure." It's a running joke in the family. Darian is on her fourth dining room table since marrying Jackson and moving in here over seven years ago, as the family keeps growing.

Jackson looks between Carter and Lance. "Will it impact our fishing trip this spring?"

Jackson has been planning a big fishing trip off the coast of the Carolinas for months with his three sons and his three sons-in-law. He's incredibly excited about it.

Carter and Lance look at each other and shrug. Lance answers first. "I think Skylar will be just about eight months then. None of the other kids went early. I should be okay, but obviously, if she's having problems, I won't be able to go."

Jackson nods and turns to Carter; worry is written all over his face. Reagan rubs his arm. "I'll be fine. You should go."

"Babe, you'll be thirty-eight weeks. I can't leave you."

"I'll stay with my mom." She turns to Jackson. "Can you have a chopper on standby just in case to ease his mind?"

He nods. "Of course."

She turns back to Carter. "We're good. I want you to go."

He sighs. "We'll see. We'll discuss it as it gets closer."

Jackson opens the outdoor refrigerator and grabs a few

bottles of champagne. I don't know how many glasses he pours, but it's a lot. Everyone except Reagan and Skylar toast to the growing family. It's crazy that they're due only a few weeks apart.

I ask Reagan, "Which room in the Daulton mansion will be the nursery?"

They have the biggest house I've ever seen in my life. They built it a few years ago. It's got things in there that I didn't know houses could ever have. They must have spent a small fortune.

Reagan answers, "The one at the far end that overlooks the pool area. We realized it needs a little bump out, so we'll ask Collin to do what we're envisioning. He's the best and obviously knows our house well."

My heart races at the mention of Collin's name. We met at Reagan's birthday party four years ago. He took me into a closet and gave me the best sex of my life. Nothing since has remotely come close. But he won't come near me or look at me. I have no idea why. He disappeared right after we had sex that night. He had asked me to come back to his place, but then he just left without a single word.

We've only seen each other a small handful of times at Carter and Reagan's major events, but he doesn't ever acknowledge my presence. What a dick. A sexy dick, but a dick, nonetheless.

We have a fun afternoon and evening. Jackson removes his hands from Aunt Darian's body long enough to grill steaks for us. He's always all over her. It's a running joke in the family. It doesn't bother Jackson or Aunt Darian, and it certainly doesn't deter him.

Just before we sit, Cassandra's sister, Beth, and her seven-year-old son, Luke, walk out back to join us. Beth is much younger than Cassandra. She's probably about thirty-five, though she looks like Cassandra with dark hair and exceedingly light blue eyes. They're both beautiful.

Beth tells us that Luke got into trouble at school for starting a massage train. I nearly spit my drink from my nose.

"Did you say *massage train*?"

She nods. "Yes, why?"

"Do you know what it is?"

"Well, as I understand it, it was a train of kids each giving a massage to the person in front of them and receiving a massage from the person behind them." She shakes her head. "Luke loves to find ways to touch the girls. He's kissed most of them at this point. They now call him Cassanova O'Connell. I keep getting calls about it."

Cassandra smiles proudly. "He's a chip off his aunt's old block." She looks at him. "Luke, you can only touch the girls if they say it's okay. You understand that, right?"

"Duh. I know Aunt Cassandra. They all fight over me." He shrugs. "What can I say? I'm irresistible to them."

Half the table laughs while the other half looks on in shock. He's seven.

Beth turns to him. "Who taught you the word *irresistible*? Who told you that you're irresistible to girls?"

He has a sheepish look. "Um, Uncle Trevor. He said I get it from him."

All heads turn to Trevor. He shrugs. "What? I know what it's like to be irresistible to the ladies. The struggle is real."

Cassandra just laughs at her husband. She laughs at everything he says.

I chime in, "Well, as long as it's actually massages. That's not a *traditional* massage train." I gave a big smile as all of the adults catch on.

My father growls, "I assume you've only *heard* of this, right?"

I look around in an obviously guilty way. Ruffling his feathers is a hobby of mine. "Umm, sure."

My cousins all laugh. Melissa smiles in amusement.

Luke pulls Beth's shirt as he wiggles in his seat. "Mama, this bathing suit is smashing my dick."

We all start laughing at the language coming out of that little mouth.

Beth looks mortified. "Luke, please don't ever use that word in front of your mother, or at all. If your bathing suit is too small, just say so and we'll get you a new one."

Trevor smiles. "That happens to Brandon too, Luke. He's built very much like his father in that department. How about I'll take you shopping for bathing suits built for special men like us?"

Luke's eyes light up. "Okay, Uncle Trevor. That would be awesome."

That's sweet of Trevor. Luke's father, Beth's ex-husband, is barely in the picture. Trevor ends up doing a lot of father-like activities with him.

After dinner, everyone with kids leaves to get their respective little ones to bed, leaving me with Reagan and Carter, Aunt Darian and Jackson, and Melissa and Dad. I know an outsider might find it strange that exes like Melissa and Jackson can spend so much time together, but I don't know any different. Melissa is even close with Aunt Darian. They hang out, along with Cassandra, all the time. The three of them drinking to excess and cackling like schoolgirls is a common occurrence.

The seven of us are in the hot tub. Did I mention that my family is extremely touchy-feely with their significant others? *All* of them. Not only am I the odd woman out, but the rest of them are also glued to their spouses.

Reagan rubs my arm. "Are you dating anyone?"

My father lets out a small growl.

Melissa and I smile at each other in acknowledgment of how crazy my dad is about my love life. Frankly, he's crazy in general. He has major temper issues. Melissa does a good job keeping him under control. It's no small feat. Though she loves to rile him at times too. I don't need to know why.

I shake my head. "Nope. I'm still a virgin, sitting in my tower waiting for Prince Charming to rescue me."

Everyone except Dad laughs. He mumbles, "I don't know what you're all laughing at. That sounds good to me."

Reagan smiles at me. "You know that Kyle in accounting has a huge crush on you. He's cute."

I give an over-exaggerated fake yawn. "He's boring. Do you honestly see me with an accountant? He's too young anyway."

Carter raises his eyebrow. "I'm pretty sure he's at least twenty-seven or twenty-eight. He's been with us for a few years."

"And? I like older. *Much* older." I wink at Carter. Reagan gives me a conspiratorial smile. She knows I have a crush on her husband. She's so damn secure that it doesn't bother her in the least. I love that about her.

"I prefer a man that works with his hands." I let out a small moan. "Something about rough hands does it for me." I wink at Carter again, looking him up and down. "And muscles. *Big* muscles."

Reagan laughs, but my father growls again.

Melissa lightly slaps his chest. "Stop acting like a Neanderthal. She's an adult and can date who she wants."

I nod. "Thank you, Melissa." I look at my father. "I'll date who I want, where I want, when I want."

And that's how it's been for me for as long as I can remember. I started having sex in high school, with college guys. As I got into my college years, the men got older and older. I don't know why I'm more attracted to older men, but I am. I don't have relationships. I'm the hit-it and quit-it type.

CHAPTER TWO

FIFTEEN YEARS AGO

JADE

I walk in the front door from school and throw my backpack against the wall of our small kitchen, leaving a mark.

My mother lets out a breath in defeat. "What happened now? Are the boys still making fun of you for your height?"

I cross my arms. "I don't care about that shit."

"Jade! Language. You're seven. You can't go around saying words like that."

"I don't care about that crap."

She shakes her head. "That's not much better."

"I don't care when kids make comments about my height. I like being tall. They're just jealous."

"Then what is it?"

I can feel the tears start to form, but I try to be strong and hold them back. I never let anyone see me cry. "There's a father-daughter dance next Friday. I'm the only kid without a father."

Her face drops. She walks over to me and wraps me in her comforting arms. "I'm so sorry, sweetie. I'll go with you."

I shake my head. "No. All the kids make fun of me for not having a father as it is. It would be worse to show up with my mother. I don't even have an uncle...that I know of."

I give her a skeptical look. She won't tell me anything about my father's family. He may not be in my life, but why can't his family be in my life? I know he has a big one.

"I'm sorry, sweetie. Do you want Frank to take you? I'm sure he'd love to do that with you."

I drop my chin in astonishment. "Your loser boyfriend? Absolutely not. I'd rather go with a stranger. When he bends over, you can see the crack in his ass."

"Jade! Mouth! He's not a loser." She looks up and says to no one in particular, "The mouth on my seven-year-old."

I'm starting to lose the will to hold back my tears. I can feel my lip trembling. "Can I see his picture again?"

She looks at me like I'm pathetic and broken, which I may very well be. "Sweetie, I don't think it's a good idea. It always upsets you."

"Please. I'm already upset." I sigh. "I don't look like you. Do you know how hard it is to not know where you came from? I like seeing his picture. At least I know who I look like."

Tears form in her eyes. "You came from me. I know we don't look alike, but you came from me." She mumbles, "You got his temper though."

I look up at her wide-eyed. She's never given me any information about my father before, despite my asking. She always says she didn't know him well, and what she did know was most likely drug-induced behavior.

"He had a temper?" For some reason, it makes me happy to know this. At least I know where it came from. My mother is always so calm. I'm not.

I see a small smile form on her lips as she nods. "He did."

"Please, Mommy, can I see the picture?"

She blows out a long breath, but then goes to her bedroom to retrieve it from wherever she keeps it hidden from me. She walks back into the kitchen and hands it to me.

Tears trickle down my cheeks like they do every time I look at the only photo of him I've ever seen. He's very handsome. He has blond wavy hair and the same blue eyes as me. We have the same nose too. Even though he's sitting, I can tell that he's tall.

I look up at her. "Why didn't he want me? What's wrong with me?"

She squeezes me in her arms again. "Sweetie, there's absolutely nothing wrong with you. You're amazing. It wasn't that he didn't want you. Drugs are powerful and terrible. They make you crazy. They take away your ability to make good decisions. He wasn't a bad man. He just made bad decisions. For that reason, I told him he couldn't be around you if he was still using drugs. Your safety is the most important thing in the world to me. When I was using drugs, I made foolish decisions too."

At least my mom is honest with me about drugs and her previous addiction.

She smiles. "Jade, I love you enough for two parents. You're my everything."

I know she does. I nod. "Thanks, Mommy."

THE NEXT FRIDAY, I watch out the window as all the girls in the neighborhood, wearing their best dresses, head to the dance with their fathers. Most of them are holding flowers.

I've done this at least two times before. It never gets easier.

Mommy hands me a pint of my favorite ice cream, Rocky Road, along with a spoon. "Do you want to watch *Princess Bride* or *Loverboy*?"

I shake my head. "No. Fuck 'em. Let's get dressed and go to the dance."

"That's my girl. Watch your mouth though." She smiles. "Let's meet back down here in ten minutes in our fanciest dresses. Wear your favorite red one."

I nod.

ON MONDAY AT SCHOOL, I'm hanging upside down on the monkey bars when I see a man in a car watching me. A familiar-looking man. A big, blond-haired man with blue eyes that perfectly match mine.

I flip down so I'm right-side up and can see more clearly. That's him. That's my father. Instead of happiness, rage fills my body. A rage I've never known before.

PRESENT

"Jade, tell me what you remember about that day."

I sigh, on a video call with my therapist, Dr. Pearl. "I feel like we've been over this a thousand times. You know everything about me. There's nothing left to tell you."

My mother made me start seeing Dr. Pearl when I was eight years old. I was unaccepting of my father, and she thought I might need a professional to talk to about it. I saw her weekly for years. Once my father and I reached a better place five or six years ago, we moved it to monthly check-ins.

She's a petite woman with a short, dark bob and needs glasses to see the screen for our call. The dark hair has become grayer throughout the years, but her haircut is always the exact same. She's always well put together. In all these years, I've never seen her in anything other than a cardigan sweater buttoned only at the very top.

"Yes, Jade, but each time you tell the story I learn something new. You hold back on purpose. I know you like to mess with me."

I let out a laugh. I do like to mess with her. Though I secretly like her and often feel a sense of relief after talking to her.

"Fine. I remember locking eyes with him. For seven years I dreamed of seeing him. I thought the reunion would be a happy one where I ran into his arms, he twirled me around, and told me that he loved me and would never leave my side again. Where we became best friends and made up for lost time. But in that moment, looking into eyes that looked so much like mine, all I felt was anger. Deep anger. I swore I would never let him or anyone else hurt me like that again."

"Why did you feel anger instead of happiness or relief?"

"Why? Because he abandoned me. He left when she became pregnant with me. He didn't care about me. It fucking hurt."

"He was sick, Jade. Drug abuse is an illness."

"He left me. He chose drugs over me. He loved them more than he loved me. There's no other way to see it."

"That's not how it works, Jade. I think he's proven in the past fifteen years just how much he loves you."

"I know he loves me now, but the damage was done. I'm fucked up. Plain and simple. You're never going to cure me. I'm sorry to be a black mark on your permanent therapist record, but I'm incurable. Beyond repair. Mark me as damaged goods."

"How so?"

"Isn't it obvious? I didn't go to therapy school, but even I can identify my issue. I struggle with relationships. I don't let people in."

"Look at how welcoming you've been to all the new family in your life over the past four years. You have wonderful relationships with all of them. I'm proud of you for letting them in so willingly and openly. I anticipated more of a struggle when you first told me about them."

"Do I get a therapy gold star for that?"

She smiles. "I'll mail one to you."

I laugh. At least Dr. Pearl sometimes humors me.

"With men. I've never had a serious relationship with a man. What's the point? They're going to disappoint me. They'll leave like he did. I just beat them to the inevitable punch."

"Have you considered that maybe you haven't met the right man?"

"No. I'm *never* getting married."

"And you still haven't ever had a real conversation with your father about it?"

"Nothing more than the small handful of times he joined our sessions when I was younger."

"Perhaps you'd be able to move on if you finally have it out with him. Maybe then you could have a healthy relationship with a man."

"I doubt I'll ever want to have a boyfriend. I rarely make it to a second date. Even if I do, the minute they want something more than a roll in the sack, I jump ship."

"You're *always* the one to end it? You've never been in a position where you wanted more, and he didn't?"

"I hate when you ask questions you know the answers to. One guy. You know the one. The toe-curling guy. The one who helped me learn that I like it a little rough." I wink at her and watch her squirm. It amuses me to make her uncomfortable. I try to do it at least three or four times a session.

"The best sex guy who you claim bailed on you."

"I claim? It's more than simply bailing. I turned my back and he disappeared. Literally five minutes after he was inside me. Talk about a hit-and-run. It was a hit and sprint."

She sighs. I love frustrating her. "That whole story makes no sense. I know you, Jade. You're not giving me all the facts." She looks down at her watch. "I have another patient to call. I'm noting that we'll start here next time."

"Ooh. I can't wait."

"Sarcasm is the lowest form of wit. You're too smart to resort to that."

"Sarcasm is my love language. I love you, Dr. Pearl." I blow her a kiss and give her a big fake smile.

She just shakes her head. "Go back to work. I'll see you next month."

I laugh as I close the window on my computer.

There's a knock at my office door. I yell, "I'm not decent. Don't come in."

The door opens and Thor walks in. "You're the least decent person I know. If I have to wait for you to be decent, I'll never get to see you."

"Not true. I don't mean to brag, but I'll have you know that my therapist just told me she's sending me a therapy gold star. I might have to display it on my desk."

Thor laughs. "You must be a gold mine for a therapist."

I nod. "Totally. You've got an awful lot to say for a woman whose parents named her after a fictitious superhero. You must have deep issues. Maybe not feeling like you've lived up to the name?"

She laughs again. Yes, Thor is a woman. Her full name is Thorunn, but she's so good at her job, handling it like a superhero, that everyone calls her Thor. Of course, that also means everyone assumes she's a man until they meet her, but we have fun with it.

Thor is an attractive blonde woman, and she's equally as tall as me. It's nice to have another tall friend. I'm always the giant around my friends. She's the head of the design department and has been for over ten years. She's my boss, and we have a great working relationship. She's in a slightly different place in life than me, with a husband and two kids. But we get along well in the office, and occasionally after work for drinks.

"I don't have issues. I *am* a fucking superhero. Now, I did come into this den of sin for a reason. Skylar needs modeling for her Matthews proposal. She said she'd rather you do it than Neal, but I told her you're already overloaded. It's entirely up to you."

I flip my hair. "God, it's so hard being the best.

Everyone wants a piece of you."

She coughs, "Trained by the best."

I smile. "I'll give you that one. It's fine. Add it to my pile. Dominic's proposal is almost done." Dominic has the same job title as Skylar. He's in his early forties and is sexy as hell, with dark hair, olive skin, piercing brown eyes, and a broad chest that always makes his shirts look like they're going to pop off him. I wish they would.

She narrows her eyes at me. "Stop mind-fucking Dominic. He's twice your age."

"What? Me? Never." I smirk at her. "Only pure thoughts of what's underneath those tight suits he wears. They're a little snug in the crotch, if you catch my drift."

She bites her lip. "You're not wrong."

"And what's with his eyes? It's like they bore into your soul. I'm usually into blue eyes, but his brown eyes are the sexiest I've ever seen. I wouldn't mind them staring at me while he fucks me on my desk."

She shakes her head. "You're deranged." I giggle. "Speaking of those who engage in inappropriate office behavior, did you see how high the pool has gotten as to whether Reagan and Carter will announce a pregnancy by year-end."

"Hmm. That's a little over two months away. What's it up to?"

"Twenty-to-one odds they announce before Thanksgiving. Ten-to-one by Christmas."

"I'll put five-hundred dollars on before Thanksgiving."

"You wouldn't have any insider information, would you?"

"Nope." I wink multiple times.

She smiles. "I guess we'll both be betting on before Thanksgiving."

CHAPTER THREE

FOUR-AND-A-HALF YEARS AGO

COLLIN

"What do you mean Reagan broke up with you? You guys are in love. I've seen it with my own eyes. You're endgame."

Carter practically collapses in my arms at my apartment door. He's a mess.

I close the door and help him to my couch. "What happened?"

He plops down and I sit next to him. "She thinks I've been faking my feelings to get her business for my father."

"Your father? You hate him. You would never do that."

"I know." His head is down in his chest. "I did something stupid regarding her business before we started dating and now she thinks I'm a fraud." He legitimately has tears rolling down his face. He whispers, "Collin, I can't lose her. I love her. I can't even breathe without her. She's my world."

I rub his back. "I know, buddy. We'll fix this. I'll do whatever I can to help. I know you love her, and I know she loves you too."

"I more than love her. She's all I see. Do you know what it's like to be in a room of people but only be able to see one? To have everyone and everything else fade into the background?"

I shake my head. "No, I don't."

"That's what it always feels like with her." He starts sobbing. "She makes me a better man. She calls me on my shit. I need her. I can't live without her. And now she hates me. She won't talk to me. She can't bear to look at me."

There's a devil on my shoulder right now telling me that if I ever wanted a chance with Reagan, this is the moment.

I close my eyes for a second to gather my thoughts. While I'm no angel, I value Carter's happiness above my own. He's my best friend. My family. I know that I'll do anything I have to do to help him get Reagan back, so I quickly brush that devil aside.

I console him until he calms down enough to have a thorough conversation. "Tell me everything that happened."

He proceeds to tell me what transpired. After some back and forth, we form a plan. It will be a huge sacrifice for him, but he's willing to do everything and anything to get her back. I can't imagine loving someone so much that I'm willing to give up what's most important to me... What he's about to give up.

A few days later, I watch from a window as Reagan runs into Carter's arms. They hug and kiss like they'll never let go of the other. Then she says something, and he starts hysterically laughing, because of course, in this emotional moment, she cracked a joke. She's Reagan and she's perfect.

I know he has a ring in his pocket right now. He's going to ask her to marry him at some point soon. I'm happy for my best friend. I'm happy that I was able to help him make this happen. I'm selfishly jealous that he found the perfect woman. I don't think another one like her exists.

PRESENT

I crack my eyes open on a Saturday morning. I hear a noise coming from inside my condo.

My bedroom door opens, and Carter appears in jeans, a T-shirt, and a leather jacket. That's usually his motorcycle-wearing uniform.

He quickly scans my room. "Are you alone?"

I nod. "Unfortunately. Why are you here?"

"It's a nice day. I thought we could go for a ride."

"I'm not riding bitch with you. You're sexy, but I'm not holding onto your flabs while we ride one of your bikes."

He rubs his stomach. "Are you jealous of my sexy abs?"

I pull the sheet down to my waist, revealing my perfect, muscular stomach. "You should be jealous of mine."

"Ugh, pull the sheet back up. I don't need to see that dad bod."

I let out a laugh. "Why are you really here?"

"I want to go for a ride with you. Of course I had another bike dropped off. I don't want your smelly, scrawny arms around me."

"I don't suppose you brought the Dodge Tomahawk, did you?" It's a half-a-million-dollar bike and goes up to four hundred and twenty miles per hour. It's the most perfect bike ever made, and Carter has one.

He smiles and dangles a set of keys in front of him. "Nothing but the best for my best friend. I got a new bike that I'm going to try out, so the Tomahawk is all yours for the day."

My eyes nearly bug out of my head. "You're seriously letting me drive it?"

"You bet, brother."

I spring out of bed in excited anticipation.

He covers his eyes. "Ugh. I don't need to see your junk."

I look down. Whoops. I forgot I was naked. I puff out my chest with all the bravado in the world. "Admit it; you've never seen one this big."

He lets out a laugh. "You've seen my dick, Collin." I hate to admit it, but he's right. He has a fucking third leg in his pants. I thought I had the biggest dick ever known. He might beat me. Just barely though.

He peels his eyes back open and looks closer. "Did you get your dick pierced?"

I nod. "A few months ago."

"Why?"

"Do you have any idea how much women love it?"

"Wasn't it painful?"

"It didn't feel good, but it's worth it now. Stop staring at my perfect dick. Get the fuck out of my bedroom. I'll be out in five minutes."

"Gladly." He turns and leaves my bedroom.

I dress similarly to him, in jeans, a T-shirt, and a leather jacket, and then walk out of my bedroom a few minutes later. "Where are we going?"

"Let's shoot down to Atlantic City. It's a nice day out. We can have breakfast on the boardwalk and then be home by early afternoon."

"That sounds good."

That's about an hour from here. There would normally be traffic on a Saturday morning in the summer, but not in the fall. Once we're out of the city, it's a fast, open ride the whole way down.

We climb aboard the bikes and make it down there in less than forty-five minutes. We practically race the whole way. I win. This bike goes so damn fast. It's amazing.

We park near the boardwalk and sit down outside at one of our favorite spots. When Carter was still single, we spent a lot of time in Atlantic City. We'd go to clubs and stay in casinos. Reagan is always game to party down here, but it's not quite the same as prowling for women with your best friend.

The waitress approaches and we order our food.

I look at him. I feel like he brought me here to talk about something. "What's on your mind? Why are we here?"

He laughs. "I can't just want to have breakfast with you?"

"Hmm. No. What's up?"

"I have news to share with you." A huge grin breaks out on his face. "Reagan's pregnant. We're having a baby."

"Oh, thank God. I thought maybe you were shooting blanks and she was going to need me to come in for the close."

He scowls at me. "Asshole. She didn't want to rush things. She wanted to establish herself as the CEO before thinking about starting a family. Selfishly, I haven't minded having her to myself for the past few years. I've loved every minute."

"Ugh. You're so pussy-whipped."

He smirks. "Yes, I am. Proud of it."

I hold out my hand and smile. "Congrats, man. I'm happy for you guys. I hope the baby looks like her...or me."

He shakes my hand extra hard. "I hope it looks like her too."

Our food arrives and we begin eating. "Carter, why did you bring me here to tell me? Did you think I wouldn't be happy for you?"

He shakes his head. "No, nothing like that. I just wanted to have a nice day and tell you. I feel like I'm entering a different phase of my life, but I want you to know that no matter what, you'll always be important to me. Obviously, Reagan's family has become my family, but besides them, in all the ways that matter, you're my only original family."

A scrunch my nose. "Your mom still hasn't come around?"

He shakes his head. "No. She sides with him. I'll never understand it. It's hard to have a relationship with her when she won't get away from him. I won't ever let my kid around that abusive fucker."

"I'm sorry. Well, you can always count on me. I'll always be by your side. You know that, right?"

He nods. "Thanks, Collin. You don't know what that means to me. I don't know what I'd do without you."

"You're already going soft, and the baby hasn't even come yet."

"I can live with that."

"How's Reagan feeling?"

"You know Reagan. She hasn't missed a beat."

"Is she showing yet?"

"No, but I think her tits are bigger?"

"Jeez, I didn't realize they could get bigger."

He throws his napkin at me. "Stop looking at my wife's rack."

"It's a pretty good rack."

He smiles like he's imagining them. "Yes, it is."

I roll my eyes and he laughs. "Oh, and Skylar's pregnant too. She's due two weeks after Reagan. I think Reagan is happy to share this with her. Skylar can help her."

"Fuck, Skylar is fertile. Glad I didn't get mixed up with her."

"Yeah, because that was your decision," he says sarcastically.

I can't help but chuckle at that. I did hit on Skylar all the time, years ago when she was single. She wanted no part of me though.

"What about you? Do you think you'll ever get married and start a family?"

I shrug. "It's not like I'm set against it. I just don't

know if I believe the right woman is out there. I'm picky. You know I have particular tastes. You're lucky. You found a perfect woman. I won't settle for less than perfect." I smile. "I want the Dodge Tomahawk of women."

"I get it. You'll find your Dodge Tomahawk one day. I did. How's work going?"

"It's fine. We're busy, so I guess that's good. My family still thinks I'm a moron that needs to be coddled and watched, but I'm actually pretty good at what I do."

"You're the best. That's why we use you."

"Thank you. I'm honestly just bored of doing the same type of low-grade house over and over. Your house was the best project I've ever done because you asked for something different. Something I could dream up in my head. Something no one else has ever seen before."

"Our house is spectacular. You did an amazing job. You're very talented. Speaking of which, we want to add a little bump out to the room that will be the nursery. Can you squeeze us in?"

"Of course. I'll take care of it right away. It might be nights and weekends since my days are jammed up. Is that okay?"

"Whatever you can swing. Thank you."

We head out and ride back into the city. It was nice spending this time alone with him.

I mention that I may go out with my brother tonight. He said they'll meet us out if Reagan is up for it.

CHAPTER FOUR

COLLIN

I'm going out with my youngest brother, Braden, tonight. He's still single too. Mac and Shane are married with kids. Mac is the oldest, then me, then Shane, then Braden. Mac and Shane's wives constantly try to fix us up with their friends, but that's not happening for me. Braden is much sweeter than me, so sometimes he accepts, but I never do. I have certain tastes and those uptight women won't be into them. I like wild women with no inhibitions.

I dress in dark blue jeans and a blue sweater. I brush my still wet from the shower hair, which admittedly has gotten a little long, curling at the nape of my neck, and nearly reaching my eyes in the front if I don't wear a hat or brush it.

I think this look is back in style though, so I'm in no rush to deal with it. My friends and family make fun of me for it every chance they get, but I like it and I'm not changing it anytime soon.

I'm also not as clean-shaven as I used to be. I like the scruffy look. Women definitely like the scruff, especially when my face is buried between their legs.

I text Braden that I'm on my way and will arrive at the bar, Hole in the Wall, in about ten minutes. He responds that he's arriving now and will scout the talent, meaning he'll look for hot women.

Hole in the Wall is a traditional Irish pub, but its authenticity draws a lot of people and it's become a bit of a hangout for the over-thirty crowd. We've been going there for years. Clubs now are inundated with people in their early twenties. Before Carter met Reagan, we used to hit the clubs every weekend. I'm thirty-eight now. I'm over that scene. Braden is only thirty, but he prefers to hang out with me rather than with some of his friends closer to his age.

I see Braden as I walk through the door. He's much fairer than me, looking every bit the Irish lad he is. We have the same blue eyes, but his hair and skin are a little lighter. He's around six feet in height, leaving me a few inches taller than him.

It's crowded tonight, which is expected for a Saturday. Music is playing and the drinks are flowing. I love this place.

I see him already talking to two women. A shorter brunette, who's a bit hidden by their positioning, and a tall blonde, with curves in all the right places, evident in tight jeans and a midriff-baring top. Her back is to me. If the front matches the back, I'll be elbowing Braden out of the way.

Braden notices me as I approach. "There he is. My slightly less attractive older brother."

I grin as I approach, placing my hand on the

blonde's exposed lower back. "He means, significantly *more* attractive."

When she turns her head, I realize my mistake and immediately pull my hand away. "Jade? What are you doing here?"

She smiles. I can't believe I never connected the dots that she and Reagan are related. They have the same mischievous smile, and the same shade of expressive, blue eyes. Jade may be a bit taller, but the resemblance is uncanny.

She looks me up and down. "I'm looking for a fairy tale, Collin. You know, a man who doesn't fuck me in a closet and then disappear two minutes later. Who doesn't go out of his way to ignore me for four years." She shakes her head. "I know, I'm so needy, aren't I?"

Her smile never wavers. Her friend and Braden start laughing hysterically.

Her friend asks, "This is *that* guy?"

Jade nods her head, still freaking smiling. "It is. Carter's bestie. I find myself wondering if Carter knows what happened."

My face immediately drops. "He doesn't. And it's going to stay that way."

She winks at me. "It will cost you a few rounds of drinks." She turns to her friend. "Pandora, this is Collin. Collin, this is Pandora."

I start to open my mouth, but Jade places her fingers over it. "I know you're about to bust out with some stupid Pandora's box joke. Save it. We've heard them all."

Braden lets out a laugh. "Damn, Collin, you've met your match."

I give an over-exaggerated fake smile and hold out

my hand. "It's nice to meet you, Pandora. Ladies, can I get you drinks? Pandora, perhaps a juice box?"

Pandora rolls her eyes. Jade giggles as she loops her arm through mine. "I'll go with you. We should catch up, *old friend*. It's been a little while. Four years to be exact."

I should remove her arm, but I don't. Admittedly, I don't mind her touch. The past four years have been good to Jade. *Very* good. Her body has filled out in all the right places. She's womanlier now. Confident too. She was gorgeous and bold when I met her, but there's an added layer of confidence present now that wasn't as strong then.

I listen enough to know that she graduated from college early and is killing it at Daulton and Lawrence Holdings. She's obviously very smart.

Before we get to the bar, I turn to her. "Listen, I'm sorry I left so abruptly that night, but when I found out you were only eighteen, and that you're Reagan's cousin, I freaked out."

"I never lied to you about my age."

"I know. I just assumed you were older based on the way you looked and the fact that you mentioned working with Reagan and Carter. I'm sorry for freaking out. That was wrong. I regret it. You were just so young. Honestly, I felt like a perv."

She laughs. "I came on to you, Collin." I see a drop of emotion on her face before she masks it. "It's not a big deal. I'm used to men bailing. It's kind of a theme in my life."

Oh fuck. What does that mean? I run my fingers through my hair and notice her watching. I roll my eyes. "I know, it's longer. I don't need you giving me shit too."

She moves close to me and runs her hands through it. "I like it." She tugs hard on the back. "If it were this long four years ago, it would have given me something to grab onto that night." She leans into me, our bodies touching. She scrapes her nails down my neck, giving me chills.

I've attempted to erase that night from my mind, but I'd be lying if I said I was successful. The attraction and sex were electric, and I know I would have taken her home for more if the evening didn't go the way it did.

Her close proximity is turning me on. She smells like a fruity mix. I can't place the exact kind. It's intoxicating.

I quickly scan the bar. Every man's eyes are on her. She's insanely beautiful, so that's not a surprise. I wish we didn't have our history. I'd be very receptive to this aggressive behavior. My cock is receptive, whether I want him to be or not.

I grab both of her wrists and hold them behind her back with one hand. I've never been with a woman as tall as her. In her heels, I need only bend my head down slightly for us to be nose to nose.

I run the thumb of my other hand across her bottom lip. "If I remember correctly, your hands were indisposed at the time. There would have been no hair pulling." I tug her hair. "Except maybe by me."

I run my hand down the front of her neck and apply a little pressure. I whisper into her ear, "Remember how I controlled your body? Your pleasure?"

Her breathing picks up. Her nipples harden. I can feel them against my chest. She whispers back, "I remember."

I inhale deeply. "I can smell how aroused you are right now."

"I am."

My cock is hard, pushed up against her. She swivels her hips a bit, creating some of the friction we both clearly want. I'm so drawn to her. Is it acceptable now that she's twenty-two, four years older than she was then? Unfortunately, I'm also four years older.

I slowly kiss up her neck and she whimpers.

I'm about to brush my lips along hers when my phone vibrates in my pocket. I pull away from Jade and take it out, looking down at the text message.

"Oh shit. Reagan and Carter will be here in a minute."

I take a few deep breaths to calm myself down. I really want to take her somewhere and have my wicked way with her, but obviously that's off the table.

She gathers herself for a moment too before asking, "Are you going to ogle Reagan the whole time?"

I snap my head up. "What the hell is that supposed to mean?"

"It means that while they may be blind to it, I'm not. You have a thing for Reagan. I've watched you stare at her like a lovesick puppy for years."

"I don't know what you're talking about. She's my best friend's wife."

"Whatever helps you sleep at night, Collin."

"What about your obsession with Carter?"

She smiles in victory. "So you *have* noticed me the few times I've seen you throughout the years?"

Shit. How could I not? She's gorgeous. But now I'm totally busted.

She shrugs. "Unlike you, I make no attempt to hide my crush. Carter is the hottest man I've ever seen, present company included. Reagan knows I feel that way. She's confident. It doesn't bother her in the least."

I tilt my head to the side. "You're an intriguing woman, Jade McGinley."

"I'm more intriguing when I'm naked." She looks me up and down. "I bet you're significantly more intriguing naked too."

I stare at her. I don't know if I hate her or am impressed by her. She stares right back in challenge. We're sharing the same air. The mutual attraction between us is unmistakable.

Out of the corner of my eye, I catch Reagan and Carter walking in, draped all over each other. Their flushed faces and messy hair tell me that it was an eventful ride here. They take a private car service whenever they go out, leaving them with time in the backseat to do as they please.

I quickly walk away from Jade and make my way over to them.

"Hey, beautiful."

Reagan kisses my cheek. "Hey, Collin."

"You're pretty too, Reagan, but I was talking to Carter. No one is more beautiful than Carter Daulton." I bat my eyelashes at him.

Reagan laughs. "My bad." She leans into Carter. "I

can't say I disagree. He's a beautiful man, with an even more beautiful..."

Carter covers her mouth and I laugh. Reagan never misses an opportunity to work into conversation how large and perfect Carter's dick is. She's even named it *the anaconda* and often refers to it as such.

Reagan looks over my shoulder toward the bar. "Is that Jade?"

I nod. "Yes, I just walked in a few minutes ago and she was talking to Braden."

Reagan's eyes light up. "Ooh. They'd make a cute couple. How old is Braden? Thirty?"

I reluctantly nod. I don't like that idea at all.

Reagan continues, "She does like them a little older. We should all sit together."

I realize that Braden now knows I had sex with Jade. I don't need it coming out tonight.

"Sure. Why don't you guys get a table? I'll gather the troops. Jade has a friend with her. Order a round of drinks."

They nod and head toward a table, which I notice has been roped off in anticipation of their arrival. Reagan always has her assistant call ahead and get them a table wherever we go. It's a nice perk.

I turn back and see that Jade has rejoined Pandora and Braden.

I walk over to them. "Carter and Reagan have a table. They saw you, Jade. They want everyone to join them." I give Braden a stern look as I move my finger between me and Jade. "Not a fucking word about this. I mean it."

Braden nods in understanding. We may joke around, but he knows how important Carter is to me. He would never want to do anything to jeopardize my friendship with him. I should probably worry about Jade's mouth, but if she hasn't mentioned it in the past four years, I doubt she's going to do so now. At least I hope she won't.

We make our way to the table. I see Braden grab Pandora's hand. I feel a sense of relief. I don't want him anywhere near Jade.

Reagan and Carter are sitting in the middle of a circular booth. Braden and Pandora slide in on one side, leaving Jade and me nowhere to sit except next to each other on the other side.

Jade slides in first and she and Reagan embrace. She looks at Jade. "I didn't know you were going to be here. I thought the club scene was more your vibe."

"Meh. Those guys are all the same. Either young, dumb, and full of come, or old, creepy, and rich. Those guys think they can buy you. We needed a change of scenery."

Reagan elbows Jade. "I thought you liked older men. I'd think old, creepy, and rich would be right up your alley."

Jade smiles. "Once they're collecting social security, that's a bit extreme. Even for me. I'm talking sixty-year-old guys. I like my men around, say, thirty-nine." She winks at Carter. "How old are you?"

Through gritted teeth, Carter says, "As you know, I'm thirty-nine."

Reagan and Jade just laugh. They're both nuts.

Reagan says, "Thor told me she thought you were dating someone."

Jade shakes her head. "She's just messing with you.

No, you know I'm not a big fan of dating. Remember, I have daddy-abandonment issues. At least that's what I'm told."

I can't help but ask, "Why do you have daddy-abandonment issues? Declan worships the ground you walk on." I've seen him with her. He's very much involved in her life.

"I didn't meet my father until I was seven. It wasn't exactly a happy reunion. I kicked him in the balls for years before I remotely let him in. I have all sorts of trust issues with men. I usually love them and leave them before they can do the same to me." She squeezes my leg under the table. "Though occasionally they beat me to the punch."

I swallow hard. Braden's eyes look like they're about to pop out of his head.

I need to change the subject. "Carter, did you like your new bike today?"

Carter's whole face lights up. He tells us about his new motorcycle. He has several dozen. Reagan loves them and hangs onto every word he says.

The waitress continues bringing us drinks. Everyone but Reagan is downing them. She's sticking to water.

At some point, Jade rests her hand on my thigh. I don't know if she's doing it on purpose, but I admittedly don't hate it. Sitting next to her, taking in her scent, with her hands on me, it's all got me a bit confused about what I'm feeling right now. This might be the first time in five years that I'm at a table with Reagan and my attention is on a different woman.

I'm looking at Jade, but not totally paying

attention to the conversation, when I hear her say, "Better for blow jobs."

Everyone starts laughing. I missed the joke.

"Sorry, what's better for blow jobs?"

Jade smiles. "One of my friends has Invisalign. She said her boyfriend likes her to wear it for blow jobs."

I nod. "Totally. I can confirm that. It keeps their teeth out of play and is even soft when their teeth do brush against you. I'm a fan. Nothing worse than a woman who uses too much teeth. When I'm old, I'm only dating women with dentures so they can take them out at night. I'll want a gummy woman in my bed."

Everyone is laughing. Jade moves her hand higher on my thigh, and leans over to whisper, "Maybe the wrong women are sucking your dick, Collin."

She turns back to the group and says, "Fruit Roll-Ups too. If you wrap their dicks in a Fruit Roll-Up and lick it off, men seem to dig that, and it makes it much tastier for you."

I can't help but lean over and whisper, "Maybe you're sucking the wrong dicks, Jade. I have something tasty for you."

She licks her lower lip and my cock stirs. She looks down and notices.

I see a small smile creep onto her lips as she turns her head back toward the group and moves her hand higher on my thigh, brushing against my cock.

I can't deny that I'm incredibly attracted to her. It's almost visceral, completely out of my control. But then I look at my smiling best friend and his wife. They would never be okay with a scumbag like me dating Jade. Between the age difference, my history with women, and some of my needs, Carter would never forgive me when things inevitably go south.

As much as I want it in this moment, I know it can't ever happen. I grab her wrist and reluctantly remove her hand from my thigh.

CHAPTER FIVE

10 YEARS AGO

JADE

I get home from school and Mom is crying at the kitchen table. I place my hand on her back and she startles. "Oh, Jade, I didn't realize you were home." She wipes her eyes to attempt to clean them of the evidence of her tears.

"What's wrong, Mom? Why are you crying?"

She shakes her head. "Oh, nothing. Max broke up with me." She mumbles, "And he took our television."

I sigh. "Mom, every guy you date steals from us. Maybe you're looking in the wrong places for men."

She has a remarkable knack for picking losers. Steve stole our DVD player. Frank made off with our couch. Yes, our couch. He managed to come in and take it when no one was home. And now Max stole our television. The fancy, new one that Declan bought for us. It was the nicest thing we've ever owned.

"I'm never dating. It only leads to heartache and pain. All men are scum."

She squeezes my hand. "Don't say that. I believe there's someone special out there for everyone. You just have to keep your eyes open." She gives me a small smile. "We all get our happily ever after at some point."

I know she believes that. She's very into fairy tales, thinking Prince Charming will one day come and sweep her off her feet. I don't believe in any of that. I'm a realist. I know what men are capable of. Declan wanted no part of me for years. Every man in my mother's life has hurt her and disappointed her. The boys at school are all jerks. I'm never going to let myself care enough to be hurt like she always is.

I sigh at what I know is coming. I've seen this program before. She's now going to lay in bed for a month crying. All for an out-of-work loser who treated her like shit and looked a little too hard at me. It feels like she spends half her life crying over men. That will never be me.

I hear a knock at the door. As if this day couldn't get any worse, I open it to see Declan. Shit. "What do you want, Declan? It's not a good time. I can't deal with you today."

He gives me a small smile. "We have dinner plans tonight. I came early to see if you wanted to go shopping for any school clothes. You seem to grow every week. It can't be easy to keep up."

I look down at my slightly too short jeans. He's not wrong. I don't seem to ever stop growing. I'm the tallest kid in my class, by a lot. And that includes all the boys.

"As fun as shopping with my sperm donor sounds, I can't. And we have to cancel dinner. I need to be here for Mom. She's a mess. Max broke up with her."

"Good. He was a loser. And I didn't like the way he looked at you."

I let out a laugh. "I can't disagree with you on that." I point to the now empty space on our television console. "He stole our TV on the way out."

I see rage fill Declan's face. It's a familiar look. One I often see in the mirror.

He attempts to gather himself. "His last name, please."

"Why? What are you going to do?"

"Jade, give me his last name."

I wonder if I should give him the name. And then I think why the hell do I care if Declan does something to him? I don't owe Max anything. "Shwender. He lives over on Kings Lane."

Declan nods, turns, and leaves.

For the next hour, I take care of Mom. I make her favorite foods, hug her while she cries, and even manage to get her in the bath. I pour her a glass of wine and tell her to just relax.

While she's in the bath, there's a knock at the door again. I open it to see Declan with our television under his arm. I see blood all over his knuckles.

"Is Max still alive?"

"He was breathing when I left." He smiles. "Though his future ability to bear children is now in question."

I can't help the small smile that forms on my face. "A guy like that shouldn't procreate anyway. Most people shouldn't." I certainly never will. "Did you get any video? I wouldn't mind seeing that asshole go down."

"Watch your mouth. No video."

I open the door wider. He walks in and reconnects the television.

Afterward, while he's at the sink washing the blood off his hands, there's another knock at the door.

I open it to a delivery man with several bags of food. I turn back to Declan and raise my eyebrows.

He shrugs. "If we can't go out, we'll have dinner here."

"Dinner for thirty people?"

He gives me a small smile. "I wasn't sure that your mother would be up to cooking for the next few days. Now you'll have leftovers."

I nod. "Thanks, Declan. We appreciate it."

PRESENT

"Mom, are you home?"

I hear her voice coming from the living room. "Yes, sweetie, I'm in here."

Even though Mom moved to New York City when she got married a few years ago, she kept her small house in Philadelphia. She likes to come here and paint alone. She said she will always consider Philly her home and wants to visit me a lot. I told her I have plenty of room in my condo for her, but she insists on keeping this place. She texted me last night to let me know she's in town and asked me to come over in the morning.

I walk into the living room. She's sitting in her favorite chair, curled up with a book. She's an avid reader. Always has been. I guess I get that from her. Perhaps all the romance novels she reads are the reason she still believes in fairy tales and happily ever afters. I just read them for the sex scenes.

My mom is an extremely attractive woman. We look

nothing alike. She's about eight inches shorter than me with brown hair and big brown eyes. She's kept herself in great shape, with an amazing body. She never had issues finding interested men when I was growing up, I just don't think she was ever looking in the right places. There were a long series of losers until she met Rick about nine years ago. They dated for five years before they got married, the first marriage for both of them. He's a nice enough guy. A little boring for me, but he's good to her and that's all I really care about. I'm happy that she found someone, especially someone who doesn't treat her like shit.

I thought they might consider having a baby, but that hasn't happened. She got pregnant with me at twenty-two, my current age. She's only forty-four, so it's not completely out of the realm of reason.

"Good morning." I hold up a coffee cup from her favorite, unique-to-Philly, café.

Her eyes light up at the sight. She stands, kisses my cheek, takes it from me, and inhales the aroma. "Hmm. Thank you. You're my favorite daughter."

"I'll let my imaginary sisters know."

She smiles. "Have a seat." I do as she returns to her chair. "How are you? Catch me up on everything."

"Work's good. Busy, but good."

"I can't believe how much you've accomplished at such a young age. I'm so proud of you."

"Thanks, Mom."

"How's your dad?"

"He's fine. I saw him last week at Aunt Darian and Jackson's. Oh, Reagan and Skylar are both pregnant. They're due at around the same time in the late spring."

"How nice for them. Skylar is really churning them out." I see her smile, but I sense pain too.

"Mom, did you ever want to have more kids? I'm sure you still can."

"At one point I did, but I think that ship has sailed."

"Why? You're still young enough. You and Rick could have a baby." He doesn't have any kids of his own.

Tears well in her eyes.

I reach over and take her hand. "What's wrong?"

"Sweetie, I wanted to let you know that I'm leaving Rick."

Tears start falling down her cheeks. I get down on my knees in front of her and wrap my arms around her waist. "Oh, Mom, I'm so sorry. I thought you were happy. I didn't realize you were having problems. Did something happen?"

She leans her head on top of mine. "There's nothing scandalous that went on. There's just something missing from our relationship. The passion wasn't there. If I'm being honest with myself, it never has been. I knew it from the beginning. I feel like if I don't make this break now, I'll regret it down the line. I know I wanted some stability, and Rick provided that, but he's almost too stable. I want someone I can't live without. That gives me something I can't imagine getting anywhere else. Does that make sense?"

I look up at her. "Of course. You want to be happy. You deserve that." I smile. "You want someone that makes your toes curl."

She giggles. "I suppose I do. You don't think I'm being foolish? Chasing a ridiculous fairy tale?"

I shake my head. "No, not at all. If you want a fairy tale, make it happen. You should grab life by the horns and do what makes you happy. Are you okay financially? I'm happy to help. Reagan and Carter pay me stupid crazy money."

She runs her hand over my cheek. "No, sweetie, I'm

fine. Thank you for offering though. I may not have the money the rest of your family has, but I'm getting by just fine. I've had a few good years with my paintings."

Mom is an artist. Her paintings are amazing. They didn't always put food on our table, so she made and sold jewelry too. A few years ago, her paintings started to sell like crazy. She's significantly more comfortable now than she was when I was a kid.

"Okay, but don't ever hesitate to ask."

"I won't. Thank you. What about you? Are you seeing anyone?"

I let out a laugh. "Have you ever known me to truly *see* anyone?"

She sighs. "No, I suppose not. It's not healthy, Jade. One day, you're going to meet a man. You need to give in at some point and let yourself trust someone."

I stand and cross my arms. "Because so many men have come through for us in the past?"

"I know I didn't set a great example for you growing up. I tried to change that with Rick, but he's just not my Prince Charming."

I shake my head. "I'm sorry, Mom, but I don't believe in Prince Charming. Every man we've ever known has let us down. They're the inferior sex for a reason."

"Jade, that's not true. It's been fifteen years. Your dad has shown you love every day for those fifteen years. Your relationships with men are unhealthy. Have you been talking to Dr. Pearl?"

"Yes. I'll have you know that I'm doing quite well. She offered me a therapy gold star."

"I imagine she was humoring you."

I shrug. "Maybe."

"Please, sweetie, when the right man comes along, be

open. Don't be like me who always looked in the wrong places. I'm forty-four and I've never experienced true love. It's a lonely place to be. Put yourself out there."

"I'm young. I'm having a good time right now and that's all I want. I enjoy no strings sex."

"Is it at least good sex?"

Yes, my mom and I are open about sex. When you have two single women in a house, and your mom is a young one, it tends to happen.

"Meh. It's been a while since it's been truly great." About four years.

She scrunches her face. "Me too."

We both giggle. She rubs my leg. "What are you up to this afternoon?"

"I'm supposed to go shopping with Melissa, but I'll cancel if you need me."

She shakes her head. "No, it's great that you have that time with her. You've definitely adopted her sense of style."

Melissa dresses right off a Paris runway. She always wears high-end clothes. Always. When she takes me shopping, the boutiques fall all over themselves to make her happy.

"That's quite a compliment."

She smiles. "I meant it as one."

"It's nice to have another tall woman to go shopping with. Finding long clothes isn't as easy as you'd think."

"I know. I shopped for you for many years. It's good that she can help you find things to wear to work and all the fancy events you're invited to with your family."

I have a pang of guilt. It's true that in the past four years I've had a huge uptick in my lifestyle. It's not just me making more money, it's everything that comes with my new family.

They're incredibly wealthy and equally philanthropic. There are always black-tie charity events. Jackson flies us all over the country in his private jet. He takes us on vacations. Melissa has a bottomless bank account and never hesitates to do or buy nice things for me.

I scrunch my nose. "Mom, you're okay with me spending time with Melissa, right?"

"Oh, sweetie. I'm sorry if I made you feel bad about it. I'm thrilled that you have a nice relationship with her." She smiles. "I'm happy you don't have an evil stepmother."

"I don't, but what I do have is a crazy father."

She lets out a laugh. "Yes, you do." She holds up her coffee cup. "God bless Melissa for dealing with him and managing him the way she does."

I meet her cup with mine.

"Ooh, Jade, that looks gorgeous on you."

It's a designer-fitted pink pantsuit. I love it. I look down at the price tag and bite my lip. I shouldn't spend this much on clothes.

She clearly notices. "It's my belated twenty-second birthday gift to you."

I put my hands on my hips. "You got me a diamond necklace for my birthday."

She thinks for a moment. "Umm, that was from your dad. This is from me."

I let out a laugh. "No, it wasn't. This is too much. I can't accept it. Thank you, but no."

"It's not too much. I have to bribe you to make sure you continue to go shopping with me. I've never had a fellow tall shopping buddy, and I never had a daughter."

It's remarkable how much I resemble my stepmother. I maybe have an inch on her, but we otherwise look the part with blonde hair and blue eyes. She's stunningly beautiful. She looks like a young Kim Bassinger despite being in her mid-fifties.

I roll my eyes and she nods to the saleswoman that we'll take it.

I sigh. "Melissa, it's not right. I can't accept this."

"Jade, please. I can't bring my daughters-in-law to this place. Cassandra doesn't have time. She has a woman come to her office to fit her for her clothes. Jessica wears scrubs all day and is barely five feet. And Kylie is a kindergarten teacher. These clothes don't exactly work for her lifestyle." She rubs my arm. "I truly think of you as my daughter. It genuinely gives me pleasure to buy you nice things. Let me spoil you. You deserve it."

I bite my cheek to hold back tears. "Shit, Melissa. You know I never cry. You'll be on my shitlist if you make that happen."

She smiles. "It's settled then." She turns to the sales lady. "Celeste, we'll take it." She points to everything I tried on and whispers, "We'll take everything."

I shake my head. "You're crazy."

"Wouldn't I have to be to marry your father?"

I laugh. "Fair enough. How's Dad? I feel like he's been extra grumpy lately. Is he on his man-period?"

She laughs. "He's grumpy with you because you *love* to push his buttons."

I can't help but smirk at the truth in that statement. "Admit that it's fun. You push his buttons too."

She gives me a devilish smile. "Sometimes it is."

I change back into my regular clothes. We sit and sip champagne while the saleswoman packs everything Melissa bought. I can't imagine what today cost her. I feel like I'm living in an alternate universe sometimes.

I ask her, "Are you excited about your trip?"

They're going to the South of France for a few weeks. Dad is a photographer and has an assignment there. Melissa is going with him.

Her eyes light up. "Yes, I'm so excited. I've traveled more with him in the past few years than my entire life combined. I love it so much."

"You're fluent in French, right?"

"I am." She's fluent in several languages.

"It sounds amazing. I want to travel a bit more now that I'm making real money. I've never been abroad."

"You're welcome to come with us."

"I couldn't take that much time off work, and I lived with you two for a year. I thought it was the honeymoon phase, but it doesn't seem to have ended. I think I'll take a pass. Maybe I'll go with a friend sometime soon though."

She lets out a laugh. "Fair enough. Anytime you want to go, let me know. I'll help make it happen."

"Thank you."

"Are you seeing anyone special?"

I shake my head in exasperation. "You always ask this, and the answer is always the same. I'm not looking for someone special."

"I'll keep asking. One day, your answer will change."

"Never."

CHAPTER SIX

COLLIN

I wake up Sunday morning and am planning to head over to Reagan and Carter's house today to work on the nursery bump-out.

I look at the other side of my bed. It's empty. It's been empty all week. That's not the norm for me. Seeing Jade, touching Jade, and smelling Jade has my cock only looking in her direction. I didn't even go out this weekend. What's the point? No one interests me. It's all the same shit.

I think about her running her fingers through my hair. That in and of itself was worth all the crap I take for letting my hair grow longer.

I grab my hardened dick and start pumping. I close my eyes and remember her scratching her nails down my neck. I want her to do that all over my body.

I think about when I was holding her wrists behind her back and touching her neck. She was so turned on by it. I could feel it. I could smell it.

Her tits are much bigger than when we were together. Her hard nipples were pressing on my chest. She got turned on when I was rough with her. Four years ago, she definitely loved how rough I was.

I wish I could remember her taste. I know it was good. I remember wanting to take her home for more of it. I think about tasting her again. It would have happened if Reagan and Carter didn't bring me back to reality last week. We were a hairsbreadth away from kissing. I could feel her breath mingling with mine.

I flash back to four years ago. The image of her panties in her mouth and her dress around her waist, with those long legs. I would give anything to see that again. To see the rest of her too.

I ran my thumb over those plush lips last week. All I can think of is having them wrapped around my cock while those naughty blue eyes look up at me.

My cock explodes all over my stomach. I sit up and run my fingers through my hair. Fuck, Collin, get it together. It's not happening. It can't.

I need coffee. I throw on sweatpants and go to the bathroom to brush my teeth and clean my stomach. I look at myself in the mirror. I stare for a moment. There's something off. I stare a bit longer. I realize it's my smile. I've always been a happy, jovial person. Lately, I haven't. I have nothing special in my life. Nothing that gives me joy. Nothing to look forward to.

I go through the motions in everything. I do it at work and I do it in my personal life.

I hate to even think it, but I don't like working with my family. I like construction. No, I love construction. I love dreaming of something and then watching it come to life. But I hate the way my family does it. It's like we have five or six sets of plans and do the same things over and over. I get that there are efficiencies in that, but it's boring. There's no pizzazz or creativity in what we produce. I'm not proud of the mundane homes we build. And my family has no respect for me. I'm never heard when it comes to the business.

It's a hard pill to swallow, but I know there's nothing I can do about it. I have no formal education. When Carter was off getting an Ivy League education, my father had me in an apprenticeship, learning construction from the ground up. He said I should know how to do everything so when my time came to manage people, I'd know whether they were doing it properly.

I walk into my kitchen, and Braden is standing at the coffee machine. I motion to him. "By all means, just walk into my place. Help yourself."

His place is a little smaller, but we're in the same building. It's nice to have my brother here. Despite the eight-year age difference, I'm closest to him. Mac is an overbearing prick, and Shane has the exact opposite personality as me, as in he has none. Braden and I have always gotten along well.

"Sorry, I ran out of coffee."

"It's fine. You saved me from having to make it and wait for it to brew. Thanks for being my barista bitch."

"My pleasure, Master Fucks-a-Lot."

"Ooh. I like that name. It suits me. Start calling me that more often."

He laughs as he pours me a cup and hands it to me. I nod. "Thank you."

He looks my shirtless body up and down. "Jeez, Collin, you're getting big. How much are you working out?"

I shrug. "I guess more than normal. It keeps me sane and keeps me from punching Mac in the face."

He lets out a laugh. "I hear that. He's on a power trip. He's a fucking miserable son of a bitch, isn't he? He's turning into Da."

"I can't argue with that."

"For what it's worth, Collin, I think the ideas you bring to the business are good ones. Mac has no imagination. No vision. No strategy to grow the business. It's like Da told him to hit the repeat button and that's exactly what he's doing. Except we live in different times. People don't want the same house as their neighbors anymore. They want something different. Something special."

"I know. I agree. I just wonder how long the business can survive if it doesn't grow and change."

He places his hand on my shoulder. "We have a family dinner tonight. Why don't you bring it up? I'll have your back."

I shrug. "I've mentioned it before. They've all seen Carter's house. It hasn't swayed them in the least."

Braden's eyes light up. "Carter's house is the most amazing thing I've ever seen, Collin. How can they see it and not want to offer the things you did in there?"

"I don't know. I'll bring it up again. I have nothing to lose. We'll see what happens."

JADE

Reagan and Carter are out for the day, but she needed me to drop contracts from the office at her house. I asked if I could lay out by their pool. Even though fall is in full swing and it's generally sweater weather, today is a warm day and I'd like to take advantage of it. She was happy to have me use the pool and told me to invite friends if I wanted. She's so generous. I'd rather use the time to catch up on some reading though. Jade Dollston, Carolina Jax, and L.A. Ferro have new novels out, and I'm dying to read them.

I head over there in my bikini and cover, excited for a quiet afternoon alone by the pool.

I turn into the driveway and see a pickup truck. When I pull in behind it, I notice a bumper sticker that reads, *Makes Frequent Stops... At Your Mother's House.* There's only one person on this planet who would have that bumper sticker. Collin Fitz.

I smile as I think of him. He looked edible last week when I saw him. His hair is longer, and he's got scruff now that he didn't have when we met, nor the last time I saw him. I think it was the first time in four years that I wasn't staring at Carter the whole night. It was Collin occupying my thoughts. Dirty thoughts. I couldn't help but feel his big, muscular quads. I saw his dick harden at my touch. He's fighting the mutual attraction, but I know it's there. I know he's into me.

He's perfect for me. He's older, sexy, confirmed to be good in bed—great in bed—and I know he won't want any kind of relationship. I hate when guys get clingy and want you to have an official *girlfriend* title. That's usually when I bail. Collin would never want that from me. He's a player.

And maybe this time, I'll be the one to hit-and-run. I wouldn't mind a little retribution...after a lot of great sex.

Unfortunately, he's afraid of upsetting Carter. That or the age difference bothers him. He probably doesn't want to blow his chance at Reagan, though he has none. She's permanently spoken for. In the small handful of occasions I've seen him through the years, I've watched him stare longingly at her. I know what It looks like because that's how I usually stare at Carter.

I enter their code and quietly make my way inside the house. I assume Collin is working in the soon-to-be nursery. I tiptoe upstairs and down the hallway. I can hear both his miter saw running and Imagine Dragons playing.

I'm not prepared for what I see when I peek my head into the room. Collin's back is to me. He's in jeans that hug his perfect ass, a light gray wife-beater shirt, a backward baseball cap, and he's sweating. He's got a tattoo covering most of the upper half of his left arm, but I can't make out what it is. His arm muscles are bulging. I'm not sure I realized how muscular he is. He's fucking hot.

I can feel my breathing pick up and my heart racing. My bathing suit bottoms are soaked, and I haven't gone near the pool yet.

To make things worse, at some point he turns to the side, lifts the bottom of his shirt, and wipes the sweat from his face. His abs are cut from up above. His pathway to paradise, from his belly button into his jeans, is practically taunting me. It's like an arrow pointing to where I want to be.

I do what any normal, red-blooded woman would do when seeing this. I remove my bathing suit cover, ball it up, and throw it at him from the doorway.

It lands right on his head and falls down in front of him

into his hands. As if in slow motion, he turns his head to me. I'm standing there in my white bikini. I see his lips mouth, "Holy shit."

I've got my hands on my hips, with all the confidence in the world. I know I have a good body. A great body.

We both stand there in a silent stare-down. Neither of us is talking. Neither of us is moving. Neither of us has removed our eyes from the other. You could cut the sexual tension with a knife right now.

He lifts my cover to his nose and takes a deep inhale. He's staring at me like he's going to rip my bikini from my body. I'd be okay with it if he did.

"You got anything to say, Fitz?"

He studies my body thoroughly in no rush to respond. He eventually does. "I'm trying to decide which Bond girl you look like right now?"

"What are my options? Maybe I can help."

I see a small smile form on his lips. "Obviously Halle Barry from *Die Another Day*. You've got the body."

"I can live with that."

"Part of me wants to call you Pussy Galore from *Goldfinger* just because of her name."

"I understand the appeal. It makes a lot of sense."

"But their bikinis weren't white. As a *Bond* purist, I'm thinking more along the lines of Ursula Andress."

"From *Dr. No*?"

"You know your Bond movies. That one is older than both of us."

"I do know my Bond movies."

"She's the OG Bond bikini girl and she wore that famous white bikini. I'm not sure she wore it as well as you, but she wore it well."

"I guess we have our answer."

He nods. After several long moments, he asks, "What do you want, Jade?"

Without missing a beat, I respond, "To lick the sweat off your body."

He momentarily closes his eyes. "We can't. For a million reasons, we can't, not the least of which is that they could be home any minute."

"They won't be home for hours. I just spoke with her."

He blows out a breath. He's got some sort of internal struggle going on right now. "I'm sixteen years older than you. Carter is my best friend."

"No one has to know."

I see him contemplating. Why is he denying us what we both clearly want? The mutual attraction and desire running through both of us is more than apparent.

I can't help but push this along. I slide my hand into my bikini bottoms.

His eyes widen. "What are you doing?"

"I need to be touched. If you're not man enough to do it, I'll do it myself."

I run my fingers through my folds. Wow, I'm turned on.

I pull those obviously wet fingers out and up to my mouth. I slowly lick across them. "Do you remember how I taste? Need a refresher?"

I slowly walk over to him. He doesn't move. As I get closer to him, I take in his scent. It smells sweaty and manly. I'm impossibly horny.

I trace my fingers all around his lips like he did to me four years ago.

He licks across his lips. His eyes flutter.

I tilt my head to the side. "I'll call you Daddy if you want."

He roughly pulls my body to his. Just before his lips meet mine, he says, "You can call me *Big* Daddy."

I smile as our lips come together. It's a mix of sweat, mint, Collin, and me. It's the sexiest thing I've ever tasted in my life.

I wrap my arms around his neck. He grabs the backs of my thighs and lifts me, so my legs wrap around him.

I'm nearly six feet tall. While I may have been stick-skinny when I was younger, I'm much more curvaceous now and am certainly more top heavy. No man I've been with has ever been able to lift me as easily as Collin seems to. *Ever.* I love it.

His tongue meets mine as the kiss turns rabid. God, he's a good kisser. We only minimally kissed the last time. I didn't know what I was missing. It's aggressive and passionate. It's wet, but not too wet. It's fucking sexy. He's sexy.

He sits me down on his workbench and breaks his mouth from mine. He gets down on his knees, violently removes my bottoms, tosses them to the side, and spreads my legs as wide as they can go.

He studies my pussy and then looks up at me. "You're practically dripping onto the table."

"A little something to remember me by. A souvenir for you."

He pulls me to the edge, crashing my pussy into his mouth, and licks straight through me.

He closes his eyes, "Just as good as I thought it would be."

He spreads my lips and practically dives in. His tongue is pointed, exploring all of me until he lands on the spot where I need him the most. Where I'm craving his touch.

He attacks my pussy feverishly. Perfectly. Expertly. I

throw his hat to the side and grab fistfuls of his hair, holding him to me as he quickly works my clit into a complete and total frenzy. I love that he knows exactly what he's doing. I've found that it's more uncommon than one would think.

He slowly slides two fingers into me and lifts his head as he pushes them in ever so deep. "Tell me how it feels. I want to hear your words. I get off on them."

Damn, he's hot.

"It feels good."

"You can do better. No more tongue until you do better."

His fingers continue to pump in and out of me, but the only thing I can feel from his mouth is his hot breath teasing me. He keeps his lips close, but never touches me. I want his mouth on me. I *need* his mouth on me.

I look down at him. My eyes meeting his. "My pussy is on fire and wants to explode all over your face. As soon as you get your tongue back on me, it will."

He nods. "Give me all your juices. Cover me. I want to bathe in them."

He brings his tongue back to my clit, giving me everything. He sucks, circles, and swivels.

I shout. "Yes, Collin."

I'm gyrating all over his face. I want it so badly. A big orgasm is within reach.

As if he knows my body perfectly, he curls his fingers deep inside me, and my world turns momentarily dark as I come on a loud scream.

Oh my god. That was good. *Really* good. I have to blink a few times to remember where I am.

When it's clear that I'm done, Collin doesn't pull his face away. Instead, he takes things a step further and rubs his entire face all around my pussy, covering himself in my juices. I can feel his scruff against my extremely sensitive-from-orgasm flesh.

He stands and stretches his tongue as far as it will go as he licks all over his face. "Yum. I'll get to savor that taste all day."

All I can think in the moment is that he may be the hottest man in existence.

He reaches into his back pocket and pulls out his wallet, removing a condom.

Having partially regained my wits, I sit up and unbutton his jeans. I slowly unzip them, place my hand inside, and pull out his cock.

My chin drops. I didn't see him last time. I felt how big he was, knowing he was the biggest I'd ever had, but I didn't see it. I may have chickened out if I saw this monster.

I look up at him, the shock likely written all over my face. He smirks. "There's a reason I told you to call me *Big Daddy*."

I can't help but smile.

Something silver catches my eye. Holy shit. His dick is pierced. I've never seen a pierced dick in person.

He notices me staring at it. "No, I didn't have this the last time. Yes, it's going to rock your world."

Fuck. Yes.

I lick my lips and hold out my wrists. "Is Big Daddy going to tie me up again?"

He rubs his hand down my chest, expertly unclasping my bikini top with expert precision. My breasts immediately spill out. He runs his thumbs over my hardened nipples. "Did baby girl like being tied up?"

I nod.

He turns his head and scans the room. With his giant,

pierced cock hanging heavy, he walks over to a bundle of wood secured with a thick string. He pulls a pocket knife out of his jeans and slices the string, the wood pouring out all over the floor.

He violently rips the string from under the pile, his countless muscles flexing while he does so, and walks back over to me.

I place my wrists together and hold them out. In some kind of expert sailor fashion, he binds them. It's tight, but not uncomfortably so.

While he tears open the condom and rolls it on himself, I lean forward and lick his sweat-slickened arm.

"Hmm. I've been dying to taste that."

"What does it taste like?"

"It's manly. Salty."

"I've got something else salty for you."

I spread my legs wide. "Bring it, Big Daddy."

"Tell me what you want. Use your words."

"I want your monster cock inside me."

"Haven't you learned yet? Be more descriptive."

He's very into me describing things in detail.

"I want that giant cock of yours to pound into my wet pussy until I forget my name."

I lift my eyebrow in challenge. "Do you think you can handle that?"

He smiles as he brings his tip to my entrance. I'm licking my chops in anticipation of what's to come. I want him so badly. I'm practically shaking in anticipation.

"Hold your hands up." I do. He slides his head between my arms and grabs my ass with both hands and pulls me close so that just his tip breaches my entrance.

He whispers. "I remember this ass. It took every ounce of restraint for me not to fuck it."

I mouth, "Get inside me."

He brings his thumb to my mouth. "Open up."

I do and he starts to slide his thumb in at the same time his cock slides further into me. He's big. It's immediately overwhelming my senses.

At the same slower pace, he continues entering both my mouth and pussy until his cock is halfway in.

He stares at me in the eyes and rubs his thumb over my tongue. He takes the opportunity to sink his entire big cock into me. All the way into me.

I suck in a breath at the surprise intrusion, my body attempting to loosen up to his enormity.

He slides his thumb out to my lips and rubs them. "I dreamed of these lips around my cock after I saw you the other night. I jerked off to them, to you, just this morning."

I have no words right now. I'm not sure I want to tell him that I've been touching myself thinking of him too. I feel so full, I can barely speak.

He's still inside me as he begins to pepper my neck with kisses. "Fuck, Jade. I nearly forgot how tight you are."

I breathe, "It might be that you're huge, not that I'm so tight."

I can feel him smiling into my neck as he kisses his way to my lips. He takes them softly and sweetly, not what I was expecting. I love that he keeps me on my toes.

I can't use my hands, but I use my arms to pull his head to mine, kissing him back. I suck his Jade-salty tongue into my mouth.

As I begin to loosen, he begins his movements inside me. If I thought it was going to be as slow and sweet as the kiss, I was mistaken.

He lifts me by the ass, pushes me against the closest wall, and proceeds to fuck my brains out. Literally, I think everything that was once in my head is now gone and turned into a puddle that's dripping out of my pussy.

My legs are locked around him as I do my best to keep up with his inhuman thrusts. His kisses are no longer slow and sweet. They're wet and aggressive, with a bit of teeth and an ounce of pain. Good pain.

His mouth moves all over me, not just my lips. My neck, shoulders, chest, and breasts. He's definitely going to leave marks, biting across me. My back might have marks too from being pounded into the wall over and over.

"Collin, so good."

He starts to speak, but before he can, I correct myself. "Your colossal cock is making me see stars."

He's so deep inside me. Every thrust is a burst of pleasure to my body. The piercing is only adding to the gratification. I can feel it further stimulating my insides. Holy shit. How did I go four years without this? How did I go my whole life without this?

The depth, the rubbing, the pace, it's all so damn overwhelming. I can barely feel my legs. I'm dripping down onto him. I can wholeheartedly say that I've never been this wet in my life. I can hear the sounds of it as he slams into me over and over.

He holds me up with one arm and grabs onto one of my breasts with his other. "These tits weren't quite like this last time."

No, they weren't. I've definitely filled out more since the last time we were together.

He moves that big hand up to my neck and wraps it around me. He looks me in the eyes, and I nod.

He applies a small amount of pressure to my neck. As soon as he does, my eyes roll to the back of my head, and I come in a way I never have before. I'm so far gone; I don't think I could tell you my name right now. I think it starts with a J. It might end with an E. I couldn't tell you what's in the middle. But I can feel my come pouring out of me onto him.

"Fuck, yes." He squeezes my neck just a drop more and then holds himself deep inside me as his cock manages to swell, filling me while he comes.

I struggle to breathe as the reality of how hard he's squeezing my neck sets in. He immediately releases it as I gasp for air.

We both breathe heavily but don't otherwise move. My whole body is numb from the orgasm.

We're silent as we both regain our senses.

He's the only man that's ever touched my neck. I was surprisingly into it four years ago, and again today. I don't know why.

Eventually, I lift my arms over his head. I run my fingers and eyes up and down his left arm tattoo, able to see it more clearly now. It's a crown and heart with hands. "What does this mean?"

That question seems to snap him out of our post-coital bliss. "Nothing I'm interested in discussing."

He sets me down and pulls out of me, and then removes the condom and leaves the room, likely to dispose of it.

He walks back in with a wet washcloth. He gets down on his knees and wipes between my legs. The water is warm. He's incredibly tender about it.

What the hell is happening right now? I've never seen a man do this.

When he's done, he looks around the room and gathers my bathing suit and cover. He not only brings them to me, but he helps me back into them.

I'm at a loss for words. I just move my arms and legs as he needs in order to dress me.

When he's done, I hold up my bound wrists. He nods. "Right. Sorry."

He removes his pocket knife again and slices the string off me. We stare at each other. I have no idea what to make of it, but now it's awkward. I don't need his rejection for a second time.

He starts to speak, "Listen, Jade..." but I hold up my hand.

"Don't bother. We both know what this was. I needed to be fucked, and you gave it me." I walk to the door and wave as I leave the room. "I'm heading to the pool. Have a good day, Collin."

I quickly walk down the hallway, downstairs, and out to the pool. There are several towels on a shelf. I take one, lay it down, stretch out, open my book, and try to forget about the sex god upstairs. I hope I played it cool, not showing that it was the best sex I've ever had. Why is he so damn good at it? Why does he turn me on so much? I simply saw him and then acted like a dog in heat.

I consider myself fairly experienced for twenty-two, but nothing I've ever done comes close to what just happened with Collin. That second orgasm might permanently mark my soul. It will be the orgasm that all others are measured against. I thought it was amazing four years ago. Today took it to a whole other level.

I take a few long breaths to try to remember what it was. A release. A release of sexual tension from the other night. Maybe four years of sexual tension. I know we both felt it at the bar. Perhaps now we can both move forward.

I hear him working for a few hours, and then silence. I guess he left. I hate that I feel a small pang of hurt that he didn't bother to say goodbye. That's not me. I'm the one who says goodbye to men. I said goodbye to him earlier though, so I'm happy about that.

A little while later, I see Reagan walking toward me. She stops at my lounge chair. "Hey. Thanks for bringing me the paperwork."

"Of course. Thanks for letting me use the pool. It was nice to get a quiet afternoon to myself."

"Was Collin here when you were? I forgot he was working on the nursery today."

"Oh, yeah, I think so. He was upstairs hammering away." I inwardly smile at the truth of that statement. He was hammering all right.

She looks me up and down. "Do you know that you have teeth marks on your boobs?"

I look down and notice them for the first time. I smile as I shrug. "All signs of a good time."

She lets out a laugh. "It's going to take one hell of a man to rein you in one day."

I shake my head. "I'll never be reined in."

CHAPTER SEVEN

COLLIN

I'm having dinner at Mac and Ashleigh's house tonight. My whole family will be there. I decide to go a little early to spend quality time with his kids. He has an eight-year-old son, Liam, and a four-year-old daughter, Lucy.

I let myself in and see Ashleigh in the kitchen cooking. I adore Ashleigh. She's the sweetest, kindest woman. She's petite, with brown hair, green eyes, and a cute face of freckles that come out more in the summer.

I kiss her cheek from behind. "Hey, beautiful."

She turns and smiles at me. "Ooh. Keep talking."

"You're sexy, a great cook, a wonderful mother, and Mac says you're very yummy."

Her cheeks redden adorably at that last bit.

She smiles. "He didn't say that."

I nod with a huge grin. "Yes, he did."

"Do you want to taste something yummy?"

I look around like I'm making sure we're alone and joke, "Okay, but don't tell Mac. Also, don't tell him that I'm a better taster than him. He gets jealous."

She laughs as she lightly slaps my arm with her dishrag. "I meant the stew, dopey."

No one makes better Irish Stew than Ashleigh.

I smile. "Hell, yes."

She feeds me a heaping spoonful. "Hmm. Amazing. You're the best."

I hand her the bottle of wine I brought. She looks at it. "Snoop Dogg wine? That's my favorite."

"I know. It's offensive that you love it so much, but I know you do." I wouldn't call myself a wine connoisseur, but I know this isn't quality wine, by any stretch of the imagination.

She giggles. "Thank you. I appreciate the indulgence."

I look around. It's unusually quiet. This house is never quiet. "Where is everyone?"

"Mac is picking Liam up from baseball practice. He'll be back in a few minutes. Lucy is in the playroom. You're the first to arrive. Everyone else should be here soon."

I turn to exit the kitchen toward the playroom. "Sorry, I need to go see my best girl."

I hear her shout, "What about me?" as I walk away.

As soon as I walk into the playroom, Lucy looks up at me and a huge smile spreads across her adorable face, melting my heart. She runs straight into my arms shouting, "Uncle Collin!"

I pick her up and twirl her around. "How's my favorite niece?"

"I'm your only niece." My brother, Shane, has one son.

"And? You're still my favorite." I whisper, "No matter what, you always will be. Don't tell anyone else."

She giggles. "I won't. Want to know a secret?"

"I *love* secrets."

"You're my favorite uncle."

I can't help the goofy smirk on my face at her admitting that to me.

"Can I braid your hair, Uncle Collin?"

I nod. "I was planning to braid it before I got here, but I didn't because I thought you might want to."

Her face lights up. "Yay!"

She sits on the couch, and I sit on the floor in front of her. She brushes my hair for a long time and then carefully braids it using all kinds of colorful items. While she's working, she tells me about her friends at school.

At some point, I hear Mac and Liam walk in. Mac stops short when he sees what's going on in the playroom. "This is what happens when you have girl hair, Collin."

A bat my eyelashes at him. "I'm secure in my masculinity. It also helps me maintain my favorite uncle status."

Lucy kicks me. "That was a secret."

"I won't tell anyone else except Uncle Braden and Uncle Shane."

She gasps. "No, you can't tell them. They'll be sad." She holds out her pinkie. "Promise me you won't tell them."

"Hmm." I reluctantly lock my pinkie with hers. "I

guess I promise not to tell them." I cross the fingers of my other hand and wink at Mac.

My brother rolls his eyes. "Lucy, everyone else is only a few minutes behind me. They'll be here soon. Can you help Liam set the table?"

She finishes my last braid. "Okay, Daddy."

She leaves the room and Mac sits on the couch. I lift myself up and sit on it too.

He flicks one of my braids. "Your hair is ridiculous. Get it cut."

"The ladies don't seem to mind it."

"I'm sure your bevy of sleazy women don't mind at all. It's not your hair they're after."

My mind immediately drifts to Jade. She's not remotely sleazy. Just the opposite. The sex we had this afternoon was out of this world. She's so damn sexy. Completely uninhibited. So responsive. The things I could do to her. The things I want to do to her.

I got next to no work done the rest of the afternoon today. I kept watching her stretched out by the pool. Jade McGinley in a bikini should be illegal. It probably is in a few states.

I went to the back door to say goodbye when I was leaving, but then stopped myself. I can't give in to that temptation again. She brushed me off when it was over. That's probably for the best.

"Earth to Collin."

I look up. "Sorry. What?"

He examines my face skeptically for a moment. "You drifted. Very unlike you. I don't suppose it means you've met someone?"

I shake my head. "Hell no."

"You're lying. You're terrible at it. You always have been. You scratch your neck when you lie."

"No, I don't." I look down to notice I'm scratching my neck. Shit. Maybe he's right.

"Who is she?"

"No one."

"It better not be Reagan. You need to get over her. She's married to Carter. Your best friend. Our biggest client. She's pregnant with his child. Time to let her go. Oh god, I hope you didn't do something we'll all regret. That would be just like you."

"Fuck you, Mac. I haven't done anything, and I never will. And stop fucking referring to my best friend as a client. You know it bothers me. It sounds calculated. I was friends with Carter long before he was our client. If he decides to never again be our client, he'll still be my best friend."

"Whatever. You have a lush condo in the city thanks to the business he gives this family. Keep it together for once."

My family has no faith in me whatsoever. I may have earned that in the past, but not in the last few years. I've kept my head down and worked hard. Maybe I party to excess on the weekends, and indulge in women, but that's on my own time. I've been a contributing member of our family business for years.

"I'm over my crush. I just want a woman *like* her. Not *exactly* her. She's a good friend just like he is. I don't see her that way anymore."

I think for the first time in five years, that's actually the truth. Maybe I'm getting over my crush. Maybe I want to get over and under another blonde-haired, blue-eyed stunner.

"So then who were you just thinking about?"

"No one. I just have a few things on my mind."

We hear the door open and what sounds like a stampede rolling in. In reality, it's my mother, father, Braden, Shane, his wife, Lydia, and their six-year-old son, named after my father, Nolan John. We call him NJ. He looks just like me. It's fodder for many jokes.

I give my mother a huge hug. As soon as I lift my head, my father smacks the back of it. I rub it. "What the hell, Da, that hurt."

In his heavy Irish accent, he says, "You look like a damn sissy with your hair like dat. Take dat shit out. Get some scissors, for Christ's sake."

"Da, don't say words like *sissy* in front of the kids. Or anywhere, for that matter. It's not okay."

I get that my father is old school. I get that he grew up in a different time in Ireland, but it's the twenty-first century in America, and it's not acceptable. I can't imagine my brothers, or their wives, want their children to hear that. I wouldn't if it were my kids.

I look around at my brothers. Nothing. What a bunch of pussies. Everyone lives in fear of my father. I do see Braden start to speak, but I shake my head at him. Why have two black sheep in the family?

Instead, I relieve my mother of the three loaves of soda bread in her hands. It's her specialty. "Thanks, Mom. Why didn't you bring any for anyone else?"

That earns me a significantly less hard smack to the back of my head from her. "You make sure to share with everyone. Of all my boys, you always ate the most."

I smile. "It's because your cooking is so good. It's

probably why I'm the best-looking and most muscular."

My brothers all moan in displeasure.

I get down and high-five NJ. "How's it going, handsome?"

He runs his hands through his hair. "I'm trying to grow my hair like yours. Daddy is trying to make me get it cut."

I whisper in his ear, and he smiles. My brother, Shane, looks at me skeptically. I think a small part of Shane hates that not only does NJ look like me, but he also has a touch of my outgoing, silly personality, not Shane's more demure personality.

After saying all the hellos to everyone, we all sit down to eat. My father looks around until his eyes land on Mac. "How's business?"

My father semi-retired last year. I say semi in that he is supposedly fully retired, but still manages to find his way into the office and job sites at least three times a week to bark orders at everyone.

Mac answers, "Business is great. The Underhill house is on schedule. The Wolf mansion is breaking ground next week. Carter and his wife keep buying properties and knocking them down. It's a constant stream."

My father nods. "Who's overseeing da Wolf mansion?"

Mansion? Hardly. It's slightly bigger than a normal house. It's not a mansion. Carter and Reagan's house is a mansion.

Mac gives me a disapproving look and then turns back to my father. "I want it to be Collin. For some unknown reason they like him, but he's insisting on doing the work on Carter's nursery himself."

My father shakes his head. "No, Collin. Send one of da young guys to do dat small project. You're needed at da Wolf's. If they want your irresponsible arse, then dat's what dey will get."

I shake my head. "I want their nursery to be perfect. It's Carter's first child. I don't trust anyone else. I've been working nights and weekends to get it done quickly. Give me two more weeks and then I'll get to the Wolf job."

Mac and my father both sigh. My father scowls at me. "And get a damn haircut before da job starts. Those are high society people. Dey don't want a thug in their house every day."

Lucy gasps. "No, I love Uncle Collin's hair."

I wink at my family. "All the ladies do."

I'm met with a sea of eye rolls.

I think this is my opening. I clear my throat. "Listen, everyone. Carter's house has been featured in a ton of magazines. Half the calls we get are from the publicity. I think that if we want to keep growing the business, we need to consider doing more custom work. Not just builder-grade, colonial homes. Innovative homes. Technologically advanced homes. Homes that don't look like any others."

Mac has a look of disgust. "You're not a businessman, Collin."

"I didn't realize dropping out of high school and working most of your career as an electrician made you Jeff Bezos."

Da scrunches his nose. "Who's dat?"

"The owner of Amazon. He's a billionaire."

Mac shakes his head. "Collin, just do your damn job on the weekdays so you can continue your playtime on the weekends. Leave the business decisions to the real adults."

Braden pounds his fist on the table. "That's such bullshit, Mac. You know Collin is talented. You've seen Carter's mansion. You know full well it's nicer than anything you could have ever done. Give him a little credit."

Mac narrows his eyes. "Credit? Credit for simply being lucky and having a rich best friend. We can't trust Collin with clients on Carter's level. Carter might be okay with Collin's antics and mouth, but normal people aren't. Dad left me in charge. We stay the course. It's kept us in business for forty years and it will keep us in business for forty more."

My father nods his head. "Mac is in charge now, boys. What he says is da way it will be."

And that's the end of the conversation.

We finish eating and the kids all head off to the playroom. They chat a bit more about business. I mostly stay quiet. It's not as if I'm ever heard or my suggestions ever considered.

Ashleigh and Lydia talk about the kids and their upcoming activities. I make a mental note to get to their various sporting events. Of particular significance, Lucy is starting t-ball this spring. I can't wait to see her out there in her little uniform.

My parents both smile at all of it. They support their grandkids in everything. They miss nothing. Some of their friends spend winters in warmer climates, but my parents refuse to do so. They don't like to miss anything for the grandkids. Games, recitals, school plays, all of it.

My father eventually turns his attention back to me. "When are ya gonna find a nice girl like Ashleigh and Lydia and settle down? You're gettin' a bit old to be running around like ya do."

"I'm not really the nice girl type. I'm also not sure I'm the settling down type."

I see Braden trying to hold his laughter. He loves that I'm the big target when it comes to love and marriage. It keeps him out of the line of fire.

My father shakes his head. "Dey have plenty of nice friends. You should meet some of dem."

"Hmm. I think Braden has interest in them. He likes nice girls more than I do."

Braden narrows his eyes at me and then turns back to them. "Actually, I just started seeing someone."

This is news to me. "Who?"

"You met her the other night. Pandora."

I smile. "Did you open her box yet?"

That earns me another smack to the back of my head. I really need to stay more than an arm's length away from my father.

"Don't talk dat way in front of ya mother or ya sisters-in-law."

I mumble, "Sorry."

Ashleigh winks and smiles at me. I swear I have days where I think she's the only one in our family who gets me.

After dinner, my father, brothers, and I traditionally go off to the study to drink whiskey. NJ fell and hurt himself, so Lydia and my mother are dealing with him.

My father turns back as they're walking out of the room, "Collin, ya comin'?"

"I'm not leaving Ashleigh to clean everything by herself. I'll be there in a bit."

Ashleigh smiles. "Thanks, but I've got it. You can go with them."

"I'm not totally useless. I'll at least help you clear the table." I whisper, "I'd rather hang with you."

"Thanks, Collin. I appreciate it."

Everyone leaves except Ashleigh and me as we begin clearing the table. At some point, she looks up at me, "Why do you let them talk to you like that? They're wrong about you. I tell Mac to lay off, but then he gets all jealous and crazy wondering why I'm protective of you. He can be a nut at times."

"Well, I *am* much better looking than him."

She rolls her eyes. Everyone rolls their eyes at me.

"He's so much like my father. It's amazing," I say.

She sighs. "I know."

"Everything is good between you two, right?"

She nods. "Of course. I just..."

"What?"

"We're in a bit of a disagreement right now and you know how Mac is about getting his way. I want to go back to work, and he doesn't want me to go."

"He's such a caveman like my father. Do you want me to talk to him? You were a teacher, right?"

Her face lights up. "I was and I miss it. If you don't mind, I would love for you to talk to him. Lucy starts full-day Kindergarten next year. I need something to do."

"Consider it done."

"Thank you." She grabs my arm. "You're a good

man, Collin. And I personally think you're right about the business."

"Thanks, Ash. It means a lot that you believe in me."

"I do." She's quiet for a moment. "I know my friends are a little vanilla for you. I get it. If you change your mind, know that they ask about you all the time."

I give her a small smile. "Thanks. They're just not my type. I'm sorry."

"I understand. I can't help that I want you to meet someone who makes you happy. You have so much to offer. I just know that one day you'll meet someone who checks all the boxes, whatever they may be."

I'm quiet. Too quiet.

Her eyes widen in shock. "Collin, did you meet someone?"

I let out a long breath. "There's someone I'm interested in, but she's off limits to me."

"Why?"

"I don't really want to say."

She looks at me with so much compassion. "You know I'm always here if you need to talk. I won't judge you."

I nod.

"For what it's worth, I think you're an amazing man. Anyone, regardless of the circumstances, would be lucky to have you. Why do you think all my single friends want you?"

"Because I'm hot and ridiculously good in bed?"

She laughs. "Well, maybe the hot part. I couldn't say much about the rest of it. But you're an awesome guy. Don't let your father or your brothers convince you otherwise. And if there's a woman you want, and she wants you, I say go for it. Fuck everyone else. Since when do you care what other people think? It's one of the things I love most about you. It makes you special. You swim against the current. You don't always go with the flow. You're uniquely you and I adore you."

She's right. Why am I denying myself what I want?

I smile. "Ugh. If I only I met you before Mac."

She giggles and mumbles, "I don't know if I could handle you."

That might be true, but there's one woman I think is up to the task.

CHAPTER EIGHT

COLLIN

I'm in Carter's office with him and Reagan. When I come here, I try to dress a little nicer than my normal work clothes of jeans and boots. Well, I'm still in jeans, but they're my weekend jeans and I'm wearing a button-down shirt, nice shoes, and a jacket. No tie. I don't do ties.

I'd be lying if I said I didn't put in a drop of extra effort just in case I ran into Jade. I can't get her out of my mind. There's something so enticing about her. Obviously she's ridiculously sexy, but it's her whole demeanor. She'll say and do anything. She's a little wild and very funny. She has no filter. I love that.

Ashleigh was right. Since when do I care what other people think? Well, I guess I care a little about what my family thinks. If I didn't, it wouldn't bother me that they have no faith in me. I know I care what Carter thinks. Mostly, I care about our friendship. It's the most genuine thing in my life.

That's the problem with starting something with Jade. Carter won't like it. He'll hate it. And when it goes to shit, which it will because that's my M.O., what does that mean for my relationship with him?

Reagan asks, "What do you think?" She's showing me a bunch of properties they want to buy, have me rebuild, and then sell.

"I like the office building and the two larger single-family homes. The Wander property has endless potential. The rest don't seem worth the hassle for you guys. There's not enough money in it for you. You guys have mega-money. Why bother with the small potatoes?"

They smile at each other like they have a secret. They always manage to communicate without talking. I've watched over the past five years as their two minds have become one. They're that in sync with one another. I can't imagine that ever happening to me. I can't imagine being so incredibly in sync with another person that you have all the same thoughts and can finish each other's sentences.

Carter places his hand on my shoulder. "We want to set up this business with you. Not Fitz and Sons Construction. Equal partners. Reagan and I will own half, and you'll own the other half."

"What? I don't have this kind of money. I can't contribute."

Reagan nods. "You contribute time and expertise. We can't manage the rebuild on these properties. We'll fund it and you work on managing the projects." She hands me a folder. "Here's all the paperwork for a new company. It will take some time to set up, but this is what we're thinking."

I look at Carter in question. He smiles. "Collin, you're incredibly talented. You didn't just build our house like a regular contractor. You designed it. You worked with the architect and engineers. I've never seen anything like it. It's special. It's innovative. You have a unique mind for this. Your family might not see it, but we do. I know you're not completely happy working with them. You can start to build something on your own. Maybe one day soon, if you choose, you can completely break free from them."

I'm in shock. "What? Are you serious?"

They both nod.

I have tears in my eyes. "Fuck, Carter. You don't have to do this."

"I know, but we want to. We're investing in your talent. We believe in you. That's what Daulton and Lawrence Holdings is at its core. Finding talent and helping it to blossom into something bigger. This company helped do that for Reagan's father and helped do that for Jackson. It's our mission. Maybe this deal looks a little different and is a bit more personal, but the general principles are the same."

I run my hands through my hair. "I'm at a loss for words. I don't want anything to interfere with our friendship. What if things go south?"

Carter nods at the folder. "That's why we have the paperwork. Have an attorney look through it all and let us know."

"I trust you. I don't need that."

He smiles. "Do it. I insist."

I let out a breath. "Okay. I guess if you think it's best. Thank you. I'm...I'm blown away right now."

Reagan shrugs. "Thank *you*. You're helping us too.

We're submitting the bid for the Wander property immediately. Why don't you head down to Jade's office with the information on the property. She's a genius at taking what's in your mind and getting it out onto virtual modeling so everyone else can experience it."

"Okay. I will. Thanks again. Are you sure you think I'm up for this? It's not just an excuse to see my pretty face more often?"

They laugh. Carter answers, "We're excited about it. Now leave so I can take advantage of my wife before her next meeting."

She gives me a big smile and nods. "I like when he takes advantage of me."

I laugh as I leave. I may make a quick stop in the bathroom to make sure my hair looks good before I go see Jade.

I approach an administrative person's office to ask where Jade's is. She points me in the right direction.

Her door is closed when I arrive. I knock.

She yells, "I'm naked, don't come in."

I immediately open the door. She's fully clothed sitting behind her desk. "Ugh. What a letdown. I was hoping for naked."

Her face lights up. "If I knew it was you, maybe I would have been naked. Come in and close the door behind you."

I walk in, close the door, and hold up the property files. "Reagan asked me to give this to you and let you know my vision for its rebuild so you could do some virtual modeling."

"I see. Are you doing a project with us?"

"Yes, this one and likely a few more."

"Will you and I be working together for the duration?"

I shrug. "I don't know. I've never done virtual modeling on any project. Our family business doesn't have that technology. How long does it take?"

"For only one property?"

"For now."

"A single-family home?"

"Yes."

"As long as you're fairly descriptive, it doesn't take me long. This isn't a skyscraper. It's a relatively small house."

"It's a ten-thousand-square-foot mansion. It's hardly small."

She smiles and points to some files on her desk. "Each one of those represents a building with at least a million square feet."

"Gotcha."

"I can do this for you quickly though. I'll take notes today and then we'll meet again. If you have modifications, I'll make them. If not, we're done. It's pretty simple."

"Okay. Let's just get started. You should probably sit on my lap. It helps me think."

She smiles. I love that smile. It's full of mischief. "Collin, time is money. You're going to need to think with your big head for this."

"You've seen me. You know that my big head rests below my belt."

She laughs. "You're not wrong." She motions toward a small sofa. "Sit down. Let me grab a few things."

I sit while she rummages through her desk. She

stands and walks toward me. She's in a hot pink pantsuit. It's tailored perfectly to her long, curvy body.

I give her an obvious once-over before making my way to her eyes. "You look like sexy, businesswoman Barbie."

Without missing a beat, she says, "You look like dirty, fuckable Ken."

"Hmm. I didn't have that model. Perhaps it came out after I was done playing with dolls at around thirty years old."

She lets out a laugh as she sits next to me, placing her pads of paper, pens, and rulers on the coffee table. She moves her face into my airspace. "I'm much younger. It wasn't out until about...four years ago. He was my favorite though. I don't like boring, plain Ken."

I get right in her face. "I don't like boring, plain Barbie."

Her lips are an inch from mine. She breathes, "I guess we're a match."

I nod. Our lips are about to meet when something on her desk buzzes. A voice says, "Ms. McGinley, you said to remind you when your appointment with Mr. Windsor was thirty minutes away."

Jade turns her head and shouts, "Thanks, Minnie. In thirty-five minutes, show him in."

"Will do."

"Your assistant's name is Minnie? Does she live with Mickey or Donald?"

"Obviously Mickey. Daffy lives with Donald."

"My bad. Why thirty-five minutes?"

"Reagan is interviewing this guy for the vacant

CIO position. She wants me to be the bad cop with him. To test his boundaries. I'll make him wait a few minutes."

I'm not sure why that's hot but it is. Everything about her take-charge demeanor is hot.

"What's a CIO?"

"A Chief Investment Officer. He or she identifies opportunities. Businesses we should invest in. Properties we should buy and develop."

"I see."

She nods toward the file. "We should get started."

We spend the next thirty-five minutes going through my vision for the rebuild. She asks thorough follow-up questions. It's clear she's good at what she does and is passionate about it. I suppose she wouldn't hold this position at her young age if that wasn't the case.

Precisely thirty-five minutes after her assistant rang, there's a knock at the door. She stands and straightens her jacket. "Time for me to squeeze his balls."

"Ooh. Where do I sign up for that?"

She waves her hand. "Bye, Collin. I'll let you know when this is done. Give me a little time. I'm slammed."

"Bye, Jade. Let me know if you need to be slammed more."

***

JADE

I knock on Reagan's door and hear her say, "Come in."

I walk in and she looks up and smiles. "What's up?"

"I just met with Windsor."

"And?"

"And you didn't tell me it was Beckett Windsor."

She gives me her devilish smile as she taps her chin with her pen. "It must have slipped my mind."

I narrow my eyes at her bullshit. "It slipped your mind that we're interviewing a billionaire entrepreneur to work *under* you and Carter? The man who was once named the most brilliant mind in the business world? The one that doesn't have to work another day in his life?"

"He's bored. He's not ready to hit the golf course and early bird special circuit yet. He doesn't want the hassles of running his own company anymore, but he still wants to play the game."

"Anymore? He can't be more than forty-five or fifty. It's not like he's got one foot in the grave."

"I know. That's what appeals to me. There's a lot more gas left in his tank. He's obviously got a proven track record of finding small businesses with the potential to become big ones. He wants to keep busy, and he likes what we do and how we do it. I just want to make sure he can handle being the worker bee, not the queen bee."

"Cause you're the queen bee."

"I'm the motherfucking queen bee. He needs to be okay with that."

"So you just wanted to see how he'd manage talking with a twenty-two-year-old who has an unusually high-level position for her age."

She gives me a guilty look. "If he big-timed you, I'm going to pass on him. If he can't play well in the sandbox, it's not worth the hassle to me. Tell me what you talked about. I want to know about his demeanor. I trust your opinion. That's the main reason I sent him to you. I knew you wouldn't suck his dick just because of who he is."

"Pft. He should be so lucky for me to suck his dick."

She smiles. "Tell me about the meeting."

"I wouldn't say that he big-timed me. Honestly, he was more interested in discussing the artist of the paintings in my office."

"Your mom's paintings?"

"Yes. I didn't tell him it was my mother. He said it reminded him of an artist he once knew, though he seemed to carefully choose his words."

"I nearly forgot that he's a big patron of the arts. He supposedly has a very impressive collection. What did you say about it all?"

"I gave vague information. Mostly just where he could find her work. He asked me how I ascended to my role at such a young age. It wasn't judgmental, just curious. He said that he likes the risks you and Carter take. He likes how hands-on you are. He asked me if it's true or a facade as to how much you appear to care about the businesses you absorb."

"What did you tell him?"

"That you're fake as fuck, and he should run for the hills."

She laughs. "What did you really say?"

"I legit said that, but he laughed. At least he has a good personality. He was charming, but not in a sleazy way. He wasn't a snob if that's what you're worried about. He said he misses helping the little guy get into the arena with the big boys."

"I'm glad to hear that. Anything else worth reporting?"

"He's extremely attractive."

She shrugs. "I know. That doesn't matter though."

"Maybe to you, but the rest of us enjoy the eye candy in this office. Keep hiring hot guys."

She laughs. "I'll do my best. Hotness aside, are you a yes or no on Beckett Windsor?"

"I'm a yes."

CHAPTER NINE

JADE

I'm lying on my couch after work in a tank top and shorts with a glass of wine. I look around at my condo. I can't believe I live in such a big, nice place. How did this become my life?

I have a huge, modern, brand-new condo. Melissa helped me decorate, so it's beautiful and elegant.

Most of my friends are still in college with mounting student loan debt and are praying to find some entry-level job. Not me. I'm a freaking executive at one of the biggest companies in the world.

When I was little, we had very little money. When my dad came back into the picture, he insisted on giving my mom most of his income from being a photographer each month. He went on long assignments, which didn't help our strained relationship, but he eventually began to establish himself. As he got more well-known, the amount he gave my mom went up.

My mother used some of it for essentials, and some to

buy a house, but put the rest away for college for me. Thanks to my mom's foresight, and my working for Reagan during college, I graduated debt free with a high-paying job. Now I have more money than I know what to do with.

I'm thinking about my conversation with Melissa. Maybe I really should start to travel a little bit. I never did that growing up. We were lucky to get a few days on someone's couch at the Jersey shore each summer. That was the extent of my travel until I was in junior high, and my dad took my mom and me to Disney World. I think Mom was more excited about it than me. She practically forced me into those damn princess photos. She was in every single one smiling with glee. Other than that trip, I never traveled.

Once the Lawrence and Knight families came into my life, that completely changed. I did a lot more domestic travel, but not overseas. I only have a passport because Jackson and Darian have taken us all away to the Caribbean a few times over the years on his private jet.

I'm deep in thought about the places I'd like to go when I hear my text tone. I look down at my phone.

> Unknown: What are you wearing?

> Me: Depends on who's asking.

> Unknown: The sexiest man alive.

> Me: Henry Cavill, how did you get my cell number? You finally got all the naked pictures I mailed you?

> Unknown: Please resend them so I can confirm your identity.

I laugh. Whoever is texting me at least has a sense of humor.

Me: You first.

I'm not prepared for a return text with a photo of a giant, hard penis. The same giant, hard penis that's been on my mind all week.

Me: Collin Fitz. It's good to see your big head.

Unknown: I love that you were able to identify me from my cock. Still the biggest you've ever had?

Me: Maybe. You also just so happen to have a very distinguishable, very pleasurable piercing. How did you get my number?

Collin: I may have swiped it from Reagan's phone when I was at their house this week.

Me: I hope you didn't steal any nudes of her. She undoubtedly has a few on her phone.

Collin: I didn't think of that. There's only one naked blonde woman on my mind right now.

Me: Hmm. Margot Robbie? She's hot. She's on my mind too. She could turn me. Though I do like D a little too much.

Collin: Any particular D?

Me: Nope. I'm all for equal opportunity D.

Collin: Are you sure about that? You
seemed mighty pleased with my D the
other day. You came all over it. I smelled
you for hours.

Everything he says is sexy. I should be smart right now and end this conversation, but I enjoy sparring with him, and I can't help that I'm getting turned on by simply staring at the picture of his dick. I'm saving that into my photos.

It's such a perfect dick. I'm remembering what it did to my body the other day. I slide my hand into my panties. Yep, I'm *really* turned on.

I can apparently still type with one hand though. I have mad skills.

Me: My lips are sealed. Your head is
already big enough.

Collin: Which head? The big one or the
REALLY big one?

Me: Send another pic so I can confirm
from all angles.

Of course he sends another photo. Damn, that's a good-looking dick.

Collin: What are you doing?

Me: Totally not touching myself to the
sight of your best attribute.

Collin: Can I watch?

Me: You're not going to take screenshots
and post them on social media are you?

Collin: I'm not sixteen. Let me watch
you. I'll talk you through it.

That's a rather appealing proposition.

Me: Promise to make it extra dirty?

Collin: Is there any other way? I'll even
pinkie promise.

I laugh at that. He must have nieces.

Me: Fine.

My phone immediately rings with a video call request. I accept and see his gorgeous face on my screen.

He smiles. "Hey, beautiful."

"I was hoping to see your other head. The better looking one."

"I'll get there in a minute. Move the phone down your body. I want to see what you're wearing. I need a full visual."

"I'm wearing a muumuu."

He laughs. "I'm pretty sure you don't own any."

I smile. That's true. I run the phone camera down my body and then back up to my face.

"Shit, Jade. Is that how you lay around your house?"

"Usually I lounge in the nude, but the weather is turning so I went for the super warm tank top and shorts."

"Baby girl, take off your shorts and panties. I want to see your pussy. I bet it's wet. You were dripping onto my cock the other day. I was smelling you on me all afternoon. I got nothing done. I almost didn't shower that night. I didn't want to wash it away."

Oh shit. I can't believe I'm doing this. I slide off my shorts and panties. I start to toss them to the side, but he interrupts. "Don't. Sniff your panties. Tell me what they smell like."

Why is that so hot? I bring them to my nose and audibly inhale.

"It smells like me. I smell pretty damn good."

"Yes, you do. You taste good too."

"Want me to find out for myself?"

He moans. "Yes. Slide your fingers inside your pussy. Move your phone down so I can watch."

I give him an up-close view as I do just that. I slide my fingers in and out a few times.

"I can hear how wet you are, Jade. Is this turning you on?"

I whisper, "Yes."

"Me too."

"Let me see. I want to see your cock."

"First taste yourself. Tell me what it tastes like."

I bring my fingers to my mouth and slip them inside. I make a little bit of a spectacle of sucking them clean.

"That's it, baby girl. Tell me. Use your words."

I pull my fingers out of my mouth. "It tastes like it wants Big Daddy."

"Big Daddy really wants to be in there again."

Oh god, I want that too. I breathe, "Show me what I want, Collin."

He moves the camera down his exposed body. I see every ripple of his chest and abs along the way. His cock is out. It's engorged and angry looking. It's laying heavy on his perfect stomach. I desperately want it.

"Touch it, Collin."

He wraps his fingers around his cock and starts moving his hand up and down on it.

"Baby girl, lay a pillow between your knees. Prop the phone up so you can use both hands and I can watch you from that angle."

That would actually make this easier for me, so I do as he instructs.

"Good girl. Now slide your fingers back in."

I do.

"Good. Now find your clit with your thumb and start circling. Find that spot that makes your body shake."

Once again, I do as instructed. I look down and see that he's stroking his cock faster and harder.

"Use your other hand and grab your tits."

I lift my tank top, baring my breasts. I'm not wearing a bra. Who wants to wear a bra when they're sitting home alone?

"Fuck, you have the best tits I've ever seen. Your nipples are so pink. I want them in my mouth."

I grab my breast and squeeze it before working my way to my nipple and doing the same.

"That's it. Do you like when I squeeze your throat or your tits?"

"Both."

"Which do you like more?"

I whisper as I shamefully admit, "My throat."

"I know you do. It's so damn hot. Place your hand around your neck and give it a little squeeze. Pretend it's my hand."

While one hand is circling my clit, I move the other to my neck and wrap it around.

"Apply some pressure. Just a little at first."

I do.

"Not directly on your windpipe. Do it on the sides. It gives the sensation of choking without completely cutting off your air supply."

So that's the trick.

"I can see how wet that made you. I can hear it. I can almost smell it. I wish I was smelling it. Tell me how it feels?"

"Oh god, Collin. I wish your dick was inside me. I'm about to come."

"Not yet."

"I need to."

He shouts, "I said not yet."

"Or what?"

"Or I'm going to teach you a lesson about who controls when you come?"

His demanding words set me off. I moan. "Oh fuck. Collin." My back arches and I come. Hard. I couldn't control it. I couldn't stop it. His words just get to me. His face. His body. His dick. All of it.

I spend a moment catching my breath, a little out of it. When I peel my eyes open, I look at the screen. He does not look happy.

He narrows his eyes. "You're going to pay for that."

I give a small smile. "Promise?"

"It's a guarantee, baby girl."

I hold up my fingers that were inside me to my mouth. "Collin, want to see what I would do if this were your giant cock?"

He nods as I see him lick his lips.

I slowly lick my fingers from the bottom to the tips. I then openly swirl my tongue to the bottom and back up. I flick the tip a few times with my tongue.

"Hmm, Collin. I can taste your precum. It's sweet and salty, just like you."

I slide my fingers into my mouth and slowly move them deeper and deeper into my mouth until I'm practically swallowing my hand.

"Yes, take me deep."

"Uhh hmm."

I move it in and out, moaning the whole time.

I hear his noises getting louder. His movements growing more out of control.

I pull it almost all the way out and give a big, over-exaggerated swirl of my tongue around the tip. "Fill my mouth, Big Daddy."

He lets out a loud grunt as white streaks shoot across his muscular stomach. I wish my tongue was running over it. I'm tempted to take a screenshot of the sexiest image I've ever seen, but I'd be a hypocrite if I did that to him.

We're silent as he catches his breath. I have no idea what just happened or how we got there. The whole thing very quickly took on a life of its own. What is it about him that makes me this way?

Maybe I should just end the call. Or maybe I could attempt to be a grown-up. Well, a grown-up who just mutually masturbated via cell phone with a man sixteen years older than her.

His big body is stretched out on what looks like his couch. He brings the phone closer to his face. I see him run his fingers through his thick hair as he lets out a deep breath. "I've tried fighting this attraction, Jade. It's a losing battle. I can't stop thinking about you. I want to be around you. I want to laugh with you. I want you in my bed. I want you over me. I want you under me. I. Want. You."

I TOSS and turn in bed all night. Of all the shocking things he said to me, him saying *I want to laugh with you* is what has me tweaked.

The two of us fucking, I can handle. Laughing with someone is what people in relationships do. We will not be entering into any kind of relationship. There's no way he wants that. He hates our age difference, he's afraid of Carter knowing, and it's Collin *fucking* Fitz. He can get any woman on the planet. He's probably already had most of them.

Maybe he meant we'd laugh while lying in bed after we fuck. Yep, I think that's it.

THE NEXT DAY at work I walk into Thor's office and close the door behind me. "Can I talk to you?"

"Of course. Is the current workload too much? I knew you were taking on too many things at once. I told Reagan it was too much, but she thought you could handle it."

I sit in a chair in front of her desk and wave my hand in a dismissive manner. "No. I'm a genius. This shit is easy. I have a man issue. As you know, I struggle more there."

Her eyes light up. "A man issue? Are you seeing someone?"

"Absolutely not." I say nothing else. I simply sit and pick at my lips nervously, remaining silent.

"Are you going to share, or do I have to guess? I imagine you came in here for a reason."

I slowly nod. I take a deep breath and begin. "A few years ago, I had amazing sex with a sort of stranger."

"What does *sort of stranger* mean?"

"It means we didn't know each other, but we ended up having...friends in common."

She nods in understanding. "Continue."

"Though we've been around each other a few times throughout the years, we have never spoken since that night. He wouldn't acknowledge my presence. I ran into him a few weeks ago at a bar. The mutual attraction was still there. There's a chemistry that's bizarrely strong. It's so powerful that it's practically a living, breathing thing. But nothing happened...."

"Good. You don't need a guy who ignored you for years."

"Until last week. We fucked our brains out. Against a wall."

Her face drops. "Oh. I see. Well, how was it?"

I blow out a loud breath. "If it wasn't the best sex of my life, then I wouldn't be sitting here, would I?"

"I'm following. How did you end things that night?"

"Day. It was during the day."

"Honestly, I'm afraid to ask how it went down."

"You should be. It's irrelevant though."

"How did it end?"

"I basically walked out without a word. I was a little freaked out. I wanted to avoid another awkward goodbye from him." I sigh. "Then he called last night, and we had crazy hot phone sex." I leave out the part about us now working together. She doesn't need to know that part.

"I have a lot of questions about the logistics of that, but most importantly, you didn't do anything on video that could be captured, did you? That would be highly irresponsible and a woman in your high position here needs to be careful..."

I smack my hand on the table. "Thor! Stop. There's no evidence. I have a real problem though. I'm asking for your help. I'm confused."

"Sorry. I feel the need to mother you at times."

"I have a mother. I need a friend right now."

"Fine. Friend hat is on." She makes fake movements with her hands over her head simulating placing a hat on it.

I continue, "After the insanely hot phone sex..."

"Was it hot or insanely hot?"

I narrow my eyes at her. "If you ask another stupid question, I'm leaving."

"You're so bossy."

"I know. After the insanely, crazy, wickedly hot phone sex, he tells me he wants to see me."

"In what way?"

"That's the thing. If he just said he wanted to fuck me, I'd be cool and the gang."

"He doesn't want to fuck you?"

"Of course he wants to fuck me. Try listening instead of interrupting."

Silence.

"In *addition* to fucking me, he said he wants to laugh with me. Do you see my problem?"

"Umm, no. If he wants to fuck you and laugh with you, it sounds like he wants to date you. And if he's Mr. Best Sex of My Life, then I *really* don't see a problem."

My shoulders slouch. "Ugh, that's what I'm afraid of. I just want to fuck him. I don't want a relationship. I don't do relationships. Relationships with men lead to heartache."

She shakes her head. "For someone who calls themself a genius, you're an idiot."

"How so?"

"First of all, not all relationships with men lead to heartache. I've been with my husband since college. He's never hurt me. Not once."

"Eddie is a unicorn."

"No, he's not. Back to you. Not all men will hurt you."

"Hmm."

"And just because he said he wants to laugh with you, doesn't mean he's putting a ring on it. It sounds like you have chemistry with this guy. He wants to see you. You're twenty-two and have never allowed for any remote possibility of a relationship. You had a damn fake boyfriend in high school to appease your mother's worries. It's time to grow up and be in an adult relationship."

"Did I tell you that I had a fake boyfriend?"

"Yes."

"Was I drunk?"

"A little."

"I don't recall."

I pretend-dated my good friend Jaime because my mother was freaking out that I didn't see men as anything other than hook-ups. She wanted to up my therapy, so I told her I was dating my friend Jaime while randomly sleeping with college guys and recently out-of-college guys.

"You told me. It's unhealthy. All your relationships with men are unhealthy. If you have what you say you have with this guy, you should see it through."

"You really think I should consider this?"

"Yes. At least attempt a remotely normal, healthy relationship. It won't kill you."

"Please don't use the *R*-word in my presence. Relationship is a dirty word. It triggers me."

I tap my head for a moment. "Maybe I'm just dickmatized."

"What in the ever-loving hell does dickmatized mean?"

"I'm hypnotized by his dick. It's a pretty fucking severe dick. He's got a lot going on down there. Hence, dickmatized."

"I don't think that's a word."

"It is. Look it up."

"Does Mr. Webster's Dictionary call it a word?"

"Mr. Urban Dictionary probably does. I'll bet money that Reagan and Skylar know what it means."

"We have a meeting with them in ten minutes. We can ask."

"Fine, but don't say it's about me. I don't need any questions about this situation from them. It opens up a whole family inquisition."

She nods.

Ten minutes later we walk into one of the conference rooms to meet Reagan and Skylar. As soon as we walk in, Thor says, "Jade is dickmatized. Do either of you know what that means?"

That bitch just sold me out. I give her a dirty look and she gives me a small smirk.

Reagan and Skylar look at each other and start hysterically laughing. Reagan turns back to Thor. "You're like an old lady. Of course we know what that means. I'm dickmatized too."

Thor turns to Skylar and raises an eyebrow in question.

Skylar gives a small smile. "My husband is built like a football player. Let's just say he's *proportionate* to his *very* large frame. I've also gotten pregnant three times in three years. So yes, I'm entirely dickmatized."

Reagan lets out a laugh before looking at me. "The big question is who has you dickmatized, Jade?"

I give an innocent smile. "No one you know. I'm sure I'll forget his name by tomorrow."

She gives me a skeptical look. "As long as it's not someone from a fifty-five-plus community."

"Just a few years shy of that. Two or three."

"Why don't you bring him to our family dinner this week? We can size him up for you."

"Umm, no. It's...new." I don't know what the hell it is. All I know is that Collin texted this morning and asked when he can see me. I told him I'd come by at around ten tonight. That hour can't be considered a date. That's a booty call hour. I'm going to make it crystal clear that we're fucking and that's it. No other nonsense.

CHAPTER TEN

COLLIN

I'm finishing up at Reagan and Carter's for the night. Jade's coming over in an hour and I want time to shower and get a few things ready for her.

I walk into their living room. Carter and Reagan are on the couch. He's massaging her feet as they talk. They don't notice me at first.

It's hard to describe their relationship. I've never been around a couple so in tune with each other. They do everything together, both work and play. If I ever believed in a soul mate, Carter found his in Reagan. If the past few years have taught me anything, it's that they are truly perfect for each other and so blissfully happy.

"Sorry to interrupt. I'm heading out for the night."

They turn their heads to me, but Carter doesn't stop massaging her feet. He unashamedly dotes on her.

In fairness, she does the same for him. They genuinely like each other. They're best friends. I've never heard either of them say anything remotely negative about the other. Separately, they're amazing people. Together, they're a force of nature.

Reagan nods. "Okay. Thanks, Collin. We really appreciate all the extra hours to get it done so quickly."

I smile. "My pleasure. I would do anything for you guys."

"Did everything go well with Jade on the Wander project? She can really help move this along."

I swallow. "Yes. I gave her my vision. She seemed to understand it. She said she'd let me know when it was done for me to look at it."

"Great. She'll have it done for you in no time. She works very efficiently. Do you happen to know if your brother is seeing her?"

I shake my head. "I don't think so. He's seeing her friend, Pandora. I believe he's opening her box."

They both laugh.

"Why do you ask?"

"She mentioned at the office today that she's dickmatized but wouldn't give a name. She said we didn't know the person. I think there's more to it. I've never seen her like this about a guy though."

I nearly break the skin in my mouth as I bite my cheek trying not to smile.

I shake my head. "Sorry. I don't think it's him. His dick isn't very much to get excited about anyway. I got all the family jewels in that department."

Carter chuckles while Reagan smiles. "Okay.

Thanks. He's probably better off. She's not very experienced."

They are so very wrong. I can't help but ask a follow-up question. "Oh, really? What makes you think that?"

"She's never dated. She's never had a boyfriend."

"Ever?"

She shakes her head. "No. Don't get me wrong, she's been with plenty of guys, she's just afraid to commit. She's the female version of you, Collin."

"Hey! I've dated."

"For more than two months?"

"Hmm. No. Fair enough. Good luck with your dickmatized investigation. I'll see you tomorrow."

I make my way home with a giant grin on my face. She's already dickmatized. I love it. I'll definitely slip that in tonight.

I get home, shower, and prepare everything. I slip into a pair of boxer briefs but nothing else. What's the point? She's the one that suggested we meet at ten. That only means one thing. Sex.

At a little after ten, I get a notification of a visitor. I tell the front desk to let her up. If it goes well, maybe I'll add her to my approved visitor list. Shit. Where did that come from?

There's a knock at the door. I hear a female voice from the hallway. "Pizza delivery."

I open the door to Jade in a long coat. I look her up and down. "Where's the pizza?"

"I said *pussy* delivery, not *pizza*."

"I'll need a taste test to see if I want to buy it."

The corner of her mouth raises slightly. "That can be arranged."

I motion for her to come in. She looks me up and down. "Thanks for getting dressed up."

I nod. "You're welcome. I assume you're wearing something similar underneath that jacket."

"Do you have a roommate?"

"I'm thirty-eight. Of course not."

"Then can you please take my coat?"

She unbuttons and removes it, tossing it at me. She throws her shoulders back as she places one hand on her hip.

Holy. Fuck. If I thought Jade in the white bikini would forever be stuck in my spank bank, I was wrong. Jade in blue, lace, see-through lingerie will now forever live there.

"Your outfit matches your eyes."

"I know."

"Your legs are the longest I've ever seen in my life."

"I know."

"You're fucking beautiful."

"I know."

I love her confidence. It's so sexy.

She reaches out and runs her fingertips along the hair below my belly button that disappears into my boxer briefs. I raise an eyebrow at her.

"I've been dying to touch that since you lifted your shirt to wipe your sweat. I'm dying to lick it too, just to confirm it truly is the pathway to paradise."

She's so forward. My dick hardens at the thought.

She notices. "I guess you'd like that."

"I would love that, but I've got other plans for you tonight."

"Is that so?"

I nod.

"What exactly do those plans entail?"

"Punishment."

"Punishment? For what?"

"For coming before I said it was time. I told you that you'd pay for that."

"You know, most men struggle to make women come. They're happy when it happens at all."

"I'm not most men. It sounds like you've been with a bunch of chumps." I toss her coat on my sofa, grab her arm, pin it behind her back, and pull her body flush to mine. "You'll learn to come when I tell you it's time." With my other hand, I run it down the side of her body. "I'm going to own your body. Your pleasure. All of it will bow to my command."

Her breathing picks up. She sucks my lower lip into her mouth, hard, before eventually releasing it.

Keeping her front tight to mine, I start walking toward my bedroom. She's now forced to walk backward, but she manages just fine.

As we approach my bed, I stop and look at her. "We need some rules."

"Like?"

"Do you have hard limits?"

"Hmm. No anal. If the unlikely day ever comes that I care about someone, it will be his."

"You're still an anal virgin. How sweet. What about my fingers?"

"Well, you've already done that to me, so I guess it's fine."

"Okay, what else?"

"That's it."

"Spanking?"

"Fine."

"Paddling?"

"Fine"

"Flogging?"

She visibly swallows. She hasn't done it. "Fine."

"I don't need to ask about being tied up or choking. You seem to like those."

She nods.

"Okay. Pick a safe word. Something that if you say it, I'll stop everything I'm doing."

"How about *stop*?"

"Nope. It needs to be something else. How about *dickmatized*?"

Her eyes widen and I smirk.

She then narrows her eyes at me. "Where did you hear that word?"

"Reagan may have mentioned that you're dickmatized."

"Why would she tell you that?"

"She thought it was with my brother."

She scrunches her nose. "He's not my type."

"I know."

"How do you know?"

"He's too nice."

"Are you ready to be not too nice to me?"

She turns around and bends over, her perfect ass taunting me. "Am I getting spanked for being disobedient?" She wiggles it.

I smile. "You think you know what's about to happen, don't you?"

She returns to me and runs her hands over my chest. "I'm just ready to take my punishment like a good girl, Big Daddy."

I look her up and down. She's the sexiest woman

I've ever seen in my life. It's taking every ounce of restraint I have to not scrap my plans and just take her hard.

I walk over to the table on the side of my bed and hit a button. The post covers disappear down, and smaller posts covered in various types of ties and cuffs are revealed.

Her chin drops. "Holy shit. Is this your red room of pain?"

"Is that a reference to the books women love that became movies no one likes?"

She nods as I make my way back to her.

I move my mouth to her ear and whisper, "He's got nothing on me. She's got nothing on you."

I loop my fingers in the sides of her panties and slowly slide them down her legs. I remove the straps on her lacy top, one at a time. I unclasp it, allowing her huge tits to spill out.

I look her body up and down. "Your body is a dream. It's about to become my playground. Lay down, baby girl."

Without any inhibition, she lays down in the middle of my bed with her arms and legs spread, ready and willing to be tied up. I attach her arms to the padded cuffs on the back posts and her legs to those on the front posts, rendering her completely immobile.

I grab the flogger, but simply place it next to her. I haven't decided whether I'll use it or not, but seeing it there, anticipating it, will turn things up a notch for her.

I straddle her body.

"Collin, take your briefs off. I want to see you."

"Not yet."

"Your dick is about to break through like the Incredible Hulk shedding his clothes."

I look down. She's not wrong.

I lean down and lick up her neck to her ear. "I'm going to break you first." I can hear her breath catch.

I lift my head and look her in the eyes. "I'm going to train you. You'll come on my command."

"I don't think that's how it works."

I smile. "So much to learn, baby girl. I'll be your teacher. Class is in session."

I kiss my way down her long body. I flick each of her pink nipples with my tongue until they begin to harden. I then circle and suck them into my mouth. When they're truly hard and ready, I move down between her legs, lightly running my fingers through her. "It would appear you're very into this."

She whimpers.

I tease her entrance with my fingers, but I don't slide them in. She attempts to move her hips so that my fingers enter her, but she doesn't have much room to wiggle with the way I have her restrained.

I run my fingers a few times from her entrance to her clit, only lightly brushing over both.

She moans, "Collin. Please."

"Oh, you have no clue. You're about to learn what it's like to beg for me to let you come."

I do the same thing over and over. She's getting frustrated. When I know she's reached a boiling point, I slowly slide one finger inside her. Just one and I do so achingly slowly.

I can feel her tighten and tremble around the finger. It's amazing how far a little teasing can go toward a body's reaction. She's in for a lot more teasing though.

I pump that one finger in and out several times. Her breathing picks up. She's getting louder. I curl that finger slightly and her body starts to shake. I can feel her starting to squeeze me harder.

Just as she's about to come, I withdraw my finger.

She gasps. "No!"

"Yes."

She bucks her hip. "Please. I promise to never come without your say-so. Just make me come."

"Not yet. Your lesson has only just begun, baby girl. Big Daddy has big plans for you."

I suck that finger into my mouth, slowly removing it. "Yum. You're delicious."

Her eyes flutter.

I run my fingertips along her body until I'm sure the impending orgasm has mostly receded. I then take two fingers and begin to circle her clit.

She rolls her hips. "Yes. Like that."

I continue circling her bundle of nerves. "You're getting wetter every second I do this."

"Hmm."

"Use your words."

"It feels like I'm about to have a tidal wave of an orgasm, so don't stop this time."

I continue my slow, meticulous circles. As soon as her body starts to shake, I pull my fingers away.

She writhes. "Oh my god. Keep going. I'm almost there."

I smile. "I know, but not until I say so."

Once it's completely receded, I kiss my way around her inner thighs. She keeps trying to adjust her positioning, but I continue to kiss around where I know she's physically aching for touch.

I eventually work my way to where she wants me, licking through her.

"Yes, don't stop. Stay there."

I lick through her over and over, bringing her back to the brink of orgasm before I remove my mouth. She starts to yell, but I move up her body and swallow it down with a deep kiss. I run my tongue through her mouth. Her tongue licks all around mine.

I pull away. "Delicious, right?"

She nods, though she looks defeated.

I reach over, grab for a condom, and remove my briefs. My cock springs free from its confines. I tear open the wrapper and roll the condom down my cock.

She whimpers, "Finally." She has no idea.

I move down her body and run my cock through her, but not into her, over and over until she's close to orgasm, when I again pull away.

"Ahhh! Collin! Enough! I can't take it anymore. Please."

I run through the entire routine of my fingers, mouth, and cock one more time. That's four more times she's brought to the brink of orgasm, only to have it taken away at the last second.

Her face is flushed. She has a thin layer of sweat. Her eyes are watering. She's barely coherent. It's time.

I circle my tip at her entrance. I look up at her watery eyes. She croaks out, "Collin, please."

I slowly enter her, one tight, wet inch at a time, until I'm all the way in. I lean forward and wrap my hand around her throat. I give it a firm squeeze. Without moving my cock in the slightest, I lean down and whisper, "Come. Now."

Her body jerks and she spasms around my unmoving cock. She's screaming down the building. Her pussy is oozing juices onto me.

I begin my movements, further drawing out her orgasm. She's squeezing my cock so tight.

Her back arches. "Oh god, Collin, it won't stop."

"That's it. Keep going." I maintain the pressure around her neck.

The spasms roll on and on as I thrust into her, over and over. Her eyeballs have rolled to the back of her head. Her whole body is jerking uncontrollably. It's the sexiest thing I've ever seen.

She eventually starts to come down from what is likely the longest orgasm I've ever witnessed. I haven't let up on my thrusts or grip on her neck at all though I think she needs a moment.

I slow down everything. She's completely out of breath and out of energy. Her chest is rising and falling at a rapid pace.

She breathes, "Holy shit. I've never come so hard. I can't move, and it has nothing to do with the cuffs. My whole body feels like jelly."

I smile. "And we're not done yet."

Her eyes widen. "What? You didn't come? How is that possible?"

I shake my head. "Not yet. And you're not done either."

"Collin, I may not be able to come again for a year after that orgasm."

I can't help but laugh. "You're going to come again in the next ten minutes, as soon as I tell you to."

"I honestly don't think I have anything left in me."

"You do. I promise. Do you trust me with your pleasure?"

She blinks a few times but then nods her head.

I pull out, reach down, and unfasten her leg restraints. I throw one leg over my shoulder as I reenter her. She wraps the remaining leg around me.

I rub her face with my thumb. "Are you okay?"

She nods again.

I begin my movements again, pushing deep inside her. Long, hard thrusts. My hips are brutalizing her and she's loving every minute of it.

She squeezes her eyes shut and tightens her leg around me. She lifts her hips, trying to meet my thrusts with those of her own. "Ah, Collin."

Without losing a stroke, I reach my head down and suck her wide nipple into my mouth. Her moaning is getting louder. She has another orgasm in her. I knew she did.

I'm getting close. Watching her get built up and brought down was hot as hell. Her eventual orgasm was fucking perfection.

I feel my spine start to tingle. I reach my thumb down and circle her clit. "Time to come, baby girl. Now."

She digs her heel into my lower back. Her body convulses and she screams as she comes again. This time I go over the edge with her.

I continue to work her through her orgasm. It's

not as long as the first, though still plenty long. She's going to be totally spent.

As her screams begin to subside, I take her lips in mine. Unlike the hard fucking, the kiss is soft. It's almost shockingly intimate. I don't usually have the desire to kiss a woman after I come, but for some reason I do right now.

At some point, she pulls out of the kiss and turns her head to the side. She croaks out, "Untie me."

"What's wrong?"

"It's over. I need to get home."

I shake my head. "No. You must be exhausted. Let me feed you. I can draw us a bath. I want to take care of you."

"No. I want to leave."

I don't understand what's happening. "Did I hurt you?"

"No, Collin. Please just untie me."

"You're upset. I don't want you to leave like this."

She looks me in the eyes, "Dickmatized."

I nod. "Okay, I'll untie you. Please just consider staying for a little while. You're going to be tired and sore. I want to care for you. It's important to me."

I pull out of her, lift off her, and then untie her wrists. As soon as she's free, she springs up and looks for her belongings. Her legs are wobbling, but she keeps moving.

"Where's my coat?"

I stand. "It's on the couch where we left it. You don't need to rush out."

"Yes, I do. I know what we are."

She doesn't bother to put back on her lingerie. She

practically sprints to my living room and slides into her coat. She places the lingerie in the coat pocket.

She heads to the door and looks back at me, standing naked in my bedroom doorway in a state of confusion. "Thanks for a good time. I'll see you around."

She walks out and closes the door behind her.

What the hell just happened?

CHAPTER ELEVEN

JADE

I texted Dr. Pearl on my way home last night. I told her I needed a session right away. She said she could talk just before her first appointment of the day, which is at eight, so we're talking at seven. I'm going to the office to do it from there and then start my workday.

I get in early. No one else is here. I grab a cup of coffee. I don't even drink coffee, but I got zero sleep last night, so I think I'll need caffeine today.

I set up my laptop in anticipation of her video call. It comes in right at seven on the nose. I accept the call.

She looks concerned. "Jade? Are you okay? Never once in over fourteen years together have you asked for an appointment between appointments. You've got me a little worried, sweetheart."

"I just missed your face."

She narrows her eyes. "I don't think that's it." She looks closer at her screen. "Are you on a sofa laying down?" She sounds shocked.

"Yes. Isn't that what you're supposed to do in therapy? Lay on the couch and confess your deepest, darkest thoughts?"

"Is that what's happening? You're having deep, dark thoughts?"

I'm quiet.

"Jade, you asked for this meeting, not me. Obviously something is on your mind. Spit it out."

"That's not very therapist-like of you. Aren't you supposed to be nice and slowly draw things out of me at my pace?"

"Jade, we're over fourteen years into this. I think we can do away with pleasantries and *normal* therapy etiquette. You've told me on multiple occasions not to *bullshit* you. This is me cutting out the bullshit. You are the only patient of mine that I'm comfortable saying this to; tell me what the fuck is going on."

"You're cursing too? Wow. I feel so special."

She yells, "Out with it."

"Okay, okay. Calm your tits. I'm freaking out. I had sex last night."

"You have sex all the time. That's nothing new."

I take a deep breath.

"It was mind-blowing, life-altering sex."

She twists her lips. "I'm not sure whether to be concerned or jealous."

I can't help but let out a laugh. She's like eighty years old. Or maybe sixty, but it's all the same to me.

"Is Mr. Pearl not giving it to you good?"

"We're not here to talk about my sex life. We're talking about yours."

"But you admit you have one."

"I'm fifty-five, not a hundred and five."

"You're only fifty-five?"

She scowls at me. "Don't start with me, Jade. It's very early."

"Ugh. Fine. Can I be frank?"

"Have you ever not been?"

I giggle. "True." I take another breath. "I may have set a world record for the longest, most intense orgasm ever recorded. It may have registered on one of those earthquake scales."

"The Richter Scale?"

"Yes, that's the one."

"And this is bad because?"

"It was so fucking intimate. I couldn't deal. I completely flipped out."

"Oh no. What did you do?"

"He was so...so...sweet afterward." I say *sweet* like it's a dirty word. "First, he kissed me. When it was over. I've never kissed a man when it's over. Then he wanted to take care of me, but I bolted. I didn't even put my clothes back on. I threw on my coat and ran out. Well, I didn't have clothes, just some sexy lingerie, but I shoved it all in my pocket and ran out the door as quickly as I could."

"Was the sex rough?"

"Yes, why do you ask?"

"For men who like it rough, gentle aftercare is often simply part of their routine."

"So you don't think it was something special he was doing for me?" That actually makes me feel better about it.

"I'm not saying it wasn't special for you, but aftercare is in fact often part of the routine for men who like it rough."

"Fuck. Lie to me. Tell me I wasn't special."

"You're legitimately the only person in the world who doesn't want to be made to feel special."

"I aim to be different."

"Can we back up for a minute? I'd like a little background on this man. Tell me about him."

"Okay, but you may not like it."

"I'm not here to judge."

"Don't piss on my head and tell me it's raining. You judge me all the time."

"I've never heard that expression."

"It's a good one. You're welcome."

"It's quite...ladylike."

"Sarcasm is the lowest form of wit, Dr. Pearl."

She smiles. "Sarcasm is my love language, Jade. Now, tell me about him."

I sigh. "He's *the* guy."

"I'm confused. Which guy?"

"The one who hit and ran on me four years ago. The one who I fucked in a closet at Reagan's party and then he disappeared seconds later."

"Let me get this straight. You were upset..."

"I was never upset."

"You were...annoyed that he left so abruptly four years ago. Then last night he wanted you to stick around so he could care for you, and now that upsets you?"

"Are you going to take away my therapy gold star? I've told a lot of people that it's coming."

She smiles. "I might have to." Her smile fades into a look of concern. "What is this about? Do you have feelings for him?"

"No, of course not. I don't do feelings."

She's quiet for a moment. "I think you might. Maybe you just don't know how to recognize it since you've never allowed yourself to care for any man in the past."

Silence.

"Do you want to see him again? Be honest. No Jade-like bullshit."

"I love when you talk dirty to me."

"Jade."

"Ugh. Fine. Yes, I want to see him again."

"Do you want to have sex with him again?"

"If you were given the greatest orgasm known to mankind, would you want seconds?"

"Fair enough. What's wrong with considering a relationship with him?"

"One, I don't do relationships. Two, neither does he."

"Well then, maybe you each found your match. Tell me more about him."

"He's hot as hell."

"Something more substantive.

"Well...he's older."

"How old?"

I mumble, "Thirty-eight."

"That's not terrible. You've certainly done worse."

"You're a fucking judgy therapist."

"You've asked me not to *blow smoke up your ass* on multiple occasions."

"Yes, I've been with older, but it's complicated. He's... he's Carter's best friend."

She closes her eyes and lets out a long breath. She eventually reopens them. "You're telling me that you've just had the best sex of your life, and have potentially developed feelings for, a man who is the best friend of your cousin's husband, your boss, who you've had a huge crush on for four years? Yes, consider the gold star off the table."

"You make it sound worse than it is. There's good news though."

"I can't wait for this."

"I think my crush on Carter has waned. We were all out recently and I didn't spend the night staring at him or masturbate to him when I got home."

"What did you do instead?"

"I stared at Collin and then masturbated to him when I got home."

"Who's Collin?"

I give her an annoyed look. "Keep up. He's the best sex guy."

"Oh, got it. And last night is the first time you've had sex with him in four years?"

I bite my lip.

"Oh boy. What did I miss?"

"After the night I saw him out, we had hot sex in Carter and Reagan's house when they weren't home. Then we mutually masturbated on a video call the other night. Oh, and we're doing a project together at work."

"Do I need to lecture you on how dumb it is to expose yourself in a video call?"

Why does everyone seem to focus on this?

"I've got bigger problems than that."

"I won't begin to touch on the fact that the two of you had sex in Carter and Reagan's house."

"It's not as bad as it sounds."

"I hope it wasn't in their bed."

"No, in their baby's nursery."

"You had sex in a baby's nursery."

"It's not born yet. It's not like it saw anything."

She pinches the bridge on the top of her nose. "Am I missing any other piece of this convoluted puzzle?"

"Umm, just one."

"Let me get a Valium for this."

"Dr. Pearl, I'm feeling very judged."

She smiles. "Hit me with it. It can't get much worse."

"Collin definitely has had a longtime crush on Reagan."

She closes her eyes again. "I could write a book on you, Jade. A best-seller."

"Would that get me my gold star back?"

CHAPTER TWELVE

COLLIN

I haven't heard from Jade in over a week, despite me sending a handful of texts, but today we have a meeting to look through the virtual models she designed for our project. She had her assistant call me to make the appointment.

I'm greeted by that assistant when I arrive. "Ms. McGinley is just finishing up another meeting. She'll be out in a moment."

I smile. "Thanks, Minnie."

About ten minutes later, Jade's door opens, and she walks out with a young, decent-looking guy. He's probably in his mid to late twenties.

He's looking at her practically with hearts in his eyes. It's longing. He's into her. *Very* into her. I don't like it at all. I've never been the jealous type, but that's what I'm feeling right now.

She gives him a fake smile. "Thanks for coming by,

Kyle. Next time, you can just email me these numbers. You don't need to come all the way to my office."

She's clearly telling him to fuck off. I love it. Unfortunately, he doesn't get the social cue. He rubs her arm and smiles. "But then we wouldn't get to spend time together."

Because Jade is, well, Jade, she peels his hand off her with a look of disgust. "Like I said, send an email next time. And don't ever touch a woman without invitation."

She doesn't take crap from anyone. God, she's sexy.

She turns her head to me. "Collin." She nods toward her door. "Let's go."

We walk into her office, leaving a stunned Kyle behind. Jade keeps the door wide open.

She's in a conservative black pantsuit, not nearly as sexy as the pink one she was wearing the last time I met with her.

We quietly sit on her sofa, and I turn to her. "You still look hot, even though I know you're trying not to."

She sighs. "Not here, Collin. I'm not up for this. Not today."

"Then where? You won't return my texts. What happened the other night? What spooked you?"

She stands and closes the door. She turns back to me. "Why are you complaining? Aren't you a hit-and-run guy? Shouldn't you be happy that I didn't want to stay after the sex? That I didn't need anything else from you?"

"Did you not have a good time? Was it too much? Was I too much?"

She runs her fingers through her hair in some sort

of turmoil. "It's not that. The sex was amazing. You know it was."

"Then what was it?"

"Honestly, the aftercare. That's too intimate for me. I'm not looking for intimacy. This is supposed to be sex only. A mutual release. That's it."

I start laughing.

She's looking at me like I'm crazy. "Why are you laughing?"

"I wanted to help you clean up and that's why you abruptly left and then ghosted me? That's fucked up."

"That's me. I'm fucked up."

"If I promise not to care for you, can we have a repeat of the other night?"

"You know I'm not a relationship person, Collin. Just fucking. No dinners or any relationship shit. No post-coital tenderness. Your penis in my vagina. That's it. That's all I'm capable of. That's all I want from you."

"Is your ass still off the table?"

She nods. "Yes. Consider it permanently off the table to you."

"I think you'd like it."

"Collin."

"Fine. Only pussy deliveries. Can we also order pizza?"

She smiles. "I'll think about it."

"So we're doing this? No strings sex. No relationship-like behavior. My P in your V and that's it?"

"Correct."

I smile. I hit the jackpot.

I stand and roughly pull her to me. I begin to unbutton her pants.

"What are you doing?"

"I need to touch you. To taste you. A week is a long time for me. My P didn't want any V but yours."

She doesn't move away, so I slip my fingers inside her panties and roughly sink them inside her. She throws her head back. "Ah, Collin."

"Don't pretend you don't like it, baby girl. My soaked hand tells me otherwise."

She fists my shirt as I move in and out of her, quickly bringing her to orgasm. When she's done, I button her back up and then make a show of licking each and every finger. "Sometimes I need appetizers before my pizza deliveries."

She motions toward my pants. "Are you going to have a giant boner throughout our whole meeting?"

I look down. "Probably." I sniff. "I smell your come. It drives me wild."

She bites her lip. I pull her lip out and run my fingers along it. "Are you going to wrap those lips around Big Daddy's cock tonight?"

She looks up at me with those blue eyes and nods.

I do as she wants and break the intimate moment. I sit down on the sofa and, in a businesslike manner, say, "Let's get to work."

She hesitates for a moment before nodding and bringing everything up on the screen in her office. She runs me through all of her virtual modeling created based on what I described to her last week.

When it's over, I sit in shock. "Holy. Shit. You're *really* good at your job."

She just gives me a smug look. "I know. I'm a bit of a savant."

"I didn't even know this kind of technology existed. It will help move things along so much faster. The permitting process alone will be expedited and save so much time and money."

She gives a knowing nod. "I know. That's why I get the big bucks. If you add about a million or so square feet, you'll realize the type of projects I normally work on."

"Are you big-timing me?"

"I'm just telling you how it is." She bats her eyelashes. "Do you have any modifications, sir?"

"No, but I like when you call me sir."

She smiles. "I'll see you at around ten, sir."

A FEW MINUTES AFTER TEN, there's a knock at my door. I decide to just answer naked this time. She wants *sex only*, that's what she'll get.

I yell, "Who is it?"

"Pizza delivery. Extra anchovies." I laugh at the eighty's movie reference where *extra anchovies* meant something else. Sex.

I open the door. She looks me up and down. "I like this outfit even better."

"I thought you might like it." I motion for her to come in.

She walks in, closes the door, peels off her jacket to reveal that she's also naked, and then drops right down to her knees in front of me, grabbing my cock along the way.

"That's quite an entrance."

She echoes my earlier words and, in her special sassy way, says, "I thought you might like it."

She immediately moves her head down and licks all around my balls, eventually taking them into her mouth, one at a time. She runs her hand up and down my length while continuing to pay glorious attention to my balls.

She then begins a slow path with her tongue to my tip. She licks every vein and crevice, circling and flicking my piercing a few times along the way.

She sucks my tip into her mouth while holding my balls with one hand and the base of my cock with her other. She moves my cock deeper and deeper until I hit the very back of her throat.

I twist my fingers through her silky hair and grab on for dear life.

I'm worked into a complete and total frenzy with her slow pace, moving my cock in and out of her mouth, but taking it so very deep, and sucking it so very hard. She knows when to squeeze, she knows when to suck, and she knows when to swirl her tongue. Fuck, she's good at this.

She's got me close to orgasm in no time. I give her the warning, but she doesn't move. She swallows every last drop of me as I come hard down her throat.

When she's done, she stands, licking her lips. "What's your turnaround time? I don't know how it works for the elderly. Do I have time to paint my nails?"

"You think you're so funny, don't you?"

She smiles. The beautiful smile that tells you she's up to no good.

I lift her up, throw her over my shoulder, turn toward my bedroom, and smack her ass hard. She screeches.

"You're going to pay for that comment."

She smacks my ass in return and says, "Punish me, Big Daddy."

CHAPTER THIRTEEN

TWO MONTHS LATER

JADE

The past two months with Collin have sexually been the best of my life. I've learned things about my own body that I frankly didn't know. He's opened my eyes to so much pleasure. More than I could have ever imagined possible.

I've always enjoyed sex, but now I find myself a bit addicted to the way he makes my body feel.

It's never quick. He always draws it out. And he's definitely trained me to come when he says so. There's something immensely sexy about that. He owns my body in a way I didn't know was possible.

We get together for late-night rendezvous four or five times a week. We're usually at his place, which I prefer. I can control my leaving as soon as we're done. When we're at my place, he attempts to linger. I admit that there are moments when I don't mind spending time with him. He's hysterical. He makes me laugh. But I don't want us getting too comfortable. This will come to an end at some point, and I don't need any emotions involved. At least that's what I'm telling myself.

I can admit that I often find myself wondering where I go from Collin. No one is sexier than him. No one makes me laugh like him. And no one has ever made me come as hard as he does.

I'm out at a club with Pandora and a few other friends tonight. I told Collin I'd likely come over later, but also told him that if I meet someone else tonight, I'll shoot him a text. He didn't care for that, but it's too bad. It's not like we're exclusive. We're not in a relationship. I'm not actively looking for someone else, but he needs to know that it's always a possibility. I need to keep him at arm's length.

We've had a few drinks. There are a ton of people here. I'm getting hit on, but I'm just not into them. I hate that I'd rather be in bed with Collin right now than out having drinks and fun like a normal twenty-two-year-old.

Some sleazy guy has his hands on my hips on the dance floor. I'd rather they were Collin's. I quickly push him away and let him know he's got no chance.

I feel my phone buzz. I smile. I bet it's Collin wanting me to come over right away. I think I made him wait long enough. It's time to feed the orgasm beast he's created.

I pull out my phone to see a text from my mother.

Mom: Call me as soon as you can.

COLLIN

Like a fucking chump, I'm sitting by my phone hoping Jade texts that she's on her way over. How did I end up like this? I used to be the one making women sit around waiting for me to call. Now I'm the one waiting, hoping that she makes time for me. My entire evening is dependent on Jade texting to tell me if she's coming over.

I should have gone out tonight, but I just don't have the will. Other women don't interest me anymore. I want Jade, and only Jade, in my bed.

She's exactly like I used to be. She's in and out, never stays, and barely wants to talk. It's sex—great sex—and then a quick exit. Always.

While the sex and the passion are incredible, she never wants to stick around for so much as a kiss after we're done.

Most of our fun banter comes via text while we're making plans to meet, or the moments before we get into bed. She makes me laugh. I love her brashness.

Finally, my text tone rings. I excitedly look down at my phone only to be met with disappointment.

> Jade: Sorry. Not going to make it. Rough night.

> Me: Is everything okay?

> Jade: I'll be fine. I'll suck your dick tomorrow, don't worry.

> Me: I wasn't worried about my enormously engorged dick. I want to know if you're okay.

Jade: It's my mom. Divorce is a bitch. That's why I'm never getting married.

Me: Gotcha. I assume you're with her. Give her my best.

Jade: She's in New York. She's just upset so I'm upset. It's a buzz kill. I came home early. Not up for the whole party scene tonight.

Twenty minutes later I'm knocking on her door. She opens it in sweatpants and a sweatshirt. I've never seen her dressed like this. It's cute. She's beautiful no matter what she's wearing.

She looks shocked to see me. In an annoyed voice, she says, "Collin? What are you doing here? I told you I wasn't down to fuck tonight."

I hold up a brown bag. "I know. I brought reinforcements."

She narrows her eyes at me. "What do you have in there?"

"Duh, Rocky Road ice cream."

I don't think she could have a more surprised look on her face right now if I told her there was a dead body in the bag.

"How did you know that it's my favorite?"

"You mentioned it was your comfort food once."

She has an expression on her face that I can't quite work out. Something between confused and touched. I'm hoping it's the latter.

She opens the door wider in invitation. "I'm warning you; I'm not going to be very good company. I'm in a mood."

"It's okay. Why don't we just watch a movie and eat ice cream."

She slowly nods. "Thanks, Collin. This is really nice of you. What movie do you want to watch? You can pick."

"Hmm. How about *Loverboy*?"

She stops short. "What the fuck? How do you know I love that stupid, old movie?"

"Extra anchovies. I understood the pop culture reference. And it's not that old. I was alive when it came out."

She smiles. "I wasn't. Not even close."

"If you're mean to me, I won't share any of the Rocky Road with you."

She gasps. "You better have brought your own. I'm not sharing with you."

I smile as I pull two pints and two spoons out of the bag.

We sit and start the movie. The premise is ridiculous. I turn to her. "You do realize that this movie somehow makes it okay, and romantic, that he whored himself out to hundreds of women just to make money to get back to his girlfriend?"

She giggles. "You don't think it's sweet?"

"What if it were the opposite? Am I the only feminist here? Are there any movies that glorify female hookers like this movie does for male hookers?"

She thinks for a moment and then gives me a confident smile. "Yes. *Pretty* fucking *Woman*."

I stare at her for a few seconds. "I see. I stand corrected. Carry on with your male hooker movie."

She gloats as she turns her attention back to the movie.

After she finishes the entire pint, she leans her head onto me. I don't think she realizes she's doing it. We've had sex countless times at this point, but this may be the most intimate thing she's ever done.

I wrap my arm around her and subtly take in her unique Jade scent that I've come to love so much. I realize that I'm exactly where I want to be, with the person I want to be with.

When the movie is over, I look down and she's fast asleep on my chest. I run my hand up and down her natural golden hair a few times. It's so soft. I can smell her shampoo. This is nice.

I contemplate just sleeping right here, but I know what it will do to my back in the morning.

I carefully carry her into her bedroom and lay her on the bed. Hmm. I wonder if she'll get hot in her sleep. I don't think I can get her sweatshirt off without waking her, but her sweatpants should be easy. I slowly slide them off and then tuck her into bed.

I'm about to leave when I realize that I don't want to. I want to know what it's like to sleep with her. To hold her in my arms all night. To wake up with her in the morning.

I remove all of my clothes except my boxer briefs and climb into bed. I pull her tight into my arms and fall into a peaceful sleep.

CHAPTER FOURTEEN

JADE

I wake in the morning in a way I've never awakened before. On a man's chest. A broad, sexy chest.

I try to remember what I did last night. Did I get blackout drunk? I inhale. I can smell that it's Collin's chest. Did I get drunk and booty-call him?

No, my mom called me in tears about how terrible Rick is taking the divorce. He's mistreating her. I spent an hour on the phone with her, talking her off the ledge. I ended up leaving the club immediately and taking a cab home, all while still talking to her. I haven't heard her this upset in a long time. I hate that I couldn't be with her.

It killed my desire to go to Collin's for a booty call, so I texted him to cancel. Then Collin showed up with my favorite ice cream, which may have been the nicest thing any man has ever done for me. Then we started watching *Loverboy*. I don't remember seeing the shitshow of an ending, when the male lead's girlfriend easily accepts that he whored himself out all summer.

I must have fallen asleep, and Collin put me in bed. I lift the blankets. And he removed my pants. I look over at his body. And all of his clothes.

I try to roll off him, but he squeezes me tight. He sleepily whispers, "Just a few more minutes. This is nice. You always rush out. Let me hold you a little longer. Please."

After what he did for me last night, how can I deny him this? So, I stay.

Eventually I look up. He looks so content. I can't help but turn my head and kiss his chest. I kiss it some more. And then up his neck. I keep going until I eventually reach his lips.

Without opening his eyes, he says, "My dick is cold. Do you know anywhere I can warm it? Preferably to about ninety-eight point six degrees."

I smile as I begin to kiss him.

He rubs his hands on my body as his eyes open. He looks into mine. "You don't have to if you're not up for it."

I climb on top of him. "I want to."

He lifts my sweatshirt over my head, revealing my bare chest to him. He runs his hands up and down the sides of my body. "You're so beautiful."

I run my fingertips over his scruff. "So are you."

He tugs on my panties. "These are in my way."

"Then rip them off me."

And he does.

NOT ONLY DID he sleep over, but we had morning sex and then took a long shower together. Our first. My rules of engagement are getting shaky. I just enjoy being with him.

The sex is amazing, and he makes me laugh. I love our banter. I love that he laughs at my jokes too. My usual over-the-top demeanor never seems to be too much for him.

He mentioned that he was invited to our Sunday night family dinner tonight. As long as I've been a part of this family, dinners at Aunt Darian and Jackson's house have been a Sunday night staple. I rarely miss one. I can admit that I absolutely love it. Craving family my whole life and now having a big one is everything to me. And I hit the jackpot in the one I have. They're fun and loving. I laugh my ass off at every meal.

Dad and Melissa usually pick me up on their way. They live in a giant condo in the city not far from me, while Aunt Darian and Jackson live in the suburbs about twenty-five minutes away. Obviously, I wouldn't ever ride there with Collin, so I don't.

I'm waiting in front of my building for them. When they pull up, I open the car door and my father immediately says, "That skirt is too short. Go change."

I roll my eyes and get in the car. "No, it's not. Don't be such a baby. Melissa bought me this skirt."

He side-eyes Melissa and she smiles. "What? Her legs are a mile long. She looks amazing in short skirts. It doesn't seem to bother you when I wear short skirts."

"She'd look better in ankle-length skirts. You both would."

Melissa and I both laugh at his absurdity.

On the car ride, Melissa turns back and asks her standard question, "Are you seeing anyone?"

Before I can answer, Dad says, "She's too young to date."

Melissa sighs, and we smile at each other. "No, I sit home at night and braid my friends' hair. Then we have pillow fights and fall asleep on the floor in our panties after a fit of giggles."

Melissa silently laughs. Dad says, "That sounds fun, honey."

He's clueless. "To answer your question, no, I'm not seeing anyone. I prefer gang bangs in the back of motorcycle club bars. It's more up my alley, so to speak."

Melissa smiles and shakes her head while I see my father's face redden. Melissa slaps his arm. "Declan, one day, maybe soon, she's going to come home with someone and you're going to have to manage it."

"She can get married at fifty, like I did."

I pat his shoulder. "That works for me, Dad."

We arrive to our weekly sea of warm welcomes. Collin is already there looking scrumptious in ass-hugging black jeans and a white sweater. I can't help but pinch that ass a few times when no one is looking.

We sit down for Chinese food, which is usually what we eat when Darian doesn't feel like cooking or Jackson isn't grilling. She knows what everyone likes at this point, so she preorders everything. The kids already ate and are in the big playroom Jackson had done for them.

Somehow, I'm seated next to Collin. I might have to resist the urge to touch him, though I wouldn't mind if he were to touch me.

Melissa says, "My friend Izzy is finally moving out of her house and into the city. She told Ryder and Austin that the basement furniture isn't coming with her. They freaked out. They said that they and half their friends lost their virginity on that couch, and that she needs to keep it as a memento." She looks around. "Were all of you having sex at home in high school? I didn't realize that it goes on in the house. Obviously, I know it happens for some, but at home?"

Ryder and Austin are twin sons of one of Melissa's oldest friends. They are about two or three years older than me. They're cute, I've seen them around, but they're a little young for me.

Darian manages to answer for her girls. "Harley and Reagan were. Skylar wasn't. She didn't lose her virginity until college."

Reagan smiles. "I officially have the only mother on the planet that can and would answer that question."

Skylar shakes her head. "Thanks for outing me, Mom. I'm sure everyone here needed to know that I was a virgin when I left for college."

Lance lifts her hand and kisses it. "I think it's adorable. I don't mind one bit, sweets." He winks at her.

Harley hems and haws. "I admittedly was having sex while in high school, but I'm not sure it was in the house though. I don't remember."

Reagan shakes her head. "I can name at least two guys you slept with in the house."

Harley challenges, "Who?"

"Billy Tanner in the basement after homecoming, and Steven Welsh in Mom and Dad's shower when they went to New York City for a weekend."

Harley twists her lips and then mumbles, "Oh, right."

Darian turns to her. "In my shower? Really?"

Reagan nods. "I did too. You had the best shower. It was huge, with all those shower heads and sprays."

Darian looks appalled. "I have that in this house too. Have you done it in my shower here?"

Reagan and Carter look at each other and smile.

Jackson shakes his head. "Oh god. We need a hazmat crew in here tomorrow."

A bunch of us are laughing. Melissa turns to her boys. "What about you guys? I assume Trevor was, but what about you, Hayden and Payton?"

Trevor pinches his eyebrows together. "Why do you assume I was?"

Melissa pats his head. "Honey, you were always a manwhore. I knew that was going to be the case at a very young age. When you were ten, you started coming on to my friends. It's not a great shock to me that you ended up with a woman my age."

Cassandra clears her throat. "I'm a year younger than you."

Melissa shakes her head in exasperation, as she often does with Cassandra.

Hayden says, "Trevor was having sex in college dorms and apartments of women older than Jade when he was in high school. He didn't need our house. He had plenty of other options."

Trevor turns to him. "I also had sex in the house, unlike you who saved yourself for Jess." Hayden and Jess turn to each other and smile like they have a secret. Ooh. I wonder what that's about.

Hayden turns back to the table and says, "I'll have you know that I was *not* a virgin when I graduated from high school, but I did not do it in the house."

Trevor asks, "With who? I didn't know this."

Hayden shakes his head. "None of your business."

Payton jokingly covers Kylie's ears. "I had sex in the house in high school."

All heads turn to me. Dad says, "Don't even think about answering that question."

I smile and loudly whisper, "At both houses, Mom's *and* Dad's."

Dad warns, "Jade."

I loudly whisper again, "With different guys. *Several* different guys."

I see Collin trying to hold in his laughter next to me. Under the table, he squeezes my leg.

Dad gives me the death stare from across the table. I simply smile at him.

The dinner topic changes to a more normal conversation. Well, normal for other families. Collin's calloused hand is now moving up and under the flowy skirt I'm wearing.

He leans over and whispers, "Did you wear this skirt for me? It seems like an invitation."

I give him a little side-eye and a small smirk as I spread my legs a bit. While covering my mouth with my hand, I whisper back, "The forbidden possibilities of this evening may have crossed my mind. If you keep going, you'll find that I'm not wearing any pant—"

Before I even finish that sentence, his fingers sink into me. I have to bite my lip not to let out a moan. He starts off slow, gradually moving deeper and deeper, hitting the right spot. He knows my body well at this point and is certainly using that to his advantage.

He starts pumping them faster and faster, all while maintaining a calm demeanor at the table. Damn it. Why is he so good at under-the-table finger-fucking?

Carter looks at Collin. "How's the Wander property coming?"

Collin's thumb moves to my clit while he manages to answer, "Great. We broke ground this week. Jade's model expedited things. She really knows how to take it to the next level."

Reagan looks at me with pride as I try to hide the fact that I'm about to have an orgasm at the dinner table.

I hit the table, while I manage to spit out, "So good...his ideas were sooo good."

I grab my water and down it all in one go just to hide my face. There's no way I'm not completely flushed. Please let the attention go away from me.

Fortunately, I'm heard, and they start talking about the babies and the fact that their due dates are close to the big fishing trip. I don't hear the rest of what they say because I'm biting my napkin trying not to scream into my impending orgasm.

Collin leans over and whispers in my ear, "Come now, baby girl."

I grip the table and close my eyes as I orgasm on his command like the trained puppy dog I've become. The power he has over my body is beyond comprehension.

I do my best to contain any noises that are begging to sneak out of my mouth. I try to keep my body from shaking too much.

As I begin to regain my senses, I look around, hoping I didn't give myself away. I don't think I did. Collin is smirking, but nothing else seems off. Even Dad is listening to whatever conversation is happening at the table right now. I certainly have no clue what it is.

When I'm done, Collin pulls his fingers out and sucks them into his mouth. "Where is this food from, Darian? It's finger-licking good."

I see the corner of his mouth raise again. I whisper, "You're going to pay for that."

He winks at me.

Carter's attention turns to Collin again. "Are you seeing someone?"

He shakes his head. "No. Why do you ask?"

"You're lying."

That gets my attention.

"No, I'm not."

"Yes, you are. You're scratching your neck. You always scratch it when you lie." He *is* scratching his neck. "It's endearing that you can't handle lying, so you have a tell. It's also why it's easy to beat you at poker. You're obviously seeing someone. You haven't been out in months."

Collin plays it cool. "No, Braden is still seeing that girl Pandora. You guys aren't out at all lately. I just don't have anyone to go with." He starts to move his hand to his neck, but I discreetly grab it and hold it down. "Honestly, I'm focused on the work on our new venture right now. I want it to be successful."

Carter nods, though he's clearly skeptical. "Anyway, I asked you here for a reason tonight." He grabs Reagan's hand. "We both did." He smiles at Reagan and then turns back our way. "Collin and Jade, we'd like to ask you to be the godparents for our baby."

My eyes widen. I'm speechless.

Collin stands and walks around the table to hug them both. He smiles. "I'm so honored. Thank you."

When the shock wears off, I walk around and hug them as well. I say, "Are you sure you want me? What about Harley and Skylar?"

Reagan looks at me. "I've spoken with them. They're okay with it. We'd like it to be you." I turn to Harley and Skylar and they both smile and nod in agreement.

I begin to tear. Dammit with people trying to make me

cry lately. "I'm honored. Thank you. Do I inherit your fortune too?"

They both laugh.

WHEN DINNER IS OVER, we're all sitting in the living room talking, as we normally do. I'm completely distracted by Collin and thoughts of those rough hands on my body. He's so ridiculously hot, and so ridiculously talented. My body is overheating simply being in the same room as him.

I excuse myself to the restroom. I need to splash some water on my face. It's not easy to be around him but not be with him. I hate that I feel this way. Why am I so damn attracted to him? I know why. He's hot and amazing in bed. Yep, it's the sex. The orgasms he gives me over and over again. That's it. That's all it is.

The bathroom door opens, and he walks in. Without a word, he takes my face in his hands and kisses me. His lips on mine, his tongue meeting mine, it's all so perfect and familiar now.

I can't help but rub my body on his as I wrap my arms around his waist and kiss him back.

He ends the kiss but leaves his forehead on mine. "I need to be with you. Inside you."

"I feel the same, but everyone will talk for another hour or two. They always do."

"I've had to pull my sweater down over my dick the whole time. He's ready to bust out for you."

I look down. He's not wrong. That monster isn't easy to hide.

He rubs his fingers under my nose. "Sniff." I inhale

deeply. "Your scent is on my fingers. It's driving me wild. I keep smelling them. We need to get out of here."

I move my head away from his and nod. "Follow my lead."

We separately exit the bathroom. After about five more minutes in the living room, I stand. "I had a late night last night." I turn to Dad and Melissa. "You guys stay. I'm going to grab an Uber home."

Dad stands. "It's no problem. We'll take you."

Collin interrupts. "Actually, I need to head out too. I have some things to hammer out." I catch the small smile on his lips. He turns his head to me. "Jade, where do you live? I'm sure I can drop you."

I tell him, even though he already knows.

"Oh, that's right on my way. It's no problem at all."

Dad looks at Collin with skepticism. "Straight home, Fitz. You take her straight home."

Collin salutes. "Sir, yes sir. I promise not to sell her on the black market during the twenty-minute ride home."

Dad narrows his eyes at Collin, but I kiss his cheek. "Don't worry. I'll see you later, Dad."

We both say our thank yous and goodbyes to everyone, and quickly exit the house.

The second we pull out of the driveway, I unbutton and unzip his pants, pulling out his straining hard cock.

He has the most beautiful dick. It's long, thick, and straight, with a huge head. And that piercing does things to my body I didn't know were possible. The best thing about it is that it's *always* ready to go.

I immediately take him deep into my mouth. He gathers my hair in his hand and pushes my head down as far as he can. "I want you choking on my cock. Take it deep. I know you can. I don't want you to be able to breathe."

I can't believe how much that talk turns me on, but it does. I deep-throat him the whole ride until he comes down my throat.

We practically explode through his front door, leaving a trail of clothes on our way to the bedroom. Even with our lips locked, we manage to get completely naked before we get to his bed.

He breaks the kiss and presses the button, exposing the posts with cuffs. I immediately get on my back, itching for him to tether me. "Tie me up, Big Daddy. Have your wicked way with me."

He grabs my hips and flips me over. He whispers in my ear, "I'm taking baby girl from behind tonight."

Shivers of anticipation make their way down my entire body. He locks my wrists, using the longer cuffs which give me more mobility. He doesn't tie my ankles this time. He lifts my hips in the air, so my knees are on the bed, and then smacks my ass. My pussy is weeping for him.

He fumbles around in the drawer next to his bed and places the flogger next to me. He's done that many times throughout our months together, but he's never used it. I have no idea what he has planned. I never do. I think that's half the excitement. The other half is feeling safe in the knowledge that amazing orgasms are headed my way.

I feel him behind me. He begins running his rugged hands up and down my body. "Baby girl, you are so damn beautiful. So damn perfect. The things I want to do to you."

I breathe, "Do them."

He runs his fingers through my ass. "*All* of them?"

"Hmm, almost all of them."

"Can I put a collar on you? I think you'd like it."

"Umm...okay." Shit, I've never done anything like that

before, but I do trust him with my pleasure. He's never let me down.

He pulls something out of the drawer and clasps it around my neck. There seems to be some kind of light, plastic chain attached to it.

He moves behind me, giving the chain a little tug. It slightly pulls on my neck. I get it now. He can do things to me from behind while still giving me the choking sensation. I love that this is solely for my pleasure. I can't help but smile at the thought of what's to come.

All of a sudden, his face is in my ass. Licking through my back entrance. He hasn't done this before. He's done plenty of finger play, but not this. It's such a different sensation.

He gives a small tug on the chain, and I moan.

He moves his tongue down to my front entrance and pushes inside. He gets in deep with that magic tongue of his.

With the flogger now in hand, he circles it over each of my nipples, giving each an unexpected slap that's surprisingly enjoyable.

His tongue is in my pussy, he's pulling the chain and choking me, and he's stimulating my nipples. He's like a damn octopus in how much territory he can cover.

He slides the flogger down my body until it applies pressure to my clit. That simple act has my body shaking, begging for it.

"More. Touch me more."

He applies a light slap to my clit with the flogger and I gasp at the sensation. What is happening right now? Why does that feel so good?

He pulls his tongue out of me and slides a finger in.

Then two fingers. Then three. Deep to the spot he's now intimately familiar with.

Slap.

Again, with the flogger on my clit.

"I can feel how much you liked that, baby girl. This pussy got so fucking wet for me. It loves being slapped."

I have no words, but I know he's right.

Slap.

"Use your words."

"Fuck, Collin. I can't think. I can barely speak. It's too much."

Slap.

"Let's hear them."

I breathe a few times. "My clit feels like it's throbbing out of my body. I need more. Do it again. Please."

I don't know how he does it, because last I checked he only has two hands, but he simultaneously hits my g-spot deep inside, pulls the collar, and slaps my clit with the flogger.

"If you do that again, I'm going to come. I can't hold off."

He slaps my clit again, at the same time as he says, "Come for me, baby girl."

"Oh my god. Oh god. Oh god. Oh goooooooooddddd!" My body opens up and detonates. I bite the pillow as my whole body convulses. I can't see anything. All I can feel is my body exploding and come dripping down my legs.

Before I know what's happening, Collin is underneath me, on his back, lying between my legs. I feel his tongue as he licks my come off the inside of my thighs and then he quickly latches his lips onto my clit.

Oh shit. It's drawing out the orgasm. I can't help but

grind myself into his face. He grabs my ass to encourage me riding his face.

I keep grinding, never wanting this sensation to end.

He mumbles into my pussy, "Keep going."

I ride his face until my several-minute's long orgasm eventually subsides. I pull up to my hands, trying to catch my breath.

He slides his body up the bed until we're nose to nose. He nibbles on my lips. I can taste myself on him. He groans, "That was fucking hot."

I can't do anything but nod.

"You went off. You came hard."

I breathe, "I know."

I have to shake my head to regather my sense. "I hate to add to your overinflated ego, but I'm wondering if you have a hidden third hand. I don't know how you covered as much territory as you did."

He smiles and looks down at his severely engorged cock and thrusts his hips to run it through my wetness. "I don't know about a third hand, but I certainly have a third arm."

I smile. "That third arm probably needs some attention."

He runs it through me a bit more. "You know he does."

I roll my hips over his length. "He deserves it. He's earned it. Take what you need from me. Do your worst, Big Daddy."

I assume he's immediately going to pop up and fuck my brains out, but instead he grabs my face and pulls me in for a soft, sweet kiss. His tongue slowly moves through my mouth. It's deeply intimate.

I can't do much with my hands since they're tethered, but I collapse onto his chest and kiss him back.

He moves his hands to my ass and runs his cock

through me, not yet into me, over and over, harder and harder.

I pull my lips away and breathe, "Get inside me. I need you."

He runs his hands up my body until they're at my face again. He looks at me with such sincerity. "Will you stay when we're done? I don't want you to leave. I want to care for you. I want to sleep with you. I want to wake up with you."

I shouldn't. I know I shouldn't. But he looks so sweet and he's so sincere right now. I can't help the nod that comes. "Okay."

He gives me a huge smile as he reaches over for a condom. I lift my body so he can slide it on.

I'm not going to be terribly mobile on top, with my hands and arms mostly incapacitated, but I'll do the best I can. I pull a little to try to get some more slack.

He guides me until he's at my entrance. "I've got you, baby girl."

Without breaking eye contact, he slides himself deep inside me. We're still for a brief moment, as the inside of my body forms around him. He feels otherworldly. He always does.

He brushes his lips over mine and whispers the same words, "I've got you, baby girl."

He begins his upward thrusts, quickly gaining speed and momentum. He also manages to tug on the leash, pulling on my throat.

I have no real ability to move, but he manages to fuck me from below like a man possessed. He's going deep and hard, giving me everything I want and need.

I'm able to move my hips a little, but this is all Collin. This is his show. I'm just the lucky recipient of his magic.

He licks his way down to my nipple and sucks it into his mouth, all without breaking stride.

"You're so deep, Big Daddy. Keep going."

I clench as hard as I can. His head falls back and his eyes flutter. "Oh fuck, Jade. Do that again."

I do. I breathe, "I'm about to come. Can I come? Come with me." I can't believe I just asked for permission to come. That's what this man has done to me.

He deepens his thrusts to a pace I would have thought unimaginable. He pounds into my pussy like a jackhammer. I keep clenching.

"Fuck, Jade, I'm coming. Come now."

We both yell loudly as we come together.

I'm completely lifeless on top of him as I catch my breath. He sinks his head into my neck and inhales deeply.

"I love the smell of our sex."

I can't form words. "Hmm."

This is normally the time I would insist on him untying me so I can leave. I have no desire to do that right now.

He kisses up my neck and whispers, "I'm going to draw us a bath."

"Hmm."

He slides out from under me and stands.

I collapse onto the bed and turn my head. "Unfasten me first."

He bites his lip. "You're not going to escape when I'm in the bathroom, are you?"

I smile. "Not today. My legs are Jell-O. I don't think I can even stand let alone escape." I look into his eyes. "I don't want to escape. I promise."

And that's the moment things really shift for us. He breaks out into the biggest smile I've ever seen in my life.

Just like that, my once cold heart begins to thaw. It's warming for Collin Fitz.

AN HOUR later we're still in the bath. We keep topping it off with warm water. He's taken care of me in a way I've never known possible. He's carefully washed every inch of my body. I'm not sure why I've denied myself this for the past few months. It's heavenly to feel so cared for.

I'm laying between his legs, my back to his front. He runs his lips up and down my neck. "Tell me your deepest, darkest secrets."

I smile. "I only tell my therapist those."

"You have a therapist?"

"Yes. I've been with her since I was eight years old. I was a miserable fucker to my father when he first came into my life. My mom made me start seeing her every week for years until I finally let him in. Now I only see her monthly, but I do still like talking to her about things. It keeps my head clear. It's like having a committee on life decisions. I'm not always level-headed, so she does that for me."

"What's her name?"

"Dr. Pearl."

"What's her first name?"

I think for a moment and then start laughing. "I don't know. I've been seeing her for almost fifteen years, and I don't know her first name."

"Maybe you should ask her."

"I definitely will." I lean back into him. "You don't think it's weird that I see a therapist?"

"No. Why would I think that? If it helps you, it's a

good thing. It's healthy to talk to someone. We could all probably use someone like that."

"I think I mostly like pushing her buttons. I take satisfaction in it. It entertains me."

He lets out a laugh. "I have no doubt about that."

I lift my head and trace the tattoo on his left arm. "Will you tell me about this?"

He grunts. "I hate it. It was a young, drunken night with my brothers. It's a Claddagh ring."

"What's that?"

"It's an Irish wedding band. The heart symbolizes love, the hands symbolize friendship, and the crown symbolizes loyalty. When the heart points out, like how it is on me, it technically means your heart is open, but what it really means is that you're single and ready to mingle. When you turn the ring the other way, and the heart points in, it means your heart has been captured. My brother, Mac, got a tattoo of a Claddagh ring on his ring finger right before he and Ashleigh got married. He got it with the heart pointing in. I think it was a love gesture for her."

"Aww. That's kind of sweet."

"He was kind of drunk. He's generally a miserable prick. He's lucky to have her. She's awesome." He sighs. "Anyway, I was rambling on and on about what a pussy-whipped loser he was. That it would never happen to me. So my brothers challenged me to put my money where my mouth was. They challenged me to get a huge arm tattoo of the Claddagh ring with the heart pointing out, memorializing that I'll never allow my heart to be captured."

"Is that what you want?"

"I regret the tattoo. I hate it. I was young and stupid then. I don't know if it's what I want now. Honestly, seeing

Carter and Reagan's relationship has changed my views on marriage and relationships. They have a perfect marriage. I'd be lying if I said I'd never want that with someone."

I lean back and close my eyes. "If you ever find her, let me down easy."

CHAPTER FIFTEEN

TWO MONTHS LATER

COLLIN

For the past two months Jade and I have spent a ton of time together. While the first few months were all fucking, the past two months have been something more.

We no longer have simple booty calls. We haven't defined anything, or spoken about it, but we're together. At least I think we are.

We just gradually started spending the night at each other's places. Then the evenings started earlier and earlier. We'd order food and watch a movie before moving things to the bedroom. It morphed into it being assumed we'd spend whole evenings together. All without a real conversation about any of it.

We're up in New York City for the night. My cousin from Texas and his wife are in town to gather some of her belongings that were left here when she moved from New York to Texas to be with him.

Jade and I never go out for fear of being seen, so I welcome this opportunity not only to see my cousin, but for Jade and me to get out of the house. We're staying in a hotel for the night.

We walk into the restaurant. I see Cam and his pregnant wife, Shiloh, standing by the hostess stand, their backs to us. I quietly walk up to him and whisper in his ear, "You're so damn handsome," I grab his behind, "with a perfect ass."

He turns around with a huge smile and lets out a loud Cam laugh. He gives me a big hug and then runs his fingers through my hair. "And your long locks are so damn sexy." He bites his lip and mock shivers.

Jade looks between the both of us. "Should we leave the two of you alone?"

We chuckle as I pull her close. "No, this is how we are. He's been crushing on me since we were kids."

Jade shakes her head in disgust. "You guys look a lot alike, so you're basically crushing on yourself."

Shiloh laughs. Her thick, light brown hair is pulled into a high ponytail tonight. She's extremely attractive with soft, kind brown eyes. "She got you there, Cam."

Cam smiles at Jade. "Is this your fruit?"

Jade narrows her eyes at me and jokes, "Stop telling people how good I taste."

"You do taste rather good, but he's referring to you as the forbidden fruit."

She nods in understanding.

"Jade, this is Cam and his wife Shiloh. Cam, Shiloh, this is Jade McGinley."

She hugs them both. "I've heard so much about you."

I've given her a few small details, like the fact that they were high school sweethearts who found their way back to each other after a several-year parting, but she hasn't heard everything. I chose not to tell her about the drama in Cam and Shiloh's life. Shiloh used to be unwittingly engaged to a mobster, and some really fucked-up shit happened to her. Of course, my cousin, being the badass that he is, rode in on his white horse and saved her. But the badass becomes a softy when it comes to Shiloh. He's madly in love with his wife.

We're shown to our table and have a great night with them. This is the first time we've been out with another couple. It's nice.

Jade has been smiling and laughing the whole night. She's so beautiful. She and Shiloh hit it off immediately. At some point, they leave for the restroom.

When they're out of earshot, Cam turns to me. "I've never seen you like this. You haven't taken your eyes off her the whole night."

"Look at her. Can you blame me?"

"I guess not. Obviously she's a beautiful woman." He shakes his head. "I never thought I'd see the day. The famous playboy Collin Fitz is off the market."

"Stranger things have happened. I believe the famous playboy Camden Fitz recently went off the market."

He nods in agreement. "I'm happily and permanently off the market. Has anyone in the family met her?"

I shake my head. "No, not really. Braden met her briefly before we started up, but no one has truly met her."

He looks surprised. "What's the holdup?"

A blow out a breath. "We agreed to be casual and not tell anyone about us. We don't ever go out in public. We always stay in. This is our first time eating in a restaurant in over four months together. Her cousin is the woman married to Carter. When things go south, it could get ugly. We're better off staying in the dark for now. We're fine in our little bubble."

"*When* things go south?"

"I've never dated anyone where it didn't eventually go south."

"That's the case for everyone until they meet the right person."

I'm silent at that. I've never looked at it that way.

"Collin, she's young and beautiful. She's not going to want to Netflix and chill every night for much longer. If you want to keep her around, which it looks like you do, you're going to have to get out of the house and do things with her."

I smirk. "Netflix and chill? You're like a teenager. You know, I'm the older cousin. I'm supposed to give you advice, not the other way around."

He winks. "I got the beauty and the brains in this family."

"Where are we going?"

"You're an impatient woman," I tell her.

"Tell me something I don't know."

"Relax. We're almost there."

We're in my car driving. It's a Thursday night. What Cam said last weekend really resonated with me. We need to do more than sit in one of our apartments. I certainly enjoy that time with her, but we need a change of scenery. And I really want her to see this.

We pull into the construction site. She looks at me and pinches her eyebrows together. "Where are we?"

"It's the Wander property. I thought you might want to see the shell before your vision comes to fruition. I know you get visuals in your models, but nothing beats the real thing. Nothing beats watching it come to life before your own eyes. It's such a high."

She smiles. "I love this. But it's your vision, not mine. I just memorialize it. It's your brilliance."

"How about, it's *our* vision?"

"Okay."

I squeeze her hand. "You think I'm brilliant?"

"Brilliantly talented in bed."

I pull her hand to my lips and kiss it. "So are you."

We get out of the car and walk through the opening that will eventually be the front door. I take her hand in mine. She looks at me in question. We're not exactly a hand-holding couple. "There's a lot of crap around. I don't want you to get hurt." That and I just like touching her.

She nods. "It's cool. Your hands are my second favorite part of your body."

I look at my torn, beat-up hands. "These old things? Why is that?"

"They're big and rough. There's something so sexy

about the fact that you work with them all day long. I love them on my body. In my body."

I pull her front to mine and run my hands up and down her arms. I notice goosebumps on her skin when I do. "They love being on your body. In your body."

I bring my lips to hers for a soft kiss. She runs her fingers through my hair and moans, "Collin."

I reluctantly break away. "Don't worry, I have plans for that. We'll get there. I promise."

Her eyes light up. I love her eyes. In fact, there's nothing I don't love about her. I'm in so deep with this woman.

She turns around in a circle as I give her a brief explanation of where everything will be.

She looks confused. "The sign out front reads *Fitz and Sons*. I thought you were doing this with Reagan and Carter on your own? I thought it was going to be your first project with the new company?"

I sigh. "I didn't have the infrastructure set up quite yet. I don't have the manpower or machines. That stuff doesn't come quickly, and they wanted to get moving on this project, so it's under the umbrella of Fitz and Sons. But Carter told them that I'm in charge and it's my vision. It's the only way he would agree to it. They're not really in a position to deny him anything he asks for." I smile. "I think answering to me is pissing off my brothers. I'm enjoying bossing their asses around."

She gives me that mischievous grin of hers. "I like when you boss me around too."

"Soon." I take her hand again. "Let's take a look at everything. I know it's hard to imagine when it's just a shell, but I want to show you some of the things I know you liked."

I show her all around, including a few of the things I know are her favorites. The massive kitchen, the two-way fireplaces, the movie theater, the waterfall, the outdoor jacuzzi area off the master bedroom deck, and the huge master shower that overlooks the grounds, where you'll be able to see outside from inside the shower, but no one can see in.

I point out where all the crazy technology will be. Televisions that are hidden and then appear are among my favorites.

She smiles the whole time. "Collin, it's going to be amazing. I want to come back every few weeks and see the progress."

"Deal." I'm so happy that she's excited about it. I am too.

We walk out front. I turn to her. "Wait here. I want to grab something from my truck."

I run to the truck and gather the pile of pillows and blankets I brought. I return to her and grab her hand. "Follow me. Just be careful. The ground is uneven."

We make our way to the area with the heavy machinery. I unlock the box with all the machinery keys inside.

"Are you familiar with an excavator?"

She shrugs. "I guess I've seen them."

I point to one. "This is it right here. We use them for a bunch of things like digging, lifting, and carrying heavy items. This big front part is called the bucket."

I lay out a bunch of the blankets in the bucket

before telling her to step in it. Without any hesitation she does. I quickly run to the cab, put the key in the ignition, turning on the electric, and take the remote control with me.

I then climb into the bucket with her. "Sit."

She looks at me with skepticism but does as she was told. I sit as well. I press the button and we're lifted into the air.

She gasps. "Oh my god, Collin, this is amazing."

I lift us all the way until we reach the full thirty-foot height. I lock it into place and nod at her. "You can stand now. Just be careful. We're very high up and I'm breaking about forty different construction site regulations right now."

I stay seated but hold her hand for support as she stands. She looks over the ledge and then up at the sky. "Wow. The view is incredible."

I can't see much due to the deepness of the bucket, but I look up at her. "It sure is."

She looks down, understanding what I meant. She runs her fingers through my hair and then moves down to straddle my lap.

We wrap our arms around each other. She smiles. "Are we having sex up here?"

"If you're up for it."

"Hell yes, I'm up for it. Have you done this before?"

I shake my head. "No. I've never brought a woman to a project. I never cared enough for one to see it until now."

She smiles before removing her shirt, balling it up in a fist, and throwing it over the edge of the bucket so it falls all the way to the ground. She does the same thing with her bra while looking at me in challenge.

I remove my shirt and drop it over the side.

I move my hands to her breasts. She places hers on top of them, holding them in place. "These hands will be the death of me." I squeeze her. "Hmm. So rough. So perfect."

She stands again, removing her shoes, jeans, and panties in the process. Once again, she throws them over the ledge and looks at me in challenge. I can't take my eyes off her. She's not remotely scared of being up here. She's not remotely concerned about what we're going to do up here. She's completely giving in to the moment.

She holds her arms up and twirls around, looking happy and carefree. It's cold out, but my wild woman doesn't seem to care.

She stops and raises her eyebrow. "Are you remaining clothed? What's the point of this little exercise if you remain clothed?"

I shake my head while standing and make quick work of my shoes, jeans, and boxer briefs. Fortunately, I remember to remove my wallet with condoms before tossing the clothes to the ground far below.

I stand behind her as she looks off into the night. I pull her naked back to my naked front.

She turns her head and kisses my jaw. "Thanks for bringing me here. It's nice to get out with you. I hate staying hidden. I wish we could go out together. Last weekend was eye-opening."

A pang of guilt hits me. I know it's my fault we've remained hidden for all these months. She's young and deserves to go out and have fun. Without putting any real thought into it, I ask, "Do you want to go away with me?"

She rubs her nose along my cheek. "Like for the weekend? Out of the city? We just went to New York."

"No. A real trip. Let's go down to Mexico for a week. We can relax, go out to dinner, drink, fuck our brains out whenever we want."

She turns and brings her front to mine, wrapping her arms around my neck. She looks up and smiles. "Tell me more about this *fucking our brains out* thing. That's intriguing to me."

I softly kiss her lips. "Well, we wake up to a beautiful sunrise and fuck." Kiss. "We get breakfast outside and then come back to the room and fuck again." Kiss. "We hang at the pool or beach and drink all day, and then come back to the room to shower and fuck." Kiss. "Then go to dinner, drink, dance, and fuck." Kiss. "And then we do it all over again the next day." Kiss.

"Hmm. That's only four times a day. I'm really a five-times-a-day kind of girl. Do you think you can up your game?"

I run my eyes up and down her perfect body, and then land them on my painfully hard cock. "If you're naked, I'm always *up* for anything."

"I'm going to need to sample the goods before I commit."

"I'm yours to sample."

She kisses her way down my body until she's on her knees in front of me. She grabs my cock in her hand and softly kisses the tip. She looks up at me. "You have the best dick."

"He told me that he's fond of you as well."

She licks through my slit. "And he always tastes good."

"He likes the way you taste too."

"Hmm. We'll get there. Though he might taste better dipped in a Mexican margarita."

I look down at her. "Would that be better than a Fruit Roll-Up?"

She giggles into me.

"Does that mean you'll go?"

She nods as she open-mouth kisses her way down my cock. She licks around my balls. I've never been with a woman who pays as much attention to my balls as Jade. Every time she touches me or sucks my dick, worshipping my balls is a part of it. I fucking love it.

She sucks them into her mouth while moving her hand up and down my length. I gather her hair. "I think I need to sit for this. I don't want to stumble over and plummet down thirty feet."

She pulls her head up and licks her lips. "Death by blow job would be a good way to go though, wouldn't it?"

I let out a laugh. "Fair point. Keep going."

She smiles as she slides my dick in between her lips. Her cheeks hollow out as she sucks me deeper into her warm, wet mouth.

I tug her hair. "Take Big Daddy deep, baby girl. I know you can. No one does it better."

"Hmm." She takes me deep into her throat. I can feel her throat squeezing around me. She grabs my ass, pushing me as far as I can go.

Her eyes begin to water, but she never lets up. Each time going just a hair deeper. She's got one hand on the base of my cock and the other on my ass, forcing my movements.

I wipe one of her tears with my thumb and lick it. I tug her hair so our eyes meet. I thrust my hips a bit. "Do you want to sit on this? Maybe play a little hide and seek?"

With a big mouthful of my cock, she nods.

"Good. Cause I can't stand anymore with you doing this the way you do it."

She breaks her mouth off me with a pop. When I sit, she crawls on top of me. "How do I do it?"

I lift my eyebrow. "You know you do it well."

I see a small smile form on her lips. "I went to a top-notch blow job academy. It was a private school for the gifted and talented."

"Money well spent. Let me know where. I'll give it a five-star review on Yelp."

We both laugh as I roll the condom on. She rises to her knees, placing me at her entrance. She digs her nails into my shoulders as she slowly sinks down onto me, breathing a drawn-out version of, "Fuck," as her head tilts back.

"Tell me how it feels, baby girl. Give me your words."

She tilts her head back toward me and looks me in the eyes. She affectionately runs her fingers through my hair. "Like everything else in the world fades into the background. Like we're the only two people. Like you're overtaking my entire body with pleasure. Like there's nowhere else I'd rather be. Like I never want this feeling to go away."

That was the most description she's given me yet. There was something more to it than just sexual.

I lean forward. Just before our lips meet, I whisper, "Me too." Our lips come together. Our tongues tangle perfectly like we've done this together a thousand times before. Maybe we have at this point. I've never kissed one woman as much as I've kissed her and, somehow, it never feels like enough.

She begins her movements on my body. Up and down. Forward and backward. She's in a zone, all without breaking this kiss.

More often than not, she's tied up when we have sex, but not tonight. She's taking full advantage of it. Her hands move all around my body. She tugs on my hair, rubs my chest, and scratches her nails down my back. She's leaving no inch untouched.

For a moment, it almost feels like we're doing more than just fucking, and I like it. She must sense it because she changes course.

Her movements become faster and harder. She's slamming down onto me. Her ass is slapping my thighs with each pass.

She breaks the kiss and arches her back. "Oh god, Collin. More. Give me more."

She takes my hands and runs them up her body until they're at her throat. She squeezes them until I take the cue.

I squeeze her throat hard and thrust up into her. "You like to be fucked with my hands around your throat, don't you, baby girl?"

"Yes. Harder. Tighter."

If I squeeze much tighter, she could pass out.

I squeeze just a drop tighter though and thrust up into her as hard as I can. She's still moving at a fast pace on me. Despite the cold temperatures, our bodies are hot and sweaty.

I can't hold off any longer. I know she wants to come but is waiting for me. I lean over and whisper in her ear, "Come for Big Daddy."

As soon as I say that I feel her ripple around me. I love the complete control I now have over her body. I love that a strong-willed woman like her has willingly given it to me.

She scrapes her nails down my chest, undoubtedly breaking skin, as she yells out into her orgasm. I suck hard on her neck as I groan into my own.

She collapses her forehead onto my chest, breathing heavily. "Fuck, Collin, why is it so good between us?"

"Because I'm a stallion."

I feel her shoulders shake with laughter. She lifts her head with a big smile. "You're hung like one." She bites her lip. "Is it like this for you with everyone?"

"I was a virgin until I met you."

She smacks my chest. "Seriously. Is it always this good for you?" She looks so young and innocent while asking this.

"Who says this is good for me?"

She smiles as she smacks me again.

I grab her wrist with one hand and tilt her chin with the other. I kiss the inside of her wrist and then look her in the eyes and shake my head. "No. It's never been this good for me. It's you. It's us. It's special. We're special."

She turns her head, breaking our eye contact. She struggles with intimacy. Anytime we're headed toward a form of intimacy, she always changes course. It's like she's built a wall, expecting to be disappointed. She's always waiting for it to come. I hope I don't hurt her. My track record doesn't make it promising, but I don't want to hurt her. Just the opposite. I want to be with her. I want to take care of her.

She pulls off me and collapses down onto the blankets. "Let's talk about Mexico. I've never been."

I roll down and lay next her, disposing of the condom along the way. "You'll really go?"

"A week straight of sun, margaritas, and you fucking my brains out? That sounds good to me. I've been thinking that I want to travel more now that I have some money. I never traveled growing up. Jackson's plane is the only plane I've ever been on, besides one time when my father dragged my mom and me to Florida."

"We won't exactly be traveling by private plane. Just a regular, run-of-the-mill plane, but when we land, we'll be in paradise."

She lays her head on my chest. "I can't wait."

***

I WAKE FEELING like I'm falling. I hate those dreams where you fall and can't do anything about it. I can feel Jade in my arms though. Her front to mine. I love waking up with her naked body pressed to mine. I now hate the nights we spend apart. I can't believe I've completely fallen for her. For the first time in my life, I'm thinking long-term. I just haven't wrapped my mind around how it will come out, if she even wants it to.

She puts up a tough bravado, but I know there's

more under there. I get glimpses of her soft side from time to time.

I slowly open my eyes as the falling feeling stops. I see Edgar, my foreman, smiling down at me in the bucket. That immediately deflates my morning erection.

"Fun night, Collin?"

I look down to make sure Jade's body is covered. It is. It's obvious we're naked, but she's covered.

I croak out, "Don't tell my brothers."

"Sorry, buddy. When we got here and saw the bucket in the air and clothes all over the ground, I tried calling you. When you didn't answer, I called them. I didn't know it was you up here." He turns his head to the side and looks at something. "They're walking over now."

I mumble, "Oh shit."

Within seconds, Mac, Shane, and Braden are looking down at us. Mac and Shane look pissed. Braden is smiling.

Braden studies us carefully. "Is that Jade?"

Jade stirs at the mention of her name. Her eyes peel open. She realizes she's in my arms and nuzzles into my chest. She reaches between my legs. "No morning wood? Did I suck it all out of you?"

Everyone except Mac starts laughing. It's only then that she realizes we're not alone. She turns her head and looks at everyone. She turns back to me. "I'm not normally into the whole exhibitionism thing, but I'll try anything once."

We're smiling at each other when Mac breaks us out of it by saying, "Collin, get your stripper of the week out of here. What's wrong with you? You're a goddamn child. Not to mention the code violations going on right now. Grow the fuck up."

I start to sit up, ready to pounce on him, but Jade holds me down. She turns to him, uncaring that one of her breasts pops out in the process. I immediately cover it with my hand. She practically growls at him. "I happen to not be a stripper but have plenty of friends who are. All are single moms doing what's necessary to put food on the table. None are hookers. All of them let losers like you look at their beautiful bodies just to make ends meet. Take your judgmental, limp, small dick and fuck off. Who the hell do you think you are?"

I let out a loud laugh. "Jade, this is my oldest brother, Mac. And you're right, he does have a small dick. Mine is way bigger."

Braden and Shane chuckle.

Jade holds out her hand, completely naked, in the bucket of an excavator, with my hand covering her breast, and with a straight face says, "Lovely to meet you, Mac."

He finally breaks into a small smile as he shakes her hand in return. He turns his head to me and in a stern voice says, "Collin."

"I know. Throw our clothes in here and lift us back up out of sight."

We're hit by a shower of our clothes and then a ride back to the top. When it stops, we immediately start to dress.

She looks up at me. "Your brother is a douche."

I nod. "Totally."

"I don't like how he spoke to you."

"To me? He called you the stripper."

"He doesn't know me. I don't care. You're his brother and he spoke down to you. Fuck him. You don't deserve that."

She's not wrong.

"Do you really know a lot of strippers? Let's hang with your friends more often."

She rolls her eyes. "No, I don't know any. In movies, all strippers do it to provide for their kids. I improvised."

"He really got to you."

"He treated you like shit. That bothered me. It should bother you too. Don't let him talk to you like that. No one should."

I shrug. "I guess I'm the family screw-up. I let them get their punches in. I'm mostly happy with my life. I try not to let it bother me. It's always been this way."

She zips her jeans and then gives me a quick kiss. "It's bullshit, Collin. You're better than him. Look at what you created. You're more talented than him, you're better-looking than him, you obviously have a better personality than him, and you probably have a bigger dick than him. He's jealous. Plain and simple."

I pull her body to mine and kiss her neck. "I definitely have a bigger dick than him."

She pushes me away. "I'm serious. I'm about to rain holy hell on him. Let him fucking talk to you like that in front of me again."

"Are you going to kick his ass?"

"If I have to."

"You're sexy when you get mad."

She flips her hair. "I'm always sexy."

"True. Now sit so we can be lowered down. Let's do our walk of shame."

"I'm not ashamed. I'll pimp walk out of here with my head held high."

Yep, I might have found the perfect woman.

CHAPTER SIXTEEN

JADE

Somehow, on the way off the construction site this morning, I was talked into going to Collin's dickhead brother's house for dinner tonight. I expected Collin to make some excuse not to bring me, but he seemed excited at the prospect. It surprised me.

I've never met the family of a man I'm fucking, but his brother pissed me off, and for some reason I feel the need to defend Collin. If that's how his family treats him, they're about to get a piece of my mind.

I'm in Thor's office. We're showing Dominic a few models we've designed for an upcoming project of his. He seems happy with everything, though he keeps looking at his phone.

I look at him. "Is everything okay, Dom?"

He nods. "Yes, sorry."

Just then his phone rings. He looks down and sighs. "Sorry, ladies. Do you mind if I take this quickly?"

I nod. "Go ahead."

He answers, "Digame."

"Sí."

"No? Ay, Dios mio!"

"Estoy en camino."

"Chao."

He ends the call and looks up at us. "Sorry, I need to go pick up my daughter. Everything here looks perfect. Thank you. No changes are needed."

He quickly exits the office.

I turn to Thor. "Did you know that Dom has a daughter?"

She shakes her head. "I've worked here with him for ten years and know literally nothing about him except that he's sexy as hell. I thought he was married, but I'm not sure he is anymore. He never talks about his personal life."

"Did I tell you I caught him a few months ago in a compromising position in his office?"

"No. Holy crap. Tell me about."

I smile. "He was sitting at his desk. I couldn't see anything below his waist, but I'm pretty sure a woman was under there. There was a dress thrown across one of his chairs."

She places her hand over her mouth in shock. "Oh my god. What did you do?"

I shrug. "I decided not to humiliate him. I told him I needed to grab something from my office and then I locked his door behind me when I left."

"Wow. Was it his wife?"

"I have no idea who it was." I think for a moment. "I didn't even know he spoke Spanish. Dominic Mazzello isn't exactly a Latino name."

"I guess you're right. I never thought about it. Like I said, he keeps his personal life completely hidden from us. I know nothing about him. Speaking of personal life, what are you up to tonight?"

I sigh. "I somehow got hooked into meeting Collin's family."

I think she'd be less surprised if I told her I was growing a third eye.

"That's a huge step, especially for you."

"He's met *my* family."

"Not as your boyfriend. He already knows your family. Are you officially boyfriend and girlfriend? Have you two admitted it yet?"

I shake my head. "No. We don't need labels. We're casual."

I bite my lip.

She looks at me in question. "What?"

"He asked me to go to Mexico with him. We're both sort of sick of staying hidden. We want to go somewhere that no one knows us, and we can have a good time."

"I don't know why you feel the need to stay hidden."

"Collin doesn't think Carter will understand. I think he has a little bit of shame over how we started. I'm fine staying hidden. I don't need anyone's bullshit questions and expectations. And when we're over, everyone will feel awkward. It's easier if they never knew in the first place."

"What if you don't end?"

"Of course we'll come to an end at some point. Neither of us wants a real relationship. We're having fun. We'll continue to do so as long as both of us want that."

"I hate to break it to you, but you're in a relationship. Just because you're not labeling it as such doesn't mean it's not true. You're not interested in anyone else. Given how much time you spend together, I can't imagine he's seeing anyone else. You're together all the time. You sleep with each other more nights than not. That's a fucking relationship in my book."

The same thought has crossed my mind. I'm not sure how I feel about it. All I know is that I want Collin around. I'm not ready to let go of him just yet.

"I'M NOT comfortable walking in empty-handed. Why couldn't we stop somewhere?"

Collin hands me the bag of what sounds like a few bottles of wine. "We were running late. Here, you can walk in with the wine. Happy?"

"Yes, I am." I look in the bag. "Oh my god, it's Snoop Dogg wine. I love this wine."

He makes a look of disgust. "It's nasty, but Ashleigh loves it."

"You're crazy. It's the best wine. Ashleigh is Mac's wife, right?"

He nods. "Yes."

"Does she have a stick up her ass like Mac?"

"No. She's awesome. She's probably my favorite person in the family. Actually, when I was on the fence about starting things with you, she's the one that encouraged me not to give a fuck what anyone else thought and to do what makes me happy."

"Is that what you are, Collin? Happy?"

"If you let me fuck your ass, I'd be happier."

I laugh. "We'll see."

His eyes light up. "Really?"

I smile. He's relentless with the ass thing.

We're almost at the door when he says, "Oh, my family doesn't know about my new venture with Carter and

Reagan yet. Don't mention it. They just think that Carter wants the Wander property to be like their house, so that's why I'm in charge."

I turn to him. "Are you fucking kidding me? Man up, Collin. Just tell them."

Before he can respond, the front door of the house opens, and we see Mac and a woman that I assume is Ashleigh standing there. She's adorable. She's tiny, with dark hair, green eyes, and is sporting a giant smile.

Mac nods at me. "Jade. It's good to see you again."

"Hey, limp dick." I pat his chest. "Be nice to my man tonight or you'll see my ugly side. This morning was a walk in the park compared to what I'm capable of."

Ashleigh starts laughing. "Oh my god, I love her."

I hand her the wine. "I assume you're Ashleigh?"

She nods.

"It's nice to meet you. You have excellent taste in wine. Not so much when it comes to men."

Collin and Ashleigh both laugh. Mac does not.

She peeks into the bag. "Oh my god. I love Snoop Dogg wine. It's so underrated."

I nod. "I agree. Have you ever seen how the bottle can talk to you?"

Ashleigh's eyes widen. "What? Are you serious?"

"Yep. There's a website where you hold your phone up to the bottle and Snoop on the label starts talking to you."

She looks downright excited. "Will you show me later?"

"Of course."

Collin kisses Ashleigh on the cheek. "Hi, beautiful."

She blushes. Does her husband never compliment her? I really don't like him.

She loops her arm through mine and pulls me into the

house. "I'm so excited to meet you. We've never once met anyone Collin has dated."

"We're not dating. We're just fucking."

She spits out laughing. "I see you two are a lot alike."

I was serious, but she seems to think I was joking.

"I heard about this morning. Mac was whining about it, but it sounds really hot."

I give a conspiratorial smile. "It was *very* hot."

She lowers her voice. "Did you guys really have sex in the bucket?"

"No, we just got naked and slept in it."

"Oh."

"I'm kidding, Ashleigh. Yes, we had sex in the bucket. Several times."

Her face lights up. "God, that sounds so exciting."

"It was amazing." Clearly Collin not only got all the attractiveness genes in the family, but the sex-god genes as well.

We walk into the rest of the house, and I'm introduced to the entire family. His father has a thick Irish accent. It's cute. His mother makes at least six comments about my height. It's like she's never seen a tall woman before.

I know Braden, and briefly met Shane at the construction site. I meet his wife, Lydia, but when they introduce me to their son, NJ, I can't help but toggle my head between him and Collin. I land on Collin. "Is he yours?"

Collins laughs as he wraps his arm around Lydia. "We'll never be a hundred percent sure, right Lyd?" He winks at her, and she smiles.

Shane removes Collin's arm. "He doesn't look that much like Collin."

Collin bends down to NJ and gives him a high-five. "We're the hottest guys around, right NJ?"

NJ rubs his own chin with a bit of bravado. "Our mugs get all the mademoiselles, right Uncle Collin?"

Collin winks at him. Shane smacks the back of Collin's head. Hard. "Did you teach him that?"

Before Collin can answer, the littlest, sweetest voice yells, "Uncle Collin!" as a little girl that looks like a mini-Ashleigh comes flying into his arms. He catches her and engulfs her in a big hug.

She pulls her head back and runs her hands through his hair. "Can I braid your hair?"

Collin smiles. "Of course. My friend Jade wanted to braid it before we came, but I told her that only one girl is allowed to braid my hair."

The little girl giggles.

Collin turns to me. "Lucy, this is my friend, Jade. Jade, this is the love of my life, Lucy Fitz."

Lucy smiles at me. "You're very pretty."

"Thank you, Lucy. So are you."

"Can I braid your hair too?"

"Of course you can. Uncle Collin told me that you're the best hair braider around. I need to see if it's true."

Lucy's eyes widen. She turns back to Collin and grabs his face. "Thanks, Uncle Collin." She kisses his cheek. It may actually be the cutest thing I've ever seen in my life.

We're taken to the playroom where Lucy spends some time braiding our hair. She and Collin chat like old friends. It's adorable. They're obviously close. At some point, Lucy's brother, Liam, walks in and introduces himself. He's very polite.

About thirty minutes later, we're all called in for dinner. The dining room table is set nicely.

Their family dinner can best be described as a company meeting. Their father drills each of them on their respective projects. When it's Collin's turn, his father asks, "How's da Wander project?"

Collin lights up. His eyes sparkle and he has a huge smile. "It's great. We already have the framing up."

His father looks shocked. "How did ya get through permitting so quickly?"

Collin proudly wraps his arm around me. "Because of Jade. She does the best virtual modeling I've ever seen. It got us through permitting so quickly."

"How much did dat cost ya?"

"She works for Carter and Reagan. She normally does it for bigger projects but was able to quickly do this one for us."

I mumble to Mac, "Not bad for a stripper."

I see Ashleigh silently shaking in laughter.

Collin nods at his father. "Da, this is the exact kind of change I've been trying to talk to you guys about. We need this type of technology to take things to the next level."

Mac shakes his head. "We can't afford that. We need to stick with what we know. We have a specific core competency, Collin. It doesn't make sense to change things. If it ain't broke, why fix it?"

I can't help but interrupt. "It's a matter of software and then training someone on how to use it. For single-family homes, it's quite simple once you know what you're doing."

Mac looks pissed. "You manage your business, Jade, and let us manage ours."

Collin snaps his head to Mac. "Watch how you talk to her."

"I'm sorry, Collin, but your flavor of the week isn't

going to change my opinion on our business strategy. This company has existed for forty years without her."

Collin shakes his head. "What strategy? To bury our heads in the sand? To build boring shit?"

His father smacks him on the back of the head. "Watch ya mouth. Collin, we've discussed dis. We build a certain type of home. Da same type we've been building for forty years. It's put food on dis family's table since da very beginning. We're not rockin' da boat."

Collin is silent.

His father stands and places his napkin on the table. "Boys, shall we?"

Shane, Braden, and Mac all stand and start to leave the table. They don't bother to take their plates into the kitchen. Collin stays seated. His father looks at him. "Collin?"

"I'm going to stay with Jade. I'll help clean up."

Mac shakes his head. "You're such a wimp."

He goes to smack the back of Collin's head, but I grab his wrist before he makes contact. "If you smack him again, I'm going to smack you a lot harder."

Mac gives me a nasty look. "He'll be done with you in a few days, just like the rest. You'll be yesterday's news."

"I'm okay with momentarily being yesterday's news. You have to live with the fact that you'll always be an asshole."

Braden pulls Mac away. "Come on. Let's get you a drink."

His mom offers to watch the children and she leaves the room.

I lean over and whisper to Collin, "Go with them. It's fine."

He whispers back, "I don't want to leave you."

"I'll be fine as long as I'm not with Mac. Maybe I'll let these women know that we live in the twenty-first century. Perhaps the boys will come back to find their women feeling a little differently." I wink at him.

He smiles as he stands. "I'll leave you to it, then." He starts to walk out of the room but turns and comes back to me. He bends, grabs my face, and gives me a scorching hot kiss. It's full of wet lips and tongue.

I have to fan myself when he pulls away and leaves.

Ashleigh whistles. "Damn, that was hot. I haven't been kissed like that...ever." She giggles to herself.

She stands and starts to clear the table. "Ashleigh, have a seat." She does. "Grab Mr. Snoop Dogg. In fact, grab a few bottles. We have a several things to discuss."

ONE HOUR LATER

COLLIN

I tried again in vain to get my father and Mac to see the light. They won't budge. I can't believe I'm now in a position where I'm seriously considering leaving my family's business. I guess I held out hope that if they saw the Wander property, they'd somehow change their minds about their business strategy. It doesn't look like it's happening.

We walk out of Mac's study and hear a fit of giggles coming from the dining room. We walk in.

Mac looks around. "What the hell, Ash? Nothing is cleaned up."

Ashleigh's smile fades. "Then why don't you clean it your damn self." She and Lydia start cackling.

I turn to Jade. She gives me that sexy mischievous smile of hers. I can't help but smile back. My crazy girl has stirred the pot. I can't wait to see how this unfolds.

Ashleigh practically screeches, "Collin, did you know that Snoop Dogg on the wine bottle talks to you? Legitimately talks when you hold your phone up to him." She starts hysterically laughing. "It's the greatest thing I've ever seen in my life."

Mac looks like his head might explode. "Are you trashed?"

She narrows her eyes at him. "So what if I am? You get to drink with your father and brothers every week while I cook *and* clean. Did you know that at Jade's family dinners, if the women cook, the men clean. If the men cook, the women clean. And no one relaxes until *all* the cleaning is done. *And* they *all* relax and talk together, as a family. It's not just the boys."

Mac turns to Jade and points his finger at her. "What did you do to my wife?"

Jade grins and shrugs her shoulder innocently. "Who me? The little ole stripper?"

Ashleigh says to Mac, "And by the way, I'm going back to work. I'm telling you, not asking you. You're not my boss. You're my husband. My equal. Deal with it."

Mac takes a step toward Jade, but I stand between him and her. I place my hand on his chest. "Relax, Mac. Ash is drunk. It's just dishes. We can all grab a few and have this clean in no time."

Mac nods, as everyone but Lydia and Ashleigh clear the table. The two of them can barely stand.

I whisper to Jade, "Why are they trashed, and you seem fine?"

She shrugs. "Because I can hold my liquor. Being a full ten inches taller than them has its advantages."

"What is it you said to them?"

"Just that women have had the right to vote for over a century now. Everywhere except in the Fitz household, that is."

I bring my lips to her ear. "Do you have any idea how sexy you are? Do you know how hard I'm going to fuck you tonight?"

"Hard like the bed might move a little, or hard like I won't be walking straight tomorrow?"

"The latter."

Her eyes light up. "How soon can we leave?"

"Ten minutes. Your big mouth and your tight pussy are about to get it good."

"Promise?"

"Guaranteed."

CHAPTER SEVENTEEN

JADE

I'm awakened by my alarm ringing. What the hell? It's a Saturday. Why is my alarm going off?

I pick up my phone and mumble, "Oh shit."

Collin pulls me close to him as he nuzzles his nose into my neck. "What's wrong? Don't leave yet." He runs his hands up my body.

I admittedly enjoy waking up with him. He's so loving and affectionate. I can't believe how much I like it.

I rub his big forearms. "I'm not leaving. I forgot that I have an appointment with my therapist."

He pops his head up. "The famous Dr. Pearl? Dial her up. Let's all have a chat."

I look up at him in question. "You want to talk to my therapist?"

He gives me his devilish smile. "You said you like to push her buttons. Let's have a little fun." He rubs his hands together.

I smile as I think of how Dr. Pearl will manage her way through this.

We're both naked under the sheets. I think we'll stay this way for our call. I'm now itching with excitement.

I reach into my bag and pull out my laptop, setting it up at the end of the bed. We need to give her the full effect.

Like clockwork, the video chat rings at our predetermined time. I click the accept button but slide myself off screen so all she can see is Collin, who is sitting up in bed with the sheets pooled around his waist. His delectable chest, arms, and abs are on full display for her.

The video opens, as does Dr. Pearl's mouth. She starts fumbling with her pen. "Oh my. I think I have the wrong person."

I pop my head in. "Surprise! I just wanted you to have a little eye candy this early in the morning."

Collin and I both laugh. I slide back into place and lean into his side, though I do keep the sheets covering my chest. Dr. Pearl doesn't need to see everything to gather our state of undress.

"Oh, Jade. It looks like you're busy. Did you want to reschedule our meeting for another time?"

I shake my head. "No, Collin can be here. I don't care."

She nods. "So, this is the famous Collin?"

Collin's eyes light up. "Famous? She's told you about me? Tell me everything."

Dr. Pearl looks at me for permission. "You can speak freely, Dr. Pearl." I loudly whisper, "He knows I'm fucked up. I think he's into it."

He nods. "I am. Her level of crazy is super-hot. I've heard about you too, Dr. Pearl, but she didn't tell me that you're a little hottie. You look like quite the vixen. I'm a big fan of a sexy woman in a cardigan."

Dr. Pearl's face flushes. I'm desperately trying to hold in my laughs.

She takes a moment to gather herself. She's crushing on him. It's hysterical. I don't blame her, but it's still funny to see her flustered like this.

She looks at me. "Can I ask him questions about you?"

"Fire away."

She turns her attention to Collin, fixing the glasses on her face. I imagine she wants to make sure she can see him clearly. "Collin, I understand you're a good amount older than Jade?"

He nods. "In age, yes."

"As you know, Jade doesn't have a lot of relationship experience. How are things going between you two?"

"Oh, well, I'm extremely immature, so it feels like I'm dating an older woman." He winks at her. "And I like older women."

"Jade isn't exactly a beacon of maturity. She has a rather offbeat sense of humor."

He shakes his head. Without any hesitation, he says, "Her sense of humor is my absolute favorite thing about her."

I turn and smile up at him. That was nice to hear.

"And she also gives amazing head."

I spit laughing. I turn to the camera and nod in agreement. "I *do* give amazing head." I nod toward Collin. "So does he."

He looks at Dr. Pearl with a straight face. "Do you need to see that to confirm? I don't know how the whole therapy thing works. I'm willing to show you."

She straightens her sweater. "That will be unnecessary. Thank you for the offer."

Collin turns to me. "I'm going to pour us some coffee.

I'll be back in a bit." He leans over and kisses me. I mean *really* kisses me. It's long, hard, deep, and has my toes curling. His lips suck mine in while his tongue moves around mine. His kisses are just so perfect. I have to blink a few times when it's over to remember where I am and what I'm doing.

Collin then takes things to a whole new level. He pulls the sheets off his body to stand and stretch, shamelessly revealing the full monty to Dr. Pearl. I hear her suck in a breath as her mouth opens wide and doesn't move.

As soon as Collin is off camera, he grins and winks at me. He did that on purpose to shock her.

He walks out of his bedroom completely naked. I can't help but watch his yummy ass as he goes.

When I turn back to the screen, Dr. Pearl's mouth is still wide open. "Dr. Pearl, are you okay?"

Her mouth is moving like a fish, but no words come out. Eventually, she manages, "I...I...I have no words."

I snicker. "It took fifteen years for you to run out of words. If I knew a giant cock would have done the trick, I would have shown you one years ago. I think you now understand the appeal."

She gathers herself. "He's not what I expected, Jade."

"You thought I'd go out with a guy with a small penis?"

She rolls her eyes. "Not *that* part. When you told me you were dating a much older man, I assumed a certain level of maturity. Maybe a bit of sophistication. He's...well...he's a lot like you."

"Brilliant and beautiful? Searing wit? Killer body? Professional head-giver?"

"I was thinking more along the lines of silly and carefree."

I nod. "I can see that."

"You seem happy, Jade. It looks good on you. The smile hasn't left your face since this call started."

I touch my lips and realize that I've been smiling this whole time. She's right. I am happy. I consider myself a generally happy person, but adding Collin to the mix is taking things to another level for me.

He walks back into the room with two mugs of coffee. Apparently, I'm now a coffee drinker. Admittedly, I like it. What I like the most is lying in bed with him drinking it.

He hands it to me in such a way that Dr. Pearl gets a full view of his ass. I look up to see him smirking at me.

He climbs back under the sheets. Dr. Pearl looks at him. "So, you're a button-pusher like Jade."

He nonchalantly sips his coffee. "I love pushing her buttons. *All* of them. I also love drinking coffee out of her belly button. We do that several mornings a week. Do you want to see it?"

"That's quite alright."

I interrupt, "Guess what, Dr. Pearl? Collin is taking me to Mexico next week."

She smiles. "That sounds nice. What brought that about?"

"Collin is embarrassed to be seen with me here, so we're always stuck inside. We're going to another country just so we can go out for a meal." That came out a lot nastier than I had it in my mind.

Collin takes my hand and squeezes it. "That's not totally true. You met my family last night."

Dr. Pearl asks, "You met his family? How did that go?"

"Well, I don't love how they talk to Collin, and I don't care for their treatment of women in general. Since I've never been known to hold my tongue, I let them know how

I felt. I don't think they liked it very much. I imagine I didn't gain any fans."

He looks at me. "Ashleigh and Lydia both liked you."

I nod and turn back to the camera. "The sisters-in-law liked me. I got them trashed. The rest...not so much."

Dr. Pearl smiles. "I imagine it takes people a little while to warm up to you. I'm fifteen years in and not there quite yet." She giggles.

"Dr. Pearl! Did you just make a joke at my expense?"

"I may have. You're rubbing off on me."

<hr>

AFTER THE CALL with Dr. Pearl, Collin and I spend the day together. He does take a few coffee shots from my belly button, but then we work out, go for a walk, watch a movie, and fuck like animals.

I leave Sunday morning, promising to come back after my Sunday night family dinner. I don't know what's happening, but we're at a point where we rarely spend a night apart.

CHAPTER EIGHTEEN

JADE

I wake in the morning to Collin fast asleep on his back. I have to get to work, but I can't help myself from shamelessly pulling down the sheets to look at him. His body is so damn sexy. It's undeniably masculine. There's not an ounce of fat anywhere. I could look at him for hours. I've spent so much time exploring his body throughout the past few months, but I never seem to get my fill. The desire to lick every inch of him consumes me.

I pull the sheets and blanket back up and then slide my way down under them until I'm between his legs. He's fast asleep and the big, beautiful cock is standing tall for me. I stick out my tongue and suck his balls into my mouth.

He jerks for a moment but then I feel him gather my hair. In a croaky morning voice, he says, "Hmm. That's how I like to be awakened. Keep going, baby girl. Just like that."

I continue sucking his balls but start stroking his cock with my hand.

Out of nowhere, I hear a voice in the room. Not any voice. It's Carter's. "Good morning, sunshine. Ooh. Who do you have under there?"

Then I hear Reagan's voice. "Anyone we know?"

Collin responds, "No. Why don't you two leave. There's no need to embarrass her."

I move his cock into my mouth and start sucking him hard.

I feel him quickly inhale a breath while his body jerks.

Reagan says, "She doesn't seem very shy, Collin." She and Carter both laugh.

"Get out. I'm changing my code."

Reagan says, "Will it be harder to crack than six nine six nine?"

Carter answers, "He'll probably change it to nine six nine six. We can crack that code too, Collin."

Meanwhile, I haven't stopped a thing. I've got my mouth and hand sliding up and down on his cock.

I hear footsteps get closer to the bed.

In an unusually stern voice, Collin says, "Reagan, don't. Please leave."

"Hmm. Okay. We'll let you off the hook this time. You're going to tell us all about the woman under there. The one I'm pretty sure you've been seeing for several months. The one who seems to have you off the market. The one who, judging by your bedposts, you tie up. The one who isn't deterred by our presence."

They both laugh as I hear their voices become more distant until the front door closes. As soon as it does, Collin flips us over and pins my wrists down. "You're going to pay for that."

"Ooh. I love being punished. Tell me more."

"I'm going to tie you up so you can't move and then

fuck your mouth hard. You'll be choking on me as you swallow my come."

"By all means, punish me. Give me all you've got, Big Daddy."

And he does. He ties my wrists to the bedposts, climbs on top of me, and fucks my mouth until I'm choking on him. Then he comes, hard and long, down my throat. God, he turns me on.

He wouldn't be Collin if he then didn't take care of me. Twice.

A FEW HOURS later Reagan buzzes for me to come to her office. I walk in. She looks up at me. "Close the door and have a seat."

I do as she asked. Once I'm seated, she asks, "How long have you been fucking Collin?"

I don't hesitate. I have nothing to hide. "A few months. How did you know it was me this morning?"

"I only know one woman on this planet who would keep sucking him off during our conversation, that also just so happens to have giant man feet. I saw your size twelves laying on the floor."

I let out a laugh. "They're not man feet. Just long, like the rest of me."

"You don't think he's a little old for you?"

Before I can speak, she holds up her hand. "I know you prefer older men. You've made that abundantly clear throughout the years. There's older, and then there's sixteen years older. That's a big age gap."

"We're having fun. What's the big deal?"

"The big deal is that I know neither of you have been

out on the prowl in at least five months. That sounds like more than just a good time to me. In the nearly five years I've known Collin, I've never seen him take that long of a hiatus. I also know you have a bit of a thing for my husband, Collin's best friend. And Collin has a bit of a thing for me. It all spells trouble and hurt to me."

I shrug. "I'm over my crush. We haven't discussed it much, but Collin seems to be too." At least that's what I keep telling myself.

She nods. She doesn't need to mention our resemblance for it to still be on both of our minds. It's always in the back of my mind.

"I don't want you to get hurt. He hurt Jasmine. He's hurt a lot of women in his life." He briefly dated Reagan's close friend, Jasmine. "He's not a bad guy, he's just not the commitment type. In thirty-eight years, he's never been truly serious about anyone. That means something. It's not normal."

"Like I said, we're having fun. I don't want serious either. I'm not all weepy and hung up on him." I hope. I might be a little hung up on him. I certainly don't want anyone else.

"And this is who has you dickmatized?"

I nod.

"Are you safe? Are you comfortable? I know he has... eclectic tastes in the bedroom."

"If I wasn't into it, I wouldn't still be there. It's not like I'm tied down...err...well, I sort of am, but in a good way."

We both can't help but laugh at that.

She stands and walks over to me. She bends and hugs me. "I love you. Just be careful. I don't want to see you get hurt. You don't deserve it."

I don't think Reagan has ever told me she loves me

before. I know she hasn't. I'm choked up with emotion. Feeling family love is still something I'm getting used to.

"Thanks, but I'm fine. I know what I'm doing. He and I are good. We know exactly what we are."

"Okay. If everything is good, why is it a secret?"

I shrug. "Collin is afraid of Carter knowing. He has it in his mind that Carter will lose all faith in him. He's terrified of losing Carter's friendship."

"That's ridiculous. Carter loves Collin like family. There's nothing Collin can do to change that."

"I can't speak for him. I'm just telling you what he thinks."

"It's going to come out. Please encourage him to tell Carter. I hate keeping secrets from my husband, and it will be better for him to hear it from Collin. He'll have questions."

"I'll try."

"Please do." She heads back to her desk and sits. "Beckett Windsor has accepted our offer. He starts here next week."

"Oh. Cool. I hadn't heard about it for months, so I assumed it was a dead duck."

"His daughter was having some separation issues from starting school this year. He didn't want to commit until she was settled."

"Wow. It's kind of unusual for a man of his stature to be deterred by something like that."

"You don't know his story?"

I shake my head. "No."

"His wife died five or six years ago in childbirth. He was immediately a single dad. That's why he sold his business. He said he couldn't do both and wanted to be there for his daughter. She started school this year, which is why he wanted back in the game, but not the type of hours required to run your own company."

"That's kind of endearing. He seemed so suave and sophisticated when I met him. I never would have guessed."

She nods. "Yes, I think he's a good guy who's well-intended. I'm excited to have him here."

I stand. "Great. You just keep on hiring hot guys. Let me know if you need anything."

She laughs. "You're right. There are a lot of hot guys here."

I nod. "Carter, Dominic, and Beckett? Wow. No woman will get anything done around here." I smile. "Oh, just a reminder that I'm going to Mexico next week. I'll have everything time-sensitive done before I leave."

"Oh, right. Have a great trip with your girlfriends."

I hate lying to her. I think about telling her the truth for a moment but decide against it. I'd basically be asking her to keep more things from Carter, and I don't want to put her in that position. "Thank you. I plan to."

CHAPTER NINETEEN

COLLIN

We landed in Mexico this morning and are on our way to the hotel. Jade is trying to play it cool, but I can tell she's incredibly excited. Admittedly, so am I. A week of anonymity to go anywhere and do anything we want. A week in paradise. Frankly, a week straight of being with Jade sounds like paradise to me, regardless of our surroundings.

Maybe coming here together is a big step we're not ready for, but the second I see her face when we enter the lobby, I'm happy I did it. She lights up. And when we enter our suite, it rockets to another level.

She looks around. "Collin, it's magnificent." She wraps her arms around me. "Thank you for bringing me here. I love it. It's perfect."

The bellman interrupts us. "Mr. and Mrs. Fitz, will that be all?"

Jade opens her mouth to correct him, but I cover

it. "That will be all, thank you." I tip him and he leaves.

She looks at me, "What was that about?"

I give her a small smile. "I wanted the honeymoon suite for us. I had to tell them we were on our honeymoon to get it."

She narrows her eyes at me. "I guess Mrs. Fitz is going to have a field day charging things to Mr. Fitz this week."

I smile. "It's all-inclusive but feel free."

She walks over to the huge window and looks out over the ocean. "It's beautiful here. Look at this view. I've never seen an ocean this blue. It's practically turquoise."

I come up behind her and wrap my arms around her. "It is. But you're more beautiful and you're wearing entirely too many clothes. I only brought you here so you'd wear next to nothing all week."

She lifts her arms and I remove her top. She reaches back over her shoulder and runs her fingers through my hair. She turns her head so our lips meet and pushes her tongue straight into my mouth. I can't help but moan. Her taste has become so familiar to me. It's a direct line to my cock, which is already standing at full attention. I press it against her ass.

She breaks her lips from mine. "Hmm, Collin. Get inside me."

"People might be able to see in. Do you want to move to the bed?"

She shakes her head. "No, I don't care if they watch. I want to see this view of the turquoise ocean while you fuck me from behind."

I rub my hands down her body. "I can

accommodate that request."

And that's exactly what we do. It's hot, sweaty, hard, and deeply satisfying, just as it always is for us.

When we're done, we put on our bathing suits and head down to the ocean. All heads turn to look at her as we make our way to the lounge chairs. I'm not sure if she notices, but if she does, she doesn't seem to care.

I lift her hand and bring it to my lips. "Do you realize how much attention you garner?"

She shrugs. "People aren't used to tall women. I'm like a circus freak to them. It happens all the time."

"Are you joking?"

We spread our towels on the chairs and lay down.

She shakes her head. "No. Why?"

"It's not your height, Jade. It's you. You're the most beautiful woman I've ever seen in my life."

She narrows her eyes at me. "Are you just trying to get laid?"

"I just got laid and am more than confident that I'll be doing so all week. They're not just words. It's reality. You're stunning. No one, including myself, can take their eyes off you."

She gives me a soft smile. "Thank you, I appreciate the compliment. You're pretty hot too."

"I know."

We order drinks and absorb the sun. It's nice and relaxing. At some point, I turn to her. "Will you tell me more about yourself growing up? You're so tight-lipped about it."

"Ugh. Why?"

"I want to know about you." She's damaged. I want to better understand it. "I know you had it rough. Tell me about it. Please."

She lets out a breath. "It's hard to grow up not knowing your father. I struggled with it. A lot. My mom is a short brunette. I was very fixated on not knowing the person I clearly resembled. I had a hard time not knowing where I came from." She takes a sip of her drink. "My mom got clean when she found out she was pregnant with me, but she was a strung-out junkie before that, so it's not like she ever had a stable job. She's an artist, a talented one, but that doesn't always translate into money. We moved a bunch of times because she couldn't pay the rent and we'd get evicted."

"And Declan didn't help at all?"

"All I knew of Declan my first seven years was his name and one photo. He was completely absent from my life, physically, emotionally, and financially. He didn't give a shit about me."

"I'm sure that's not true. I imagine he regrets it. Drugs are powerful."

"The love for a child should be more powerful. He made his choice. He chose drugs, not his daughter."

"What was it like when he came back into your life?"

"Bad. Really bad. I didn't accept him. Honestly, I tortured him for years. I punished him." She sighs, "But at least we finally had a little money. As his photography career took off, he did give a lot to my mom. Way more than he probably needed to. We finally had a house and were able to stay in one place. I could finally stay in one school for more than a year. We had stability."

"That means something, Jade. He cared. I know he cares about you. That's evident."

"Now. What about when I *really* needed him? What about father-daughter dances? What about having to move every six months? What about the fact that I constantly had to change schools and make new friends? By the way, it's not easy to make friends when you have shit clothes, no father, and an eccentric mother that just isn't quite like the rest."

"You have a good relationship with your mom, right?"

"She's a fucking saint. She's ten years younger than my father. She was a twenty-two-year-old addict when she got pregnant with me. She got clean and scraped her way by for me. Everything she did was for me. Can you imagine how terrifying it would be for me right now if I were pregnant, with no significant other, no money, no job, no place to live, and no family? That was her reality, and she did her best. Every day, she did her best. And trust me, I was a fucking handful."

I let out a laugh. "You still are."

She smiles. "I know. Some things don't change. She was a kid herself who made a lot of mistakes. She brought home loser after loser. If there was an unemployed asshole within fifty miles, she found him. I'm talking about countless guys who treated her poorly, loitered around the house, and stole from us. And we didn't have much. That stopped at some point. My father even beat one of them senseless after he stole the television Dad had bought for us. I think that was the final straw for my mom. She then started dating her soon-to-be ex-husband. He's vanilla and boring, but he had a real job and didn't treat her like shit."

"Wow. That's rough. You and Declan are good now though, right? You seem it."

"I suppose. I don't know that I'll ever completely trust him. I refused to call him Dad for years. But the year I lived with him and Melissa was amazing for our relationship. For the first time, I *really* got to know him. Before that, it was a meal here and there. It's not like he had custody rights. Melissa is the best thing that ever happened to him. She keeps him in check. He lacks control, but she manages to keep him under control. Her power over him is unreal."

"And that's the same timeframe you met all your cousins, right?"

She smiles. It's so genuine. "Yes. I went from zero family, to a giant crazy one. A better one than I ever could have dreamed possible. I begged my dad for a long time to let me meet his family. He never would. But it finally happened, and I'm so thankful for them. Even something as simple as Christmas has changed dramatically for me. There was a time when it was me, my mom, and a shitty tree with two homemade gifts we could barely afford. I'm sure you can imagine what Christmas at Aunt Darian and Jackson's is like. On my first Christmas with them, there were seventeen gifts for me under the tree. *Seventeen.* Do you have any idea what that means to a girl who grew up like I did?"

I never thought about it that way. I always had a lot of gifts under the tree. I grab her hand. "And you have so many people that look like you now. You went from no one that you resemble to practically a twin."

Her face drops. She sits up in her chair and turns to me. "Collin, are you into me because I look like Reagan? I know you're in love with her."

I sit up and take her hands in mine. "I'm not in love with Reagan. I never was. Did I have a crush on her for a long time? Yes, I admit that I did. It's not Reagan as much as it's certain unique qualities about her that I'm attracted to. Do you possess some of them? Honestly? Yes, you do. I love that you don't have a filter. I love that you always speak your mind. I love that you're smart and driven. I love that you have backbone. I'm attracted to you because you possess those qualities. It doesn't have anything to do with her. You said you used to notice me looking at her. Do you see it now?"

She shakes her head. "No, I don't."

"I know you don't, because it's not there anymore. I can honestly look you in the eyes and tell you that my crush is gone. You're the only one I want to look at, Jade. On the flip side, I haven't seen you look longingly at Carter in months. It's not like you ever hid it, but it's gone."

She thinks for a moment. "You're right. I don't look at him. I no longer think of him that way. He doesn't occupy my dirty thoughts anymore."

"May I ask who does?"

"You know who it is. He's tall, with longer hair, sexy scruff, a killer body, and dick built for sin. He's the star of my dirty thoughts."

"How dirty? Like, *please take my ass* dirty?"

She laughs and lays back down. "Keep dreaming, Collin."

I smile as I lay back down too. "You can't blame a guy for trying. Did you see that bar we walked by on our way out here?"

"Not that I noticed. Why?"

"It had swings instead of barstools. Long wooden swings."

She turns to me. "You have something sinister in mind, don't you?"

I smirk. "Always."

"I'm in. Whatever it is, I'm in."

I take her hand and kiss it. "I'll be the one who's in. Wear a dress and no panties tonight."

"It would appear you have a few devious things in mind, Big Daddy."

"I do. I even brought a little toy to help it along." I smile as her eyes widen.

JADE

Collin and I had a great day. We laid in the sun, swam in the warm ocean, and laughed our asses off.

We're about to head to dinner. I'm in a pink summer dress and, per his instructions, no panties. He's in cargo shorts and a blue short-sleeved button-down shirt. It matches his eyes which I'm catching myself looking into more and more often.

He walks up to me and runs his hand up my thigh. "Were you a good girl?" He moves it all the way up until he confirms that I'm not wearing any panties. He kisses my neck. "Such a good girl. You'll be rewarded."

He pulls something out of his pocket and puts it into his mouth. When he pulls it out, I realize that it's a butt plug.

I shake my head. "I told you no anal."

"A butt plug isn't just for anal sex. It enhances regular sex for both of us."

"Then you put it in your ass."

"That won't enhance sex for you."

"It will enhance my happiness though."

He smiles. "Just try it once. You said you'd try anything once. If you don't like it, you can take it out."

He's throwing my words back at me. "Fine. You can try, but I'm taking it out if I'm uncomfortable."

"Fair enough. Bend over."

I place my hands on the bed and bend over. He lifts my dress over my ass. He twists the plug in his mouth one more time before I feel it at my back entrance.

"I'm going to slip it in. I'll go slow. You'll feel a little intrusion at first, but your body will quickly accommodate it. Take a deep breath."

I do and he slowly slides it in. It doesn't hurt, I just feel full back there.

He rubs my ass. "Are you okay?"

"Yes, it's not terrible."

He gives my ass a small smack. "You can stand up."

I lift my head. "That's it?"

He smiles. "See? Not so bad."

"We'll see about that. The sex better be amazing or I'm shoving this up your ass."

He winks. "It will be. I promise."

I wouldn't admit this to him, but I'm excited about whatever he has planned for us tonight. We're over five months into this and he's never once let me down in bed. He's creative, dominant, passionate, and there's never been a single moment where my pleasure wasn't his priority. I know tonight will be no different.

He takes my hand in his. I notice that he's been doing

that a lot lately. I also notice that I like it. He squeezes me. "Let's eat."

We're having a beautiful dinner overlooking the water. It's nice to be out with him. I'm not sure I realized how much I missed going out until we got here. I definitely don't mind the cozy nights in bed with him, but I'm happy to be eating off real plates in an actual restaurant, and not from cartons on one of our sofas.

I look at him. "Tell me your biggest fear. What is big man Colin Fitz most afraid of?"

Without any hesitation, he says, "Disappointing Carter."

I was not expecting that answer. "Why Carter?"

"It's simple. He's the only person that has ever had faith in me. I don't want to let him down."

"What about your family?"

"You've seen how they are. They think I'm a joke. I admit I've given them reason to think that in the past, but in the last five years I've truly contributed to our family business. No one can see past my more youthful indiscretions or the fact that I'm not always serious. Just because I don't want the boring, traditional life they want doesn't make me bad at my job or unable to meaningfully contribute ideas."

"Carter definitely believes in you. I've seen it."

He nods. "I know he does. This new business is huge for me. It might be my only opportunity to break free of the chains of my family. To have something of my own. To have autonomy in what I create."

I smile and take his hand. "For what it's worth, I believe in you. I think you're incredibly talented."

"Thank you. That means a lot to me."

"I meant it. I hate how your family treats you. I know I

don't have a ton of big family experience, but the way they are with you isn't right. Can you imagine Reagan ever talking to Skylar at work the way your family talks to you?"

He shakes his head but says nothing else. He simply looks around. He's avoiding this conversation. Avoidance seems to be a thing for him.

His eyes eventually land back on me. "Do you want to get out of here?"

I nod. "Sure."

"Let's go let loose and have some fun."

Per his promise from earlier, we head to the bar that had swings for barstools. We walk in and I can't help but smile at what I see. It's small but crowded. It has a completely beachy vibe with pastel, distressed wood everywhere, lanterns, and the floor is sand. I've never seen anything like it.

The DJ is playing, the music blaring, and people are dancing. Everyone seems to be having a great time.

We go to the bar and order two rounds of tequila shots each, but unfortunately all of the swings are taken. We down our shots and Collin takes my hand and leads me to the dance floor.

He twirls me around while we dance and laugh. He's so fun to be with, and he's a fantastic dancer. I guess I've never been dancing with him before. I'm having the best time.

For several songs, we simply let loose and have a great time, both of us smiling through it all. We're out in public, together, with our hands on each other. It feels good. It feels great.

A slow song begins, and he pulls me into his arms, tight to his muscular body. His hands unashamedly rub all over me. I'm so turned on by his touch. Everything about him turns me on.

We sway our hips in unison. He buries his nose in my neck, as he often does. "God, I love the way you smell. It's fruity, womanly, sexy, and drives me wild. It makes me think of every inch of your body that I've explored. That I want to keep exploring. It's uniquely you and I crave it."

He starts slowly kissing up my neck until he reaches my lips. He only nibbles on them at first, teasing me.

He rubs his thumb over my face, and we stare into each other's eyes. The air has become thicker. It feels intense.

I whisper, "Collin."

He nods, whispering back, "I know," as his lips find mine. He pulls me as close to him as possible. I run my fingers through his hair, kissing him back with everything I have. This kiss somehow feels different from the rest. I don't know what it is, but we kiss and kiss, not caring that anyone else is around us.

The slow song ends and a faster one begins, but we don't stop our slow movements or our passionate kiss. His mouth, his taste, it's all consuming.

When we eventually break apart, I run my hands up his chest. "Let's go back to our room. I want you."

He runs his nose along my cheek. "Not yet. I told you that I have plans for us tonight."

He looks over my shoulder. "One of the swings is open."

He takes my hand in his and leads me over to it. He sits on the swing, pulling me onto his lap. The bartender approaches and we order more drinks.

He runs his hands up and down my thighs, knowing full well what those hands on my bare skin do to me. I wiggle a little in his lap. I can feel his breathing pick up and his cock harden under me.

He fiddles with his shorts for a moment and then whispers, "Lift for a second."

I place my elbows on the bar and lean forward, which lifts my weight off him. I feel him move my dress and then place his cock at my entrance. "Lean back." I do and sink straight down onto him.

I gasp in shock. I look down to see if I'm exposed, but Collin has fixed my dress so that nothing can be seen. I look around to see if anyone noticed. It doesn't look like they have.

This feels different from any time before. The plug must be making me tighter, because his cock feels even bigger and the piercing is rubbing me harder, in the best way possible.

He sweeps my hair to the side and brings his lips to my ear. "I can't begin to tell you how much I love being inside you. You feel so tight around my cock. I want to stay buried in your tight, wet pussy while you come around my cock."

I've never had a man talk to me the way he does. I moan, "Collin."

"I'm going to start swinging. Every time we come forward toward the bar, I'll plant my feet on the bottom of the bar and push, both away from the bar and into you. I need you to squeeze me on the way up though."

I breathe, "I'll try."

I feel so intensely full right now. With his cock inside me, and the plug, I must be tight as hell around him. It feels like I am. The sensation is different. Good different. My body is numb and tingling everywhere.

He discreetly starts to swing. Every time we go forward, he plants his feet, abruptly changing direction, and thrusting further into me.

Even though I know it's coming, each time is a shock to

my body. A *deeply* pleasurable shock.

Each time he swings back up, I try to remember to squeeze him, but this isn't exactly easy. I'm on sensory overload having him inside me, surrounded by people, with that plug adding to the sensations. I didn't expect it to feel this good. The excitement of doing this out in public is only enhancing the euphoria.

"That's it, baby girl, grip me. Fuck, Jade, you feel so good. So tight. Tell me how you're feeling?"

I barely manage, "I can't. It's too much. I can't think right now."

He tightens his hold around my waist. "Give me your words. You can do it."

I pant for a few moments, but eventually answer, "My whole body is overstimulated. You're pushing so deep. I'm so incredibly full. Full of you. I've never felt anything better."

"I can feel it. You're dripping down onto me. You're so sexy. I love how wet you are. I love that my shorts will be covered in your juices."

Shit, he's hot. He always talks during sex, with his dirty words only adding to my gratification.

Every damn time we come forward, he slams into me, hitting the right spot. I think my eyes are crossing. I can't believe I'm going to be able to come like this, surrounded by all these people.

I feel his textured hand move around my neck. He knows what that does to me. He's not even squeezing it yet, and he has me on the cusp.

I'm giving everything I have to clench around him. I want this to be good for him too. I reach back and scrape my nails on the back of his neck. He loves when I claw at him, when I mark him.

I can't imagine what we look like to an outsider. I'm holding back my screams, but my chest is heaving, and my face is undoubtedly painted that I'm being fucked.

I quickly look around. People are dancing, drinking, and laughing, not paying any attention to us.

He applies more pressure around my neck. My eyes flutter. "Oh god, Collin, I'm coming."

"I can feel you shaking. Fuck yes. Just like that, baby girl. Let go. Now."

Two more hard thrusts into me and I feel my body shake and then explode around his. My world is dark, full of one thing. Pleasure.

I squeeze my eyes shut and dig my nails into his thighs. I'm biting my lip so hard. It takes every ounce of will I have not to scream.

I feel his hot breath on my neck as his breathing increases. He pulls me tight to him as I feel him stiffen and then let out a grunt.

The swing gradually begins to slow down until it comes nearly to a complete stop, only swaying slightly. We're still. Neither of us is able to move from the position we're in. The only movements are our chests as we catch our breath.

I lean my head back on his shoulder and continue to breathe hard. We don't move for a few minutes, simply letting what we just did sink in.

That was incredible. He's incredible.

All of a sudden, I feel something substantial dripping out of me. I lift my head and turn it toward him. "Collin, I think the condom broke."

He whispers, "Shit. Jade, I'm so sorry. I forgot to put one on. I wasn't thinking."

I immediately attempt to lift off him, but he holds me

in place. "Wait a second. If you lift off me, my dick will be hanging out."

I'm so angry right now that I don't give a crap. "You have five seconds to take care of business before I leave."

He leans me forward and I assume tucks himself back in. As soon as his arm releases me, I jump up and make a beeline for the exit.

He shouts for me, but I don't miss a stride.

"Jade! Please stop."

I don't. I run. Tears streaming down my cheeks. His come streaming down the insides of my thighs.

I keep running as fast as I can toward our room. I need to clean myself. I'm desperate to clean myself.

He eventually catches me and grabs me by the shoulders. He turns me to him, clearly taken aback by my tear-soaked face. "What's wrong? I'm sorry about the condom, but you're on the pill. What's the big deal?"

I shout, "What's the big deal? I don't know what you've been out there doing. I don't know who you've been with."

He takes a step back, looking hurt. "I have no interest in anyone but you. I haven't so much as looked at another woman since we started dating."

"Dating? Is that what we're doing, Collin?"

His face is stoic.

"Dating is when people go out and do things together. All we do is stay home and fuck. You won't be seen in public with me. You're afraid of your precious Carter and the world knowing that we fuck. You're not dating me, you're ashamed of me."

I can't believe he's making me cry. I hate crying. I never cry. It shows weakness. That's what he is. My weakness.

He runs his hands through his hair. "I'm not ashamed. I just can't tell him."

"Can't or won't? You're such a fucking coward. You always take the path of least resistance, Collin. You couldn't handle sleeping with an eighteen-year-old, so you just left the party without a word. You won't man up and tell Carter about us. You won't man up and tell your family that you don't want to work with them. The easy road isn't always the right one, Collin. Sometimes you need to grow a pair. Sometimes you need to take the harder path to get to the right place."

He tries to touch my arm, but I slap it away. "Don't fucking touch me. I wouldn't want anyone to get the impression that you actually care."

I turn and sprint for our room. When I get inside, I immediately remove my dress and bra and step into the shower. I turn it as hot as it will go.

I quickly dispose of the plug and then scrub myself for an hour. I think I washed my insides as much as my outsides. My whole body is red and raw, but I don't care. I need it cleaned of him.

It takes time, but I do eventually calm down. My mind is now racing a mile a minute. Did I overact? I don't know. I'm so confused by what I'm feeling right now.

And that's the problem. I'm feeling. That's not me. How did I get here? How did I let this happen? How did I let Collin Fitz in? It was gradual. It wasn't overnight. But it's happened. I hate myself for letting it get this far when I know better.

When I eventually surface from the bathroom, I'm wearing one of the hotel robes. Collin is in the bed, in his boxer briefs, facing away from me.

I quietly slide into the bed and face away from him. It takes a few hours of tossing and turning before sleep eventually finds me.

CHAPTER TWENTY

COLLIN

I didn't sleep much last night. She's right in so much of what she said. Maybe all of it. I float along not taking what I want because it's easier than confronting anyone. While I may joke around and push buttons, I'm afraid of confrontation. She rightfully called me out on it. She might be sixteen years younger than me, but she's so much smarter and stronger than me. I don't deserve her.

I was happy she at least got into bed with me last night. I wasn't sure she would. Part of me feared she would head straight for the airport.

As daylight breaks, I roll onto my back. She's also on her back, awake, staring at the ceiling.

We're both silent for several long minutes. Both are aware the other is awake but doing nothing about it.

At some point, she rolls my way and lays the side of her head and face on my chest. "I'm sorry I freaked out on you. My biggest fear in life is ending up like my mother. Twenty-two, pregnant, and alone."

I squeeze her. "You'd never be alone."

She nods. "I'm sorry for the things I said. You've been very clear since day one what we are. I shouldn't have turned it on you. I wanted the same things. It's not fair for me to change the rules mid-game. I know exactly what we are."

It's not lost on me that she used the word *wanted*, as in the past tense. Does she want something different now? I think I do.

I want to tell her that I want us to be more, but the fact is, I'm afraid of what it will mean. I could lose the most important person in the world to me. I'm afraid I'll eventually hurt her worse than I did last night. She's right about me. I'm a coward. At some point, I need to grow a pair.

For now, I just want to be with her and enjoy Mexico. We'll see what happens when we get home.

I rub her face. "Can we just put this stuff aside for now, relax, and have a fun time while we're here?"

She looks up and gives me a sweet smile. "I'd like that."

I hold her chin so that our eyes remain locked. "I need you to know that there's been no one else since we started things. I've never remotely considered it."

She nods. "For me too."

We have a nice morning. Since we're up early, we go for a long walk along the quiet beach. We talk about everything.

I tell her how many times I've tried to persuade my family to change their business strategy, but I'm never heard. Admittedly, I keep beating that dead horse over and over, hoping they'll change their minds, but the simple fact is, they won't.

I love hearing about her passion for her job. Somehow at only twenty-two, she's doing what she loves, and at thirty-eight I'm not. It's amazing how much Reagan trusts her with such an important position and consults her on many big, company-wide decisions. Even though I've been doing my job, or some version thereof, for twenty years, my family doesn't have that same confidence in me. Their lack of faith and support is really wearing on me.

She's very encouraging of me to leave my family business and go at it alone. She believes in me and, for the first time in my life, I'm starting to believe in myself. I hate that I feel the need to leave the business my father built, but I want to be happy. I want to build what I love.

I've never had someone like this to talk to before. I have Carter, who always believes in me, but I can truly be myself with Jade. It's an intimacy and trust I've never shared with anyone, certainly not a woman with whom I share a bed. She makes me want to be a better man. The kind she deserves.

After breakfast, I suggest that she get a long massage in the spa. After the events of last night, I want her to be spoiled and relaxed.

She seems excited about it. She runs up to the room to change while I make all the arrangements.

A man named Miguel will be her masseur. He and I have a little chat about it beforehand and come to a mutual understanding.

I walk her to the spa door and tell her I'll be back

for her in two hours. I tell her I'm going to hit the gym.

At the allocated time, I quietly slip into her massage room. Jade is on her stomach with her face resting down in the round face cradle. The entire back of her body is exposed with the exception of her ass, which is covered by a towel. She is long and luscious. Her body is utter perfection.

Miguel quietly exits and closes the door behind him without Jade noticing. I add a bit of oil to my hands and start kneading her lower back, slowly working my way up to her neck and shoulders.

She moans, "Hmm, Miguel, your hands are amazing."

I can't help but smile.

I move on to her legs, starting at her feet and then up to her thighs. When I work on the left side, I get fairly high up on her inner thigh, but on the right, I brush by her pussy.

She stiffens for a moment but doesn't otherwise move.

I remove the towel and begin massaging her ass. Damn she has an exquisite ass. It fits in my hands so perfectly. I'm dying to get in there. My cock is pushing hard against my bathing suit, begging to be freed and to slip inside her.

I spread her legs a bit, and she allows it. I rub her inner thighs, working my way to her center. This time, I run my fingers through her lips. She's wet. Very wet. And she doesn't flinch.

I slide two fingers into her, and she lets out a loud moan. "Yes, Miguel, like that."

I probably should be pissed, but I'm too turned on to care in the moment.

I push deeper into her, hitting the spot I've become intimately acquainted with. The one that's making her grip the sheets on the massage table and rotate her hips.

"Oh fuck, Miguel, that's the right spot. Stay there."

I'm plunging in and out at a fast pace. With my other fingers, I apply pressure to her clit, which is swollen and throbbing to the touch.

She's getting louder and louder, pushing herself onto my fingers more and more aggressively, practically riding them.

"Oh god, Miguel, I'm coming." I feel her tighten around my fingers as she drenches my hands with her come.

She's no longer moving her body but is breathing loudly. Her face is still buried in the cradle. "Collin, get inside me. Now."

In my best Spanish accent, I say, "It's Miguel."

She lets out a laugh. "It hasn't been Miguel for fifteen minutes."

In my normal voice, I ask, "When did you know?"

She lifts her head, turns it, and smiles at me. "The second your hands touched me." She looks at me with pure heat in her eyes. "Collin, I'd know your hands anywhere. They're *very* distinct. Now why don't you oil them up a bit more and get them back on my body where they belong."

Leaning on her elbow, she nods at my obvious erection and bites her lip. "It's my turn to give you a massage. The oil might help with that."

I trace my fingertips along one side of her body. Goosebumps appear everywhere. I can see her breasts now. I brush my fingers over them. Her nipples immediately harden at my touch. I continue to move my hands all over her body until I reach the crack in her ass, applying a bit of pressure. "Oil is good for *a lot* of things."

She takes a deep breath. She rolls over onto her back and then sits up. She grabs the waistband of my bathing suit and pulls me closer to her. Just before our lips meet, she whispers, "Okay."

I pause for a moment, letting that sink in. "Okay?"

She visibly swallows but then nods.

"Are you sure?"

She breathes close to my mouth, "Yes. I want to experience it for the first time with you. I know you'll take care of me."

I bend and close the distance between us, rubbing my lips against her soft ones. Teasing them, but not yet sealing them over hers.

All of a sudden, there's a loud knock at the door. We hear Miguel shouting, "Señor, your hour is up."

I lift and turn my head, "Miguel, just charge me for another hour."

"Sí, Señor."

Jade looks at me and smiles. "I feel so special when the man I'm about to let pop my anal cherry rents a room for us by the hour."

I can't help but laugh at that. "We can leave if you want."

She shakes her head as she runs her hands down my body, unfastens my bathing suit, and pulls out my cock. She gathers some of the oil covering her body in her hand and then gives me a few pumps. "I'm exactly where I want to be, doing exactly what I want to do, with the only person I want to do it with."

I remove my bathing suit, climb up on the table, and sit between her legs, pulling her legs over mine. The tops of her legs are resting on my thighs.

She grabs the oil, squirts some on her hands, and rubs it all over my bare chest.

"I love your chest. It's so broad and muscular."

I squirt oil onto my hands and mimic her movements with my hands on her chest. "I love your chest too. I'm thankful it's not broad and muscular. Or hairy."

She giggles until I lean forward and silence her with a kiss. It's simply soft and unrushed. I move my hands around to her back and pull her hard to my body. Her oil-soaked front is rubbing on mine. My oil-covered cock is rubbing through her pussy.

"Hmm, Collin. I want you." She mumbles into my mouth, "How does this work?"

"Why don't you be on top? That way we can go at your pace."

"You can do anal with the woman on top?"

I smile. "Yes. You realize that hole is only about two inches from the other one? You can do everything that way that you can do the *regular* way."

She looks down at herself and starts laughing. "No, I didn't realize that."

I squeeze more oil into my hand. I reach down between us and find her back entrance, slowly sliding two fingers in. "Last night loosened you up a bit."

"Collin, that anal plug and even your meaty fingers are *way* smaller than your monster cock."

I smile as I continue pushing in and out of her with one hand. With the other, I tuck her hair behind her ears. "I would never do anything to hurt you. You know that, right?"

She nods.

"Tell me what you're feeling. You know I like to hear it."

"It's weird and different, yet still good and, for some reason, has my clit desperate for contact. I feel like I'll come if you brush by it."

"That's a good girl. I love when you describe how you feel."

I slowly withdraw my fingers. I gather a bit more oil and rub it all over my cock.

She grabs onto my cock. "Let me do that."

She starts pumping me tight and fast. It feels too good. I can't let it go on.

I grab her wrist and pull her hand away. "Now lift up."

She does and I position myself at her back entrance. I slide just the tip in. "Take me at your pace, baby girl. Work your way down as you feel comfortable."

I hold her ass to help guide her, but not push her. She closes her eyes, takes a deep breath, and moves down a bit.

I bend my head and suck her nipple into my mouth, hoping to distract her. She runs her fingers through my hair as she sinks down another inch or so.

I lick my way up her chest and neck, eventually reaching her mouth. I gently bite her lower lip, extending it as far as it will go.

She whimpers and sinks down the last few inches.

I release her lip. "You're doing so good, baby girl. Tell me how it feels."

"You're truly feeling like my big daddy now." I smile. "I feel full. Full of you." She exhales, "I love it."

"You *are* full of me. I love it too. Tell me more."

"My legs feel like they're vibrating. There's a tingling down the backs of them. My need for you to touch me is manic. Please touch me. I need your hands on me."

"Start moving and I will."

She gradually lifts up and then sinks back down on a loud moan. "Oh my god, that's good. Holy shit."

I start kissing her neck, as I grab her ass and guide her movements with my hands. She throws her head back as she begins to get into it, coming down harder and faster each time.

"That's it, baby girl. You're doing so good. You feel perfect. So tight. So hot. Do you want me to touch you?"

"Hmm."

"Use your words."

"Yes! Please."

"Keep moving like this and I will. I can't wait for your orgasm to milk me."

She's moving as fast and hard as she can. I bring my thumb to her clit and begin to circle it.

She grabs onto the back of my hair and pulls it. "Oh yes, Collin."

I love how into this she's getting. "Talk to me."

"I'm about to come. It's going to be huge. I can feel it all over my body. God, yes."

A few more circles of my thumb and I feel her tighten and vibrate against my cock. She screams out.

I suck her tongue into my mouth to quiet her noises, as she literally milks my cock clean of everything in there.

Her movements stop and she looks at me wide-eyed. Her grip has loosened on my hair, but she's still holding onto it. "Wow. That was way better than I thought it would be."

I let out a laugh. "I told you."

She kisses up my neck. "Now I want you to fuck me the regular way."

I pull her chest flush with mine, craving the post-orgasmic contact. "I need to rinse off first. And I need a few minutes to recover."

"Ugh. That's the worst part about being with an old man. Recovery time."

I narrow my eyes at her, and she smiles. "My recovery time is practically superhuman. Five minutes isn't too much to ask for."

"Whatever, old man."

"Are you looking for spanking, baby girl?"

Her eyes light up. "Maybe I am, Big Daddy."

CHAPTER TWENTY-ONE

COLLIN

Today is our last full day in Mexico. The week has flown by. It's been perfect. We've laughed, danced, and fucked our way through the vacation. We haven't remotely discussed us or what will happen when we get home. It's a bit of a black cloud looming, but I've been trying not to think about it. I haven't been successful.

I've been contemplating her words: *I know what we are.* We're casual. That's what we agreed to. That's all we're both capable of, right? Maybe that's where we need to stay. But when I consider what that means, when I consider not being with her, I don't like it. My head is a mess over us, but I've been playing it cool.

We're sitting at the pool today. The woman next to Jade has struck up a conversation with her. They've been chatting for over an hour. Her husband keeps drooling over Jade's body. His eyes haven't left her the entire hour.

I stand and grab the suntan lotion. "Babe, you need more lotion. You're getting red."

She looks up at me. "I am?" She looks down at her body. "I don't see it."

"I do. Let me put lotion on you. Sit up for a minute."

She does.

I climb behind her on the lounge chair so that I'm straddling it and I begin rubbing her body. *All* over her body. She turns back and whispers, "I didn't realize my nipples also need lotion."

I smile. "I take this job seriously. I'm very thorough."

"It seems you are."

I stare at the husband with a *she's mine* look. He laughs, knowing exactly what I'm doing.

Jade turns back. "Are you done?"

"Yes. I'm not getting up. Lay back into me."

She shrugs. "Suit yourself."

She lays back into my chest and I continue rubbing her shoulders. She sighs in contentment. "That feels good, Miguel." She giggles. "By the way, Belinda and Travis are having dinner at the steakhouse in the caves tonight. They invited us to join them."

"Who are Belinda and Travis?"

She elbows me. "The people we've been talking to all day."

"Oh. Sure. Whatever you want."

I turn and Belinda smiles. "We've heard great things about it."

I nod. Belinda is cute. She's got red, messy hair, and a sexy, curvy body. I can't see her eyes because she's wearing sunglasses. Travis is a big, muscular guy.

He's got dark, curly hair. I suppose he's decent looking. Not Collin Fitz level, but good enough.

Travis and I end up chatting the rest of the afternoon. He's not a bad guy. I may have misjudged him. He's an architect, so we spend a lot of time discussing design. He marvels at some of the things I've done. He takes time to look through a few of the photos I have of Carter's house on my phone. The girls chat away, and we all order several rounds of drinks.

We play volleyball in the pool, and even have a good time with a few chicken fights. It's been fun hanging out with another couple. Besides our night out with Cam and Shiloh, we haven't done any of that.

As evening approaches, we head to our respective rooms to get dressed for the evening. I walk into the bathroom as Jade is applying her lipstick.

I wrap my arms around her from behind and meet her eyes with mine in the mirror. "You're so naturally beautiful. You don't need any makeup."

She gives me a small smile. "It's just a little lip gloss. I'm not wearing anything else."

I kiss her neck. "You don't need any of it."

"You don't mind when I leave lipstick marks on your cock."

"True. Leave the lip gloss."

She laughs and we head down to dinner. She gasps as we enter the restaurant. "Wow. I've never seen anything like this."

I look around. "Neither have I." We're legitimately in an underground cave. The turquoise water is running through it. It's breathtaking.

We see Travis and Belinda already at a table

waving us over. They clean up nicely. I can see Belinda has blue eyes. She's in a tight, white, summer dress, showing off her full figure. Her red hair, which was in a bun all day, is down now in tight curls. She's very attractive.

Travis is dressed similarly to me, in khaki shorts and a nice T-shirt. He runs his eyes up and down Jade's body. I don't blame him. She looks like a supermodel. She's in a short, patterned skirt and an off-the-shoulder purple top that reveals a hint of her flat stomach.

We eat, drink, and laugh through dinner. After we order dessert, Travis says, "We have the penthouse suite. Do you guys want to come up and see it?"

Jade's eyes light up. "I bet the views are spectacular from there."

Travis nods. "They are."

Jade has no clue that we were just propositioned to swing. Belinda and Travis are obviously swingers.

I used to do partner swapping all the time and never gave it a second thought. Hell, Carter and I spent a good portion of our twenties sharing women, swapping women, and basically doing it all without any real inhibition.

Maybe Jade does realize it, and this is what she wants. It's what I did in my twenties. Maybe she should have the opportunity to do the same. Maybe we need this to prove we can be casual.

As we walk out of dinner, I whisper in her ear, "Just making sure you realize that them inviting us up to their room is their way of propositioning us for sex."

She pinches her eyebrows. "It is?"

I nod. "Yes. Is that what you want?"

"I didn't realize it. Obviously you did when we agreed to go. Is it what you want?"

"I'm fine either way. Whatever makes you happy."

She gives a tight smile. One that doesn't reach her eyes. "Let's just go see what happens."

"Okay."

We walk into their suite. Travis and Belinda show us around. It's definitely as billed. The nicest room in the resort. It's got everything you can imagine. It has both indoor and outdoor jacuzzis, a full bar, two separate bedrooms and bathrooms, a pool table, and a giant outdoor space with hammocks. Even at night, the outdoor views of the ocean are breathtaking.

Travis makes us all drinks at the bar. Belinda smiles. "Do you guys want to use the outdoor jacuzzi? You can see the ocean from there."

Jade responds, "We didn't bring bathing suits."

I whisper, "She didn't mean with bathing suits."

"Oh. Umm...sure."

Travis returns with our drinks. He takes Belinda's hand and kisses it. They walk out to the jacuzzi. They completely undress in front of us, step in, and sit down in the jacuzzi.

Belinda looks back at us. "It feels incredible. Come join us."

I turn to Jade. "We don't have to. We can leave."

She straightens her back. "No, let's stay. We should do this."

We walk outside. I want to make her comfortable, so I begin to disrobe first. With her back to the jacuzzi, Jade stares at me while I undress. I remove my shirt, tossing it to the side. I then remove my shorts and boxer briefs in one go. I hear Belinda gasp. Jade looks at me and gives me a small smile at the gasp.

I step to her and quietly say, "Do you want help?"

She nods. I pull her top over her head. She's not wearing a bra. Her back is to them, so they can't see anything yet. For now, I'm the only one that can see her big, perfect, beautiful breasts.

I slip my thumbs into her skirt and panties and pull both down at once. She steps out of them.

I look up and down her body. I move close to her and run my thumb along her jaw. I can't help but bring my lips to hers. She's irresistible.

She leans her body into mine and kisses me back. First running her hands along my chest, and then around the back of my neck.

The kiss begins to deepen when we hear a throat clear. We both turn our heads toward the hot tub. Belinda smiles. "Save some for the rest of us."

I see Jade take a big breath as she slowly turns around and steps into the jacuzzi. As I do the same, I notice a bowl of condoms on the ledge. These two aren't very subtle.

We sit with drinks and chat for a short while. Travis gradually moves closer and closer to Jade, while Belinda gradually moves closer and closer to me.

Eventually, Travis pulls Jade onto his lap, her back to his front. He runs his nose along her neck and hands up and down her sides. "You have a beautiful body."

She hesitates briefly but then says, "Thank you."

Belinda straddles my lap and begins kissing along my chest and neck. Her hand starts to grab for my cock, which couldn't possibly be more limp, but I grab her wrist. "Not yet."

She nods and continues kissing my neck, running her hands all over my chest.

Jade watches us. Her face is stoic. I have no read on her right now. But when Travis's hand cups her breast, I see her eyes turn glassy.

I can't take it anymore. "Stop!"

I look at Jade. "Do you want to do this? I don't."

She slowly shakes her head. As soon as she does, Travis removes his hands from her body.

I gently move Belinda aside and go to Jade. I pull her off his lap and to me. "I'm sorry. I don't want anyone else touching you. I can't bear it."

She smiles. "I don't want anyone else touching me either. Or anyone else touching you."

I nod in agreement as our lips meet. She lifts her nearly weightless body and wraps her legs tightly around me.

I move us back until I'm seated again, all without breaking the kiss. Her pussy is grinding on my cock. She runs her fingers through my hair and mumbles into my lips, "I want you. Now."

I motion toward our company. She stops what she's doing and turns their way. Belinda is sitting across Travis's lap. He licks his lips and says, "Can we watch you guys fuck?"

Jade turns back to me with a big smile. She shrugs, "Sure, why not? It's the greatest show on earth."

I smirk as I kiss down her body and suck one of her hardened nipples into my mouth.

I hear Belinda say, "She's got great tits, doesn't she."

Travis responds, "Yes. So do you, baby." I hear them start to kiss.

I reach down and slide two fingers inside Jade. She whispers in my ear, "I only want you on me and inside me. I hated his hands on me." She begins to roll her hips, riding my fingers with increased speed.

I release her nipple and whisper back, "I hated watching it." I grab her hand and put it around my painfully hard cock. "Do you feel how hard I am?"

She breathes, "Yes, I want it."

"I couldn't even get a semi for her. Nothing. Nada. No one does it for me like you do. It's all for you. You own me." I have no control over the words coming out of my mouth right now, but I mean every one of them. She does own me. I don't remotely want anyone else. I don't think I ever will.

"Get inside me."

"Do you want it under the water where they can't see, or on top where they can?"

My wild girl gives me my favorite mischievous smile in the world. She pulls my hair, so our eyes meet. "Show her what she's missing out on. Fuck me like you own me, because you *do* own me, Collin."

I slide out from under her. "Grab onto the side of the tub. Get a good grip."

She quickly does as she's told while I take one of the condoms and sheath myself. She positions her knees on the bench, leaving her entire ass just above water level.

I move behind her and bend my head down, licking her from front to back. I then return to her front opening, spearing into her with my tongue a few times. She wiggles her hips pushing onto my face.

I hear Travis say to Belinda, "Face them and sit on my cock so we can both watch while I'm inside you."

I continue fucking her with my tongue, while moving my fingers through her wetness. She uses the ledge to push herself and ride my face hard.

I've got her worked into a complete frenzy. I am too. My cock feels like it's going to explode. My need to be inside her right now is maniacal.

I lift my head and quickly bring my tip to her entrance as I slam into her. She yells out, "Ah, Collin!"

I give her a few seconds to acclimate to my size. I lick up her back and grab onto her nipples, squeezing them hard.

She lets out a loud moan. "Fuck me, Big Daddy."

I begin my movements inside her. It's slow and deep at first. I love that she's making noises like we're alone. Like two people aren't watching us right now.

I hear Travis and Belinda getting louder. She's getting close to her own orgasm.

I increase my pace, squeezing her hips and pummeling into her as hard as I can, over and over.

Both Jade and Belinda are loud. If anyone else is out on their balconies, they'll know exactly what we're doing up here.

I spit down into her ass. I rub it around with my thumb and immediately push it inside her back entrance. "Oh, fuck, Collin. So good. Go deep."

She's using her grip to meet me thrust for thrust as we fuck each other.

"Tell them, Jade. Tell them how it feels. Use your words."

"Fuck. So fucking good. His giant cock is so deep inside me. I can feel his piercing rubbing me. His thumb in my ass is making my whole body shake. He's a fucking God. I'm about to come."

"Good job, baby girl."

I hear Belinda and Travis both scream out into their orgasms. My girl's words sent them over the edge. They're doing the same to me.

Jade breathes out, "Big Daddy, you know what to do. No one does it better. Bring it home."

I slide my hand up her back and around her throat. I hold it there, but don't apply much pressure.

"Tell them who decides when you come."

"You do! Not until you tell me."

"That's fucking right." I squeeze her neck. I can feel her start to spasm around my cock, but she's doing her best to hold off.

I don't want her to wait any longer. "Baby girl, come. Now."

And she does. All over me. Yelling my name.

Her pussy squeezes me while her juices flow out onto me. I can't hold back as I grunt her name into my own release.

I gradually still inside her as the last bit of my come drips into the condom. I remove my hand from her throat and pull my thumb out of her ass.

I run my hands up her body as she begins to stand upright. She turns around, her eyes meeting mine. Her face is flushed from her orgasm. Her eyes are full of lust for me. She doesn't care that there are people behind me. It's just me and her. No one else exists right now.

I pull the front of her body close to mine. We share the same air as we continue to stare at each other. I run my fingertips down the side of her beautiful face.

The only face I want to look at. It hits me like a ton of bricks at that precise moment. I only see her. I only want her.

I love her. I'm in love with Jade McGinley.

JADE

We land in Philly as the sun sets. I sigh. "Back to reality."

He nods as he squeezes my hand. "I had the best week."

I lean into him. "Me too. I wish it didn't have to end."

He nuzzles into my neck and kisses it. "I feel the same way."

He looks up at me. "Can I ask you a question?"

"Yes."

"If I didn't stop things with Travis last night, what would have happened?"

"I knew you would stop it before it got too far, but I just wanted to see how long you'd let it go. Even if you didn't, I would have. I certainly wouldn't have had sex with him if that's what you're asking. Not a chance in hell."

"How did you know I would stop it? I didn't even know."

I smile. "When you said you were fine with it, you were scratching your neck. I knew you weren't fine with it."

He nods in understanding. "I did stuff like that in my twenties and a bit in my thirties. I just don't want to deny you any experiences you might want to have. If you wanted it, I would have muscled through it, even though it was killing me. That's what I was trying to do. But when he touched you, I could see in your eyes that you didn't want it."

"I didn't want it." I kiss his lips. "You're the only man I want right now."

A huge smile breaks out on his face.

We collect our bags and catch a cab at the airport. When we get to my place, he not only removes my luggage from the trunk, but his as well. I turn to him. "What are you doing? Don't you want to go home?"

He shakes his head. "I'm too used to sleeping with you every night. I can't just go cold turkey. I have to work up to it. Maybe an hour nap here or there. It will probably take weeks, maybe months, to get back to normal."

"Is that so? From one week of sleeping together every night?"

He nods. "Yep."

I'm trying not to freak out as the realization hits me too. I don't want to sleep without him next to me either.

CHAPTER TWENTY-TWO

JADE

We've been back from Mexico for a week. I have to admit it. I've fallen for Collin. What's worse is that he knows it and isn't really acknowledging it. Yes, we had our moment in the jacuzzi, but we've gone right back into hibernation. We've spent every night together, but we're at his place or mine. That's it. I feel like we're going backward. I know I can't complain. This is what I said I wanted.

I know this only ends with him leaving, but I can't seem to find the will to beat him to the punch. I suppose I'm taking it as long as I can get it. When he inevitably leaves me, I won't be okay, but I guess I'll do what I've always done, keep my chin up and push forward. Just thinking about going back to life without him makes my chest hurt. I can't imagine what it will feel like when it's my reality.

It's a warm, late spring day. Aunt Darian and Jackson opened their pool early and the whole family is heading over there this afternoon and tvening. All the boys leave for their big fishing trip tomorrow. I guess it's their grand send-off.

Collin texted that Carter invited him. He has no clue why. I suppose Collin has been to one or two of Aunt Darian and Jackson's pool parties throughout the years, but it's certainly not the norm.

As soon as I walk in, Reagan pulls me aside. "Tell me the truth. Were you in Mexico with your friends or Collin?"

"Why do you ask?"

"Because he's sitting out there with the same glowing tropical tan that you have. When Carter asked him about it, he said he was working shirtless on a job this week. I'm really struggling with keeping this from Carter. I don't like having secrets from my husband. Don't lie to me. I'm too fucking pregnant right now for any bullshit." She looks like she's ready to pop.

"Yes, Collin and I went away together. I don't know what you want me to say. I no longer care if you tell people. It's Collin that cares. He's afraid that Carter will lose his shit. He's afraid Carter will lose faith in him. His entire mental psyche depends on Carter's damn approval. I guess I don't want the hassle of my father knowing, but I don't otherwise care anymore."

"Your dad would literally flip his shit."

"I know, but I'm willing to face it. I'm not afraid."

"It's going to come out one way or the other. You're both better off getting ahead of it."

"I'll see what I can do. I'll talk to Collin about it."

THIS AFTERNOON HAS BEEN complete and utter torture. Being around Collin but not being able to touch him or have him touch me is a level of pain I've never known. It's not just the touching. It's different than at the family dinner months ago. That was physical. Now it's so much more. I'm used to having him in my space. Having him here but not having him in my space is bothering me.

I see him struggling too. It's getting ridiculous. We should just tell everyone and be done with it. Maybe things will be awkward for a bit when we break up, but we had an awkward four years, so I'm sure we can deal with it.

He's in the pool playing with the kids. Just what I need to see. Him being sweet while his muscles ripple as he throws them around. It's like the water droplets are dripping off him in slow motion. Taunting me.

I'm focused on his pathway to paradise. I know what lies underneath that bathing suit, and it's exactly that, paradise.

Reagan waddles over to me and hands me a pair of sunglasses. "Put these on. You're staring at him like you're going to fuck him in the pool in front of everyone. Other people are going to pick up on it."

I look up at her. The pain must be evident on my face. Her eyes widen and she places her hand on my shoulder. "Oh, Jade, you're hurting. Why are you doing this to yourself?"

"Do you think I should end things with him?"

She shakes her head. "No. Not at all. Just the opposite. You've clearly fallen for him. If he feels the same, just come out with it. I don't think the fallout will be as bad as he thinks it will."

"He's so non-confrontational. It's his least attractive quality."

She rubs my arm. "I'm so sorry. You don't deserve that.

You deserve someone who wants to shout it from the rooftops."

"Thanks." I stand. My mind is racing. "I'll be right back."

I need a moment to myself. I head inside to the bathroom and close the door behind me. I lean my back against the wall and take a few deep breaths. Tears are stinging my eyes. What the fuck have I done to myself? How did I let it get this far?

About two minutes later, the door opens and Collin walks in, closing the door behind him.

He makes his way to me. "Fuck, Jade. Seeing you and not being close to you or touching you is a fresh brand of hell for me."

I make my way to him and breathe, "Me too," as our bodies come together.

He pushes me back against the wall and lifts me by the ass. I wrap my legs around him. He kisses up my neck. "I need to be close to you. Inside you."

"Yes." My need to be connected to him is overwhelming.

He frees his cock from his bathing suit, quickly slides on a condom that has magically appeared, slides my bikini bottoms to the side, and thrusts into me.

We both breathe a sigh of relief as if our bodies joining is our sense of peace in the world. We're still, as his lips simply brush over mine. "Jade, I need you."

I run my fingers through his hair as I dust my lips over his scruff. "I need you too."

He pulls my head so that he can look me in the eyes. "I *really* need you."

I nod in understanding.

He starts his movements in and out of me. I don't

know how, considering we're in a bathroom up against a wall, but what we do isn't fucking. It's slow and sweet, full of tender kisses and touches. Full of emotions.

His lips and hands move all over my body, and mine all over his. I know I've never made love to anyone, and I'm not sure it can be up against a bathroom wall, but to the extent it can, that's exactly what happens.

I hate to admit it, but it's kind of beautiful and special. I've never felt so much affection during sex. It's mutual, practically pouring out of him.

He whispers into my neck, "What are you doing to me?"

I fight back the tears pooling in my eyes. I can't believe I'm about to be the kind of woman who fucking cries during sex. It's just so damn intimate.

He rubs away the tear that has trickled down my cheek. "Tell me what you're feeling, baby girl."

"Everything, Collin. I feel everything."

He nods as he continues to slowly move inside me.

We come together, swallowing each other's moans with our mouths.

After I clean up and we're tucked back into place, I can't help but turn my back to him, facing the sink. I don't want him to see the emotion on my face.

He moves behind me and wraps his arms around me, pulling my back flush to his front. I keep my head down. "Jade, look up at me."

I do and my eyes meet his in the mirror. He can undoubtedly see them still full of tears.

"What's wrong? Did I hurt you?"

I subtly shake my head and croak out, "Not yet."

He sinks his face into my neck, squeezing me tight. He whispers, "I never want to hurt you."

"Collin, I don't want us to be a secret anymore. It was fun and exciting at first, and we both had our reasons, but now it just feels dirty and painful. I know it's not our original deal, and I'm sorry I want to change things, but I want to be with you out in the open."

He nods. "I know. I agree. I'm going to talk to Carter today. Just let me tell him first. Alone. Man-to-man."

I'm shocked. I didn't expect that from him. Telling Carter is a big deal for him. "You'll do that? You'll tell him we're together?"

He kisses the spot where my neck meets my shoulder. "If I lose his friendship but gain you, it will be worth it."

Now the tears officially let loose and roll down my cheeks.

"What about the new business? What if you lose that?"

"Nothing else matters to me right now but you. I'm willing to give up anything and anyone for you. You're worth it. I...I..."

And at that exact moment, the door opens, and I hear my father's voice. "You've got to be kidding me." I turn and see him standing there with pure rage on his face. "Get your fucking pervert hands off my daughter right now."

Just as Collin lifts his head and turns it, my father's right fist connects with his cheek, sending him stumbling back.

"Oh my god! Dad, stop it!" I turn to Collin, who's leaning back against the wall, blood trickling out of his lip. "Are you okay?"

He manipulates his jaw, seeming to make sure it's still in place. "I'm fine. He's not very strong." He narrows his eyes at my father. Why is he poking the bear?

"Fitz, you're nothing but a piece of shit. I'm going to kill you."

Like the lunatics they both are, they growl and lunge at each other. They're in a two-sided wrestler's headlock with each other spinning out of the bathroom and around the house completely out of control.

They're both big, muscular men. This is a recipe for disaster. I'm screaming as they tumble toward the back of the house.

They both go down hard, now rolling on the ground, knocking things over.

"Please stop!"

My dad stands and holds up his fists like a boxer, panting heavily. "Get up, Fitz. I'm going to kick your ass for even looking at her."

"Dad!"

Collin slowly stands and wipes the blood from his mouth. They're both completely out of breath. He holds up his fists, mirroring my father's. "Bring it, old man."

"Don't ever fucking touch my daughter."

Collin smirks. "I've *been* touching her. Everywhere. *Everywhere*. For months."

Oh. Fuck.

As if right out of a movie, my father practically snarls and charges at him. He crashes hard into Collin as their bodies together barrel toward the back glass wall. I scream out as they manage to crash straight through it into the backyard and stumble directly into the pool. The wall is completely shattered. There's glass everywhere.

The whole family back there is in shock at the madness taking place in front of them.

My dad and Collin are trading punches like it's a boxing match. I'm still yelling for them to stop. Reagan looks up at my tear-soaked eyes. I see her mouth, "Oh shit."

Everyone starts screaming for them to stop, but they

don't. They're punching each other, holding the other underwater, elbowing, kicking, everything.

The kids start crying. It's complete and total mayhem.

Finally, Trevor, Hayden, Lance, and Carter all jump in the pool. Carter and Lance grab my dad's arms and pull him away. Hayden and Trevor pull Collin's arms and pull him in the opposite direction.

They're each snarling at the other. They're like animals.

Jackson shouts, "What the hell is going on?"

Dad answers, "That fucking pervert was attacking Jade in the bathroom."

I shout. "Stop it, Dad. No, he wasn't. It was completely consensual."

He snaps his head to me. "What was consensual?"

"Umm, the hugging."

His eyes practically bug out of his head. "Did you...did you...with him? That lowlife?"

I turn my guilty head away, unable to maintain eye contact.

My dad lets out a growl as he breaks free of Lance and Carter and lunges back toward Collin.

Melissa shouts, "Declan, stop!"

He freezes immediately. She's like the fucking *Declan whisperer*. Her power over him defies the laws of physics.

"Look at me." He does. "Hear them out. That's what evolved adults do."

He barks, "She's not an adult."

Melissa nods. "Yes, she is. You may not want to admit it, but Jade is an adult. She's a woman. A strong, independent woman. A woman who always maintains control. She's not easily manipulated, and she's more than earned the right to be heard. Hear her out. Hear *them* out."

I've never loved Melissa more than in this moment.

He turns to Collin, who has a mixture of blood and tears on his face. His hair is strewn about all over the place. "What do you have to say for yourself, Fitz? Tell me why your hands were on my daughter in the bathroom. Tell me why she had tears running down her cheeks."

His terrified eyes find me, and then Carter. He looks pained. "Carter, I'm so sorry. I wanted to tell you this alone, man-to-man." He looks back at my father and shocks every single person out here, including myself. "We're together. We've been together for a while. I love her. I'm in love with her."

What? He's in love with me?

I have no words for that. I don't know how to manage myself right now.

All eyes move to me. I do the only thing I can think of doing in this moment. I turn around and leave.

———

COLLIN

She just fucking walked out. I told everyone she cares about that I love her, and she left. I proclaimed my love for her in front of Carter, knowing it could end our friendship, and she left. I put it all on the line for her and got nothing in return, not even the courtesy of sticking around.

Before I realize what's happening, Declan starts charging at me again and gets in a punch. I don't even feel it anymore. Nothing could possibly hurt more than Jade leaving at this moment.

All of a sudden, Reagan holds her stomach and screams. "Ahhhh. I think I'm in labor."

Everything regarding Declan and me stops, as everyone rushes to Reagan's side. Carter quickly pops out of the pool, picks her up, and carries her inside, laying her down on the couch.

The rest of us that were in the pool wrap ourselves in towels and follow suit.

We're all surrounding her. Darian starts freaking out. "Are you okay? Should I call an ambulance?"

Reagan shakes her head. "Relax, Mom. Give it a minute."

She looks around. Declan and I are on opposite sides of the room. Things seem to have cooled down. She smiles. "Oops. False alarm. It must have been indigestion." She winks at me.

I can't help but smile back at her. She just faked labor to stop the fighting. She's truly one of a kind.

She stands and looks at Melissa. "Why don't you take Uncle Declan home?"

Melissa gives a knowing nod and grabs his hand. "Let's go, Neanderthal."

He mumbles, "I'll show you a Neanderthal later."

Trevor makes a gagging face. I can't help but inwardly laugh at that.

Reagan grabs my hand and Carter's. "Why don't the three of us go and talk in private?" She turns to Jackson. "Can we use your study?"

Jackson nods. "Of course."

Darian hands me a bag of ice. "You'll need this."

I take it from her and place it on my eye. "Thank you."

Carter and I follow Reagan into the study. I've never been in this room. It's big, with wooden planked walls. The entire back wall is shelves with books, including a ladder. In addition to the desk and chairs in front of it, there's an entire sitting area with a couch and chairs. The rest of the house is so modern. This room is more traditional. Not what I would have expected.

I sit in a big chair while the two of them sit on the couch. Carter turns to Reagan. "Did you know? Did you know about Collin and Jade?"

She nods. "I figured it out the morning we were in his room. I saw the clothes and the shoes on the floor. I knew they belonged to Jade. I confronted her at the office that day and she confirmed it."

I didn't know that.

He looks hurt. "Why didn't you tell me? We don't keep secrets from each other."

She grabs his hand and kisses it. "Baby, I wanted to. I hate keeping things from you, but this wasn't my news to share. You needed to hear it from Collin. I spoke with her earlier today. I told her I couldn't keep it from you any longer. She said she'd talk to Collin about coming clean with you."

I can't help but interrupt. "I was planning to talk to you about today, Carter. That's what Jade and I were discussing in the bathroom when Declan walked in."

He nods, though the hurt and confusion are still evident on his face. He glares at me with a look of repulsion. "How did this happen? When?"

I look at Reagan. "Do you know everything?"

She shakes her head. "No, she didn't tell me anything. I gathered that you two were in Mexico together last week." I nod in confirmation. "I also gathered that it's been several months at this point.

You both stopped going out at around the same time. I put two and two together. Jade didn't deny any of it, but I don't have any details as to when or how it began."

I swallow at what I'm about to say. I can feel my heart beating fast. "Carter, know that your friendship is one of the most important things in my life. I'll tell you everything, but please don't hate me. I couldn't bear it."

Carter runs his hands through his hair. "I don't even know what to think right now. I'm in shock."

I take one more deep breath. "I imagine you remember the party you threw for Reagan right after you two got married? Her twenty-eighth."

They both nod.

"I met Jade that night."

Carter's eyes widen. "Wasn't she a minor then?"

Reagan rubs his back. "No, babe. It was right after we met Jade. She had just turned eighteen. I remember wishing her a happy birthday in my speech that night. We even had a cake for her later in the evening and sang to her."

Carter looks back at me as realization hits him. "Did you sleep with her that night? Tell me you didn't."

"Hear me out."

Carter now starts pulling his hair. "Oh my god, Collin. She was just a child."

"Technically, she wasn't. Anyway, she approached me at the bar that night. She came on to me. All I knew was that her name was Jade, and she was your co-worker. She never mentioned her age or being related to you. Just that she worked with you guys. I assumed she was around Reagan's age, maybe a little younger. Certainly not as young as she was. Why would any eighteen-year-old be your co-worker? Why would she be at the bar ordering a drink?"

Reagan lifts an eyebrow. "You didn't notice a resemblance? It's pretty strong between her and me."

"Not that I remember thinking. She wasn't as... curvaceous as you then, like she is now. You two look more alike now than you did then."

Carter has a look of pure disgust on his face. I'm going to lose my best friend over this.

I continue, "She was a six-foot, knockout blonde coming on to me. Strongly. I didn't think beyond that. We found a room and things happened."

Carter raises his voice, "What things?"

"We had sex."

Carter places his hand over his mouth. "The way you have sex?"

I shrug. "A little bit."

"Oh my god."

"She was into it. Trust me."

Carter holds his stomach. "I think I'm going to be sick."

Reagan intertwines her fingers with his. I know she's trying to soothe him.

"Anyway, we got back into the ballroom just as your speech started, Reagan. When you called Jade up to stand with you, that was the first I heard of her being your cousin. When you then mentioned her age, I almost passed out."

Carter asks, "What did you do?"

I pause for a brief moment. "Like a coward, I ran and ignored her for four years."

Reagan whispers, "Collin, how could you do that to her? She was so young."

I close my eyes. "I know. I'm ashamed of my behavior. I wish I could do it over again. I wish I could do that whole night over again." I open them. "I did my best to avoid her for four years. I can count on one hand how many times our paths crossed at your events. I didn't speak to her at all."

Carter shakes his head. "So when did you start back up again? How?"

"That night at Hole in the Wall. It was the first time we spoke." I rub my face. "I can't explain it. The chemistry and the connection were still there. The mutual attraction was so strong. She had her hands on me under the table, but I put a stop to it. She was pushing, but I told her it wasn't happening."

Carter shouts, "So then how did it happen?"

I hold up my hands. "Relax. I'm getting there. The day I was working in the nursery, and she was there using the pool. You guys weren't around. She came upstairs and approached me. I hadn't been able to stop thinking about her since the night we were all out, and things happened."

Reagan shakes her head. "Please tell me you didn't have sex in my unborn child's nursery."

I scrunch my nose. "It was on my workbench if that makes you feel better. Hmm, maybe the wall too, but that was before the wallpaper went up."

Carter looks like he's going to puke. "She's a child."

"Stop saying that. She's not a child. She's a woman. A beautiful, smart, funny, stubborn, strong woman."

"And you're in love with her?"

"I think I am." I pause. "I know I am. We started off mutually deciding to keep it casual, but along the way, we discovered that we're kind of perfect for each other."

"Does she love you?"

"I don't know. I think she does, but she hasn't said the words. Frankly, I'm not sure that she's admitted it to herself. She's got a lot of abandonment issues with Declan not being in her life for so many years. Her mother has had a sea of bad men in and out of their lives. Men that stole from them. Men that may have come on to her. I'm sure what I did at the party didn't help matters. She makes a habit of leaving men before anyone can hurt or leave her. She's built walls around herself. She assumes all men will leave her at some point. You saw how she reacted tonight."

Reagan's eyes start tearing. "That makes a lot of sense with how she behaves. She's briefly mentioned having those types of issues in the past."

I nod.

It's silent. I think they're both processing everything I've said. I want to give them that time.

Eventually, I look at my best friend of over thirty years in the eyes. "Carter, she gives me something I never knew I needed. You once told me that you knew Reagan was the one when you felt like you couldn't breathe without her. The simple thought of sleeping without her made you sick to your stomach. There was nothing in your life you loved or wanted more than her. You'd give up anything and everything for her. That's how I feel. I didn't understand it then. I get it now. She's my Dodge Tomahawk."

He nods in understanding. "Okay."

I look at him in shock. "Okay? *Okay* as in you're okay with it, or *okay* as in I never want to see you again?"

He lets out a laugh. "Collin, you're a brother to me. Nothing you could ever do would change that. I just want you to be happy. If she makes you happy, that's the end of the conversation. I admit that I often see Jade as the seventeen-year-old with a crush, but you're right, she's a beautiful, intelligent, interesting woman now. Honestly, I don't even see other women anymore. I only have eyes for mine."

Reagan narrows her eyes at him. "Are you just trying to get laid tonight?"

He smiles. "I'll get laid regardless. You're addicted to me."

"I suppose that's true." She turns back to me. "What can we do to help? She was obviously upset when she left."

"I'll deal with her." I look back at Carter. "We're okay? Really?"

He nods. "Yes, really. I wish you had told me earlier, but I know now, and we'll get past it. Don't keep shit from me. I don't keep anything from you."

"You keep your wife from me. I've asked for threesomes for years."

He shakes his head. "Don't start. Not today. You're already skating on thin ice with me."

I smile.

"Frankly, I asked you here today for a reason."

"My good looks?"

"No."

"My charm."

"Definitely not."

"Then what was it?"

"Reagan is forcing me to go on this damn fishing trip with Jackson and all the boys."

She rubs his back. "Babe, he's been looking forward to this for a year. He'd be heartbroken if you didn't go."

"I'd be heartbroken if I missed the birth of our first child."

She shakes her head. "My doctor said I'm not dilated at all. He felt like you were fine to go this week. It's only three days. Two nights. Please go. You'll have fun. Jackson has his chopper on standby. You can be home in an hour if needed."

He sighs and turns back to me. "That's where you come in. Reagan wants to sleep at home, not here with Darian. She's uncomfortable and wants to sleep in our bed. Skylar is going to stay with her. The kids will stay with Darian. Can you sleep at our house with them? I'd feel more comfortable if you were there."

"Sleep with her? To keep her sexually satisfied in your absence? Ugh, I would have totally done that for the past five years, but now I can't. I'm taken."

"No, dipshit."

I laugh. "Are you sure? She might need the power of my vitamin D. I hear pregnant women are very horny."

"Reagan is always horny, pregnant or not."

She nods in agreement. "True story."

I scratch my chin and pretend to consider it. "Hmm. What about cuddling? Does she require that? I may be able to accommodate that."

"Skylar can cuddle with her."

"What are the logistics of two heavily pregnant

women cuddling? Their stomachs must get in the way."

He thinks for a moment. "She'll survive two nights of no cuddling."

"Hmm." I wink at Reagan. "If you change your mind about the cuddling, you'll know where to find me."

Carter gives me a hopeful smile. "So you'll do it? You'll stay with her? With them?"

I roll my eyes. "Of course I'll do it."

CHAPTER TWENTY-THREE

JADE

I walk into Mom's house and she's standing there with her arms open. I fall into them and mumble, "You heard?"

"Yes, Melissa called me. She figured you were on your way here."

I pull away. "Are you two besties now?"

"No, but we both love you and care about you. It sounds like we're not the only ones."

"She told you about that?"

"Yes. Why didn't you tell me you were seeing someone?"

I blow out a breath. "We were supposed to be casual."

"Him professing his love for you in front of everyone doesn't sound very casual to me. Why did you leave?"

I put my head down in shame. "It was too intense."

"He told you he loves you and you walked away?"

"Yes, I'm fucked up. You know this about me. That's why you've had me in therapy since I was eight."

"I had you in therapy to deal with the anger you had for your father. You wouldn't talk to me, so I hoped you'd talk to her. Jade, you could have stopped at any point. Certainly, once you became an adult. Whether you admit it or not, you want to get past whatever ails you. Whatever has held you back all these years from being in a real relationship. Do you love him?"

I sigh. "I might. But what if he leaves me?"

"What if he doesn't?"

The damn tears hit my eyes again. I've turned into a fucking cliché crybaby.

She rubs my arm. "Tell me what you love about him. Articulate it."

"He's hot as fuck."

She gives me an exasperated look. "I'm aware. What else?"

I plop down on the couch. I lean my head back and close my eyes for a brief moment. "I don't know, Mom. He likes me for me. Loves me for me. He likes my humor. He likes my wiseass comments and gives them right back to me in return. He makes me laugh. I can be myself with him, and that's what he wants. Me. Just as I am, complete with all the fucked-up parts. And the sex." I bite my lip. "Ahh. Holy shit."

She smiles. "Toe curling?"

I nod. "Everything curling. He just...he makes me feel good. He makes me feel safe. He makes me feel cherished. He makes me feel wanted. He makes me feel good enough. I know it sounds weird. Does that make sense?"

"It makes perfect sense. You're the most wonderful woman I know. Of course he loves you. Why don't you call him? Tell him what you just told me."

"That he's good in bed? He knows."

She rolls her eyes. "You know what I mean."

"I don't know if I'm ready." I whisper, "I don't know if I deserve him."

"Deserve him? Jade, you deserve the love of a good man."

I look down.

"Look at me." I do. "You deserve to be happy. If he makes you happy, then I don't know what in the hell you're doing here. You need to eventually let yourself trust a man with your heart. It's always a risk. Sometimes the risk is worth the reward. Do you trust him?"

I think for a moment but then nod. "Yes, I trust him. But what if it backfires?"

"There aren't any guarantees, but it sounds like you're in love with him as much as he's in love with you."

"Can we not talk about this right now? I can't deal with what happened today. Dad lost his shit. He broke a fucking glass wall. He's psycho."

"I knew you'd want to avoid it. Dad wanted to come here. I told him to come in the morning. Your old room is made up for you. You can shelve this for the night and then you need to be an adult and deal with them. Both Collin and your father."

I nod. "You're kind of bossy."

"At least you got one thing from me." She smiles. "Do you want to eat Rocky Road and watch either *Princess Bride* or *Loverboy*?"

I nod. "Make it *Princess Bride*. I'm not up for movies about male hookers tonight."

She thinks for a moment. "Shit, you're right. He was nothing but a male hooker in that movie, wasn't he? In retrospect, I can't believe I let you watch that movie when you were so young."

"I can't believe his girlfriend didn't dump his ass for banging all those women."

She smiles. "What a ridiculous premise for a movie. It was so popular back in the day."

We both giggle as we grab the Rocky Road and sit down to watch Princess Bride.

Before I go to bed, I get a text from Collin.

> Collin: I miss you. My sheets smell like you.

> Me: You should wash them.

> Collin: No. It gives me a boner. I'll keep them until you can refresh the smell.

> Me: I'm sorry I left. Just give me a few days to process. I need to work things out in my head. I need to deal with my father and some of our issues. I can't have you two breaking glass walls all the time.

> Collin: Okay. Just know that I meant what I said. Carter asked me to stay with Reagan and Skylar while they go on the fishing trip. You know where to find me. Good night.

> Me: Good night.

I'M AWAKENED by the sound of Dad and Melissa's voices in the living room. I walk out and Melissa immediately embraces me. "Are you okay, sweetie?"

I pull back. "I'm fine. Just a little confused. Yesterday was a bit of a mess."

She nods in understanding and turns to my mom. "Amanda, do you want to take a walk with me? We can grab coffee for everyone down the street."

"Yes. That's a good idea." Mom turns to me and nods. "We'll leave you two."

Once the door closes, Dad motions for me to sit on the sofa, which I do. He sits in a chair across from me. His eye and lip are really swollen.

"You look like Rocky."

"*Rocky One* or *Rocky Two*?"

"Does it matter?"

"In *Rocky One*, he loses. In *Rocky Two*, he wins. I think I look like *Rocky Two*."

"You're more like Rocky's child because that's how you act. Like a child. You can't go around beating up all my boyfriends."

He has a somber look. "I'm sorry for how I reacted. I saw his hands on you and your tears. I made an assumption."

"What was that assumption?"

He blows out a breath. "That he was hurting my little girl."

"I can take care of myself, and I'm not a little girl anymore, Dad."

"To me, you'll always be a little girl."

"But I'm *not* a little girl. You *have* to stop treating me like one. You have to accept that I'm an adult and I do adult things."

"Maybe you're not a child, but you're young and he's not. He's a lowlife and a player, Jade. He's not good enough for you. I would know. He's exactly like I was. Not the drugs, but the women. I liked younger women too. I know him because I was him before I met Melissa."

I shake my head. "I don't think you know him at all. He's misunderstood by most, including his own family. He's wonderful and smart. He's kind and funny. He's good to me. No man has ever been better to me than Collin. He makes me feel seen. Not just on the outside, but the inside too."

"Then why were you two a secret from everyone, including his best friend? If it feels so right, then why hide it?"

"Because we were supposed to be casual. We enjoyed each other's company. We didn't want to make a whole thing of it with the family and then have it be problematic for everyone when it ended."

"That sounds like a bunch of bullshit. He didn't want to commit."

"I didn't ask him to. The rules of engagement were mine. In case you haven't noticed, I have my own set of commitment issues when it comes to relationships with men. I don't have healthy relationships with them."

"Why is that?"

"Why? Because of you."

"Me?"

"Yes, you. You fucking abandoned me the first seven years of my life. You fucking chose drugs over your own daughter. You didn't give a shit that I existed. That I suffered. I'm terrified of relationships because I fear them leaving. Not choosing me. Just like you!"

Tears fill his eyes. "Of course I cared." He runs his fingers through his hair. "I tried to get clean. I couldn't. I did drugs for over twenty years. It consumed me. I was weak. But I always cared. There was never a second from the moment you were born that I didn't care."

"You didn't act like it. You left me for seven years. I never once saw you. It was like I didn't exist to you."

"Do you think that day you saw me at recess was the first time I sat in my car and watched you?"

I pinch my eyebrows together. "What? It wasn't?"

He shakes his head. "No. I came almost every day to watch you. For years. It was the only way I could see you. To watch you interact with other kids. Your mom rightfully wouldn't allow me around you, but I still needed to see you. Day after day I watched a little girl that looked so much like me smile and laugh with her friends, desperately wanting to be a part of your life."

I'm shocked. "Why that day? What was the final impetus to get clean?"

"Don't tell your mother."

"Does it even matter anymore?"

He nods in agreement. "I was high the day you saw me. But you saw me. For the first time ever, you noticed I was there. I could tell right away you knew who I was. I knew I could no longer watch you from the shadows. I couldn't stay away any longer. If I wanted to be around, I had to do what was necessary. That morning was the last time I've ever taken drugs. I went cold turkey. I lied to your mother about how long I was clean. It was you and my desire to get to know you, to be your father. That was my impetus. Jade, I've always loved you. I wish I did things differently, but know that in my own fucked-up way, I was in your life. I watched everything you did. Every t-ball game, every dance recital, every school play, every father-daughter dance you attended with your mother, I was there in the shadows."

My brain might explode right now from this information. I have no words for any of it. I blink a few times. "You were there, at my dances?"

He nods. "When you were five, you wore a pink dress. When you were six, you wore a yellow dress. It had a big flower at the top. When you were seven, it was red. You had clearly just gone through a growth spurt because it was too short, and I almost got out of my car and demanded you go home and change."

I can't help but smile at that last comment. Some things never change. And he's right. When I put on my favorite red dress that night, I realized that I must have grown since I last wore it. It was very short on me.

"Jade, you know that five years ago I almost made a terrible decision. I almost ended things."

I nod.

"When I found out how bad things were for Darian and the girls after my brother died, and how I failed them too, I almost did something very stupid."

I whisper, "I remember."

"You know what brought me back from the brink? You. You and Melissa. I love the both of you so damn much. I couldn't leave you. I couldn't miss out on being with her. I couldn't miss out on watching you grow into adulthood. Your milestones, your graduations, your accomplishments, and, when you're fifty, walking you down the aisle to a nice, age-appropriate man."

I put my head in my hands. It's pounding at his revelations.

My phone alarm breaks the silence. I look down at it. "I have Dr. Pearl in five minutes."

"Okay. I'll wait for you to be done so we can continue this conversation."

"No. Don't. I need some time. I've spent so long thinking you didn't care about me those first seven years. I need a minute to process this."

He stands and holds out his arms. I stand and sink into them. He whispers, "I love you. I always have. I always will."

DR. PEARL's face appears on the screen. She smiles. "Two emergency meetings in the past few months. This is crazy."

"I'm crazy. That's the problem."

"You're not crazy, Jade. Trust me. I've seen crazy. It's not you. How was Mexico? Did you have a good time?"

I can't help but smile. "It was the best week of my life." It truly was. Besides our one fight, it was magical.

"How so?"

"Collin and I had the most amazing time. No hiding. No sneaking around. We swam, we sat by the pool, we drank, we went to restaurants, we danced, we laughed, we had amazing sex. *A lot* of amazing sex. I let him pop my anal cherry."

She gives me a look of disgust. "I didn't need to know that last bit."

I grin. "I know. That's why I loved sharing it with you."

She shakes her head.

I sigh. "I loved every minute of it."

"That's wonderful. Everything sounds great. What's the problem?"

"Life. Reality." I mumble, "He told me he loves me."

"Ahh. I see. Tell me about that."

"As you know, we don't go out in public. For some unknown reason, he was invited to my family's pool party. It was so painful to have him there and not be close to him. Mexico spoiled me. We could be together and touch whenever and wherever we wanted. And I assure you, we took full advantage of that."

"I have no doubt about that."

"Being with him in secret again just sucks. I felt like we were going backward. I was struggling. I couldn't breathe. I went to the bathroom to gather myself. He followed me in. It was clear he was feeling the same torment. I know this sounds weird because we were in a bathroom up against a wall, but we made love. It was different from any other time we've had sex. It was emotional and highly intimate. I fucking cried. Can you believe I fucking cried during sex?"

She smiles.

"Stop smiling. It screwed with my head. I was a basket case. He had his arms around me trying to console me when my father walked in."

"Oh shit."

"*Oh shit* is right. He went nuts because, well, he *is* nuts. He punched Collin in the face."

She gasps as she covers her mouth. "Oh my god."

"It gets worse. They charged at each other. They started fighting and wrestling. They crashed through a big glass wall. Shattered it. Then they fell into the pool and continued fighting. My family eventually jumped in and separated them. Collin chose that moment to announce that he's in love with me. He said it in front of my whole family."

"Wow. That's kind of romantic. How did you react?"

I close my eyes. "I turned around and left."

"He put himself out there, after literally taking punches from your father, and announced to everyone that he's in love with you, and you simply left?"

"It sounds bad when you say it like that."

"It *is* bad, Jade. It was an immature response."

That's the first time she's ever said anything like that to me. I put my head down in shame. I know she's right.

She lets out a deep breath. "I'm sorry. That was judgmental. Tell me why you felt compelled to leave."

"I was freaked out. I don't know what else to say. I was scared."

"Why were you scared?"

"I don't know. I need you to tell me."

"I can guess why, but only you can decide the reason."

With increasing agitation, I say, "Don't give me therapist bullshit. You've been inside my fucked-up head for fifteen years. Tell me what's wrong with me, damn it!"

It's the first time I've ever raised my voice to her. Even at the beginning when I was really mean to her.

"In my opinion, Jade, you won't give yourself the leeway to fall in love. You made a decision one day as a hurt little girl that you'd never allow it to happen, and you're so damn stubborn, that you've stuck to it, whether you want to or not. And you know what, Jade?"

"What?"

"You don't want to stick to it anymore. You're in love with him. You've met your match. Is it permission you need to stray from your self-imposed love prison? If so, please allow me to give it to you. Let me say this in simple terms. He makes you happy. You're allowed to be happy. Stop torturing yourself."

I have tears streaming down my cheeks. "Fifteen fucking years of therapy without crying until today. I hate you."

She smiles. "You love me."

My head is down. I eventually look up. "What if he leaves? What if he hurts me? I don't know if I could take it."

"There are no guarantees in anything, but this is why you've spent years leaving men first. Leaving them before you have any emotional attachment. You sabotage relationships because you think you're not worthy of them." She leans into the camera, so our eyes very clearly meet. "Jade, you're worthy. You're amazing. I'm not surprised he fell in love with you. And you know what? I know I only spent a few minutes talking to him, but he's kind of perfect for you. Besides the fact that you're an exceedingly attractive couple, your personalities match. You both love to laugh. You both love to push buttons. You both do not understand normal societal boundaries for what you do and don't share."

I can't help but laugh at the last one. It's true. All of it's true.

"You obviously share a physical chemistry."

I moan. "That's true."

She smiles. "Have you spoken with him at all?"

"I told him I need a little time to process everything."

"How did he take it?"

I shrug. "I imagine he's a little hurt, but he was understanding. He told me to reach out when I'm ready. Carter is out of town for a few days. He asked Collin to stay at the house with Reagan. She's like thirty-eight weeks pregnant now. So I know he's over there."

"Carter trusted him to stay with her?"

I nod. "I guess."

"Do you trust him to stay with her?"

I think about what Mom said and nod. "Yes. Completely."

"I'm glad to hear that. I think it's important given the circumstances."

"Skylar's there too. She's around thirty-six weeks pregnant and her husband is away with Carter."

"It sounds like your family very much trusts Collin. Perhaps it's time for you to do the same."

Maybe she's right.

"What are you thinking, Jade? I see the wheels turning."

"He'll be with Reagan and Skylar for a few days. That gives me time to figure out what I want."

CHAPTER TWENTY-FOUR

COLLIN

I open the front door and shout, "Honey, I'm home."

Skylar waddles out into the foyer, holding a glass of what looks like lemonade. The glass is literally resting on her stomach. She yells back toward the kitchen. "Reagan, our babysitter is here."

I smile. "I'm supposed to sit on your babies? What if I hurt them?"

Skylar rolls her eyes. She barely tolerates me. It's always been this way. I used to take joy in annoying her. I think I still do.

I look her up and down. Even eight months pregnant, Skylar is hot as hell with those big lips and big green eyes of hers. "Don't you regret never fucking me before you and Lance got together?"

She tilts her head to the side, "You know, Collin, I don't have a lot of regrets in life, but if I had to name them, I'm confident not having sex with you wouldn't make the cut. Believe it or not, I never considered it a grand sacrifice."

"Our kiss was hot. I haven't forgotten it." I blow her a kiss.

I know she only kissed me the one time to make Lance jealous just before they started dating, but I never miss an opportunity to bring it up.

She narrows her eyes at me. "Nice shiner." I instinctively touch my black eye. "How does it feel to get your ass kicked by a fifty-four-year-old man?"

"He didn't kick my ass..."

"Will you two stop bickering. I don't have the patience for anything right now. I'm like a beached whale. You're both better off not pissing me off."

We turn and see Reagan. I bow to her. "I'm here to serve you, your highness. Would you like me to draw you a bath and help you undress to get in? Or, if you're taking a shower, I can be your shower bra."

She narrows her eyes. "What's a shower bra?"

"The person who holds up your boobs while you shower."

She sighs. "It's going to be a long two days."

I turn to Skylar. "What about you? You *really* look like you might be in need of a shower bra too." Her already large tits have gotten even larger in pregnancy.

She gives me the finger.

I can't help but smile.

THE PAST TWENTY-FOUR hours have been insane. They are keeping the house at arctic temperatures, and still complain that it's too hot. They eat sixteen meals a day. I've ordered enough food to feed fifty football teams, and they plow right through it.

They go to the bathroom no less than a hundred times a day each, usually needing help getting there. They're constantly thirsty. I've refilled their water bottles a thousand times.

I've given back massages and foot rubs. I've offered happy endings on the massages, but they both declined.

Oh, and Lance and Carter text me every two minutes to make sure the girls are okay.

I'm exhausted. I just need to make it through one more night. I don't know how Carter and Lance do this every day. And they seem so damn happy about it too.

Reagan and I are sitting at the kitchen table before bed because, of course, she needed a pint of Ben and Jerry's Chocolate Fudge Brownie ice cream before bed. Skylar went to bed an hour ago after downing a pint of Ben and Jerry's Karamel Sutra Core. She did not care for my comments on her flavor choice.

Reagan looks at me. "How are things with Jade?"

I shrug. "She doesn't want to see me. Or talk to me. She texted that she needs time to process. I put it on the back burner for a few days while I'm here. After Carter gets back tomorrow night, I'll go over there and try to talk with her."

"What's the main issue?"

"There are a few things. Our connection is intense. Neither of us saw it coming. We both intended it to be casual. She's freaked out about a bunch of shit, but mostly I think she's simply afraid of love. Declan not being around the first few years messed her up. I personally think she has it in her mind that she'll never let a man in enough to hurt her again. She wants me but is afraid of us. Of me. It's not like I can totally blame her with my track record."

She nods. "I get that."

"Me not wanting to be seen in public also hurt her. She was agreeable at first, but I think she would have come out to you all months ago if I was willing."

"I definitely understand her feeling that way. It was stupid."

"Maybe it was. I did what I thought was best for everyone at the time." I sigh. "At the very beginning, she was the one who was dead set on keeping things casual and secretive. As the months have gone on, I think we both realize that we're kind of perfect for each other. It's a scary proposition. I love her exactly how she is. I think she feels the same about me. I'm not sure I'll ever find another woman who appreciates my brand of crazy like she does."

She smiles. "In your weird Collin way, that was sweet."

"I guess under my extreme good looks, I'm a little insecure."

"How so? And you're not that good-looking."

I let out a small laugh. "I hate confrontation. I was terrified of Carter finding out and thinking poorly of me. He's the most functional relationship I've ever had. I didn't want to rock the boat, even if it hurt both me and Jade. I still haven't told my family that I'm going to leave the business and work with you guys full-time. I'm afraid of my father and brothers being upset with me. Jade called me out on all of it.

She told me I'm a coward and she's right. I want to try to be a better man for her."

She fiddles with her spoon for a moment. "Can I ask you a blunt question?"

"I've never known you not to."

"Is your crush on me one of the problems with her?"

That's not what I thought she was going to ask. I'm not sure how to reply.

"Umm, you knew about that?"

She nods. "Yes."

"Did Carter?"

She shakes her head. "I don't think so. We've never discussed it."

"I'm sorry. I didn't want to have a crush on you."

"I know. And you never did anything. You never made me feel uncomfortable. I just always knew it was there."

I take her hand in mine. "I hope you realize that it's nothing more than a compliment. You're kind of perfect, Reagan. Everything any man, including myself, could ever want in a woman. Carter is a lucky man."

She gives me a humble smile. "Thank you. Is it a problem in your relationship with Jade? I would hate it if it was."

I nod. "I think it's part of her trepidation. Like you, she picked up on it throughout the years. I guess it wasn't as hidden as I thought."

"It wasn't. I'm surprised Carter has missed it."

"It's because when you're around, he only has eyes for you. Do I think it plays into some of her fears? Yes. The fact that you two look alike and have similar personalities undoubtedly weighs on her. But she was in the same boat as me. She's had this huge crush on Carter for years. I think when we found each other, and really gave into it, both of our crushes dissipated. I stopped staring at you and started staring at her. I think the same went for her with Carter and me. We discussed it briefly in Mexico. I explained that it wasn't you, but more the qualities you possess that attract me. Admittedly, she has some of those qualities, but she's different too. She's her own person. I love everything about her."

She nods. "Good. I'm glad. Jade's my cousin and I love her. You're like a brother to Carter and I love you too. Nothing would make me happier than if it works out between you two. When you really think about it, despite the age difference, you genuinely do make a nice match."

"Honestly, Reagan, for the first time in my life, I want that. I've never envisioned it with any woman, not even you. But with her, I want forever. She's unlike anyone I've ever met. I'm completely in love with her. I think I have been for a while. I was just too much of a wimp to acknowledge it. There was a moment in Mexico when it clicked for me. I knew. I've just been trying to figure out how to deal with it. I really was going to tell Carter before Declan detonated the whole thing."

She smiles. "I'm happy for you, Collin. I have a feeling it will work out." She pushes herself up. "I need to get to bed. I've got three hours until heartburn sets in."

"Pregnancy sounds awesome."

"There's no fucking glow. It's just fucking hard.

I'm so ready for this baby to come...after Carter gets home."

I help her upstairs and then head to the guest room. I lay in bed with my phone, flipping through pictures of Jade and me from Mexico. We were so happy there. Why can't we have that in real life?

I decide to text her.

> Me: I'll be home tomorrow. Can we please talk then? I miss you. I'm thinking about you. Constantly. I love you.

I see dots a handful of times, suggesting she's typing, but nothing comes through. Eventually, I fall asleep.

CHAPTER TWENTY-FIVE

COLLIN

"Collin!"

I pop up thinking I just heard my name. I listen but it's silent. I must have dreamt it.

I look at my phone. It's a little before three in the morning.

The door to my room opens. It's Reagan. She looks pained as she holds her stomach. "Fuck. I think I'm in labor."

"Are you kidding me?"

"I'm not making up feeling like I'm getting stabbed in my lower back in the middle of the night, so no, I'm not kidding you. I was hoping it was indigestion, but it's not. I'm definitely having contractions."

I hear Skylar in the hallway. "Reagan, what's wrong?"

Reagan turns her head. "I think I'm in labor. We need to go to the hospital. Now."

I jump out of bed and walk toward the door. "I'll pull the car up."

Reagan looks me up and down. "Are you going in your boxer briefs with morning wood sticking out?"

I look down and attempt to cover myself with my hands. "Whoops. Sorry."

She waves her hand. "Nothing I haven't seen before."

"Not one this big."

She narrows her eyes at me. "You've been friends with Carter for thirty years. You must have seen him naked. You know he has the biggest penis on the planet. Like world-record-setting penis."

"If there's going to be a world record set, it will be by me."

Skylar shakes her head. "You two are mentally ill. You're in labor. Is this conversation really necessary?"

I nod. "She's right." I mumble, "My penis is just as big as his."

Skylar yells, "Collin! Hurry up! Damn man child."

I throw on sweatpants and a sweatshirt and run to get their Range Rover from the garage. I pull around to the front door.

Skylar is helping Reagan from the front door to the car when the ground below them gets a huge splash of liquid. It looks like a water balloon crashed in front of them.

I run to Reagan. "I think your water just broke."

She looks down at herself. "No, it didn't"

Skylar looks down. "Oh shit. That was me. My water just broke."

Reagan turns to her and shakes her head. "You're really determined to steal my thunder, aren't you?"

"Yes, I planned this. I wanted my water to break right now, with Lance out of town, all to steal your precious thunder."

"If you would keep your damn legs together, you wouldn't be pregnant for the third time in three years."

"I forgot how celibate you are. Remind me how many times a day you and Carter fuck in the office."

I yell, "Ladies! We need to get to the hospital. I'm exceedingly talented with vaginas, but I can't deliver your babies."

They both nod and slide into the car. I fire off a text in the giant family text chat string that I was added to for the weekend. It's actually a really funny chat. Trevor and Cassandra are hysterical. They shamelessly flirt and dirty talk as if no one else is on the text string.

Carter responds right away. He probably hasn't slept while away, fearing this very scenario.

> Carter: I just woke the pilot. We'll be there as soon as we can. Reagan, I love you. Please tell Baby Daulton to wait for me.

My heart breaks a little. Please, God, don't let him miss the birth of his first child. He deserves to be there for it.

> Lance: Sweets, we'll be there soon. I love you.

The cuteness is killing me. No one else responds. I assume they're all sleeping. I pray Darian gets it soon. They need her at the hospital. They need Harley too.

I drive to the hospital in world-record time. I come to a screeching halt in front. I run in yelling that I need help. I grab the closest nurse. "Please. I have two women in labor in my car."

"Are you their driver?"

"No, I'm their friend. Their husbands are out of town, and I was keeping an eye on them. They both went into labor."

"Lucky you."

"Can you help me or not? We're wasting time."

"I'll grab one wheelchair and you grab the other."

We quickly wheel them out to the car and get the girls seated.

I've got Reagan and the nurse has Skylar. I'm following her to what I assume is the maternity ward.

Reagan reaches up for my hand. "I have a contraction coming." I grab her hand and she squeezes mine in a way that I wonder if I'll ever have full use of it again, but I just let her do what she needs to.

I yell, "Bear down! Bear down!"

She screams, "What the fuck does that mean, Collin?"

"I don't know. I've heard it in movies."

"Don't talk. Ever again"

"Okay."

I look over at Skylar. She seems much calmer. Perhaps I should have wheeled her instead.

While we're on the elevator, I see her grip the armrest hard and squeeze her eyes shut. She's having a contraction but trying to play it cool.

I reach for her hand. She looks up at me and I nod,

bracing myself for a lifetime of having to jerk off with my other hand.

She squeezes it through her contraction. When it's done, she releases me. "Thank you."

"Sure thing. I'll send you a bill for my hand reconstruction surgery."

We reach the maternity ward floor and I immediately make my way to the front desk. The administrator looks at our situation. "Are...you the father?"

I nod. "Yes, my sperm is so potent that I impregnated two women at once." I wink. "Same night."

Her eyes widen.

Reagan yells, "Collin! Cut it out." She looks at the nurse. "We don't know this guy. He was our Uber driver. Kick him out of the hospital."

The nurse looks between us. "Should I call security?"

Skylar pounds her fist on the armrest. "Will you two morons cut it out." She looks at the nurse. "We're sisters. Both of our husbands are on the way. They're an hour out." She nods toward me. "He's a family friend who brought us here. Can you please find us a couple of beds? My contractions are six minutes apart. Hers are four."

I look at her in shock. "How did you know all that?"

"I pay attention. I've done this before. Multiple times."

The nurse quickly completes the paperwork and motions for me to take one wheelchair while she takes the other.

"I was able to get them a double room together. This way."

We enter the room, and a few nurses appear. They help the girls get changed, get into the beds, and hook them up to all kinds of devices and monitors. The monitors seem to know when contractions are coming. It's like seeing a giant wave in the ocean that you know is going to knock you over, but you're too far out and can't do anything about it.

They're alternating contractions. I run to whoever needs me in the moment.

At some point, the doctor comes in. He tells each he's going to examine them.

Skylar looks at me. "Get north of our shoulders. Now. Don't even think about heading south."

"Yes, ma'am."

I stand behind each when the doctor examines them. He literally sticks his hands inside them. I'm not sure whether he has the best job in the world or the worst.

I send an update to the family chat.

Me: Reagan is already eight centimeters dilated. Apparently, that means she's close. Skylar is six. Carter and Lance, how much longer? Darian? Harley? Are you there? Anyone?

JADE

I haven't slept well since I walked out of Aunt Darian and Jackson's house. Truth be told, I can't sleep without Collin anymore. I miss him.

I toss and turn for an hour in the middle of the night. I can't fall back asleep and decide to check my social media on my phone.

I pick up my phone and see a frantic text from Collin that both Reagan and Skylar are in labor. I better head to the hospital to see if they need help. I quickly throw on leggings and a sweatshirt and leave for the hospital.

Nothing prepares me for what I see when I arrive. I poke my head in the doorway and see Collin frantically sprinting back and forth between the two of them. It's like a crazy scene out of a rom-com movie.

Reagan screams, "Collin, I need another pillow."

He runs around until he finds one in the closet. He helps her lean forward and sets it behind her.

Skylar yells, "Collin, I need more water."

He grabs her empty pitcher and runs to the bathroom to fill it, brings it back to her, and then pours it into her cup. He even moves the straw to help her sip it.

Just as he finishes that, Reagan screams, "Here comes another one. Collin, I need your sandpaper man hands."

He runs over to her bed. She's on her side yelling through her contraction. He goes to her back. With one hand he holds hers, with the other he rubs and applies a lot of pressure to her lower back. "Just breathe. You're so brave. You've got this." He rubs her until it ends.

Then it's Skylar's turn. He seems to know that he's not needed in the back for her. He comes to her front. He offers one hand for her to squeeze, and with the other, he rubs her belly. Skylar squeezes him throughout her contraction.

"You've got this, Sky. Just squeeze away the pain."

I should go in and help, but I can't manage to do anything other than watch him continue to go back and forth helping my cousins through their labor.

If there was ever a doubt in my mind, it's gone now. I'm in love with him. I swore it would never happen to me, but it has. I'm madly in love with Collin Fitz.

For a solid six or seven minutes, I observe the madness, falling for him just a little more every time he does something for them.

At some point, he notices me leaning on the doorframe. He immediately stills, simply staring at me. I stare back at him. Eventually I mouth, "I love you too."

A huge grin spreads across his gorgeous face. He strides toward me, and I do the same toward him. Our bodies crash together as our mouths meet for the most perfect kiss I've ever been gifted. He wraps his arms around me and picks me up.

I run my fingers through his hair, keeping him as close to me as I can.

The rest of the world and the crazy circumstances fade away. I'm back in his arms and he's back in mine. I feel at peace for the first time in days. Maybe ever.

I can't believe how much I've missed being close to him in the past few days. It feels perfect. It feels like home. I know this is right. We're right.

"If you two fuck in front of us while we're in labor, I'll never forgive you."

We both smile as our lips part, and I slide down his body back to the ground. We turn to Reagan. She winks at us. "Though maybe it would be a nice distraction. Carry on."

We both laugh.

We can hear on the monitors that contractions are about to ramp up for both of them. Collin nods at Reagan. "You take her. Rub her lower back as hard as you can. I'll take Skylar. She's freakishly strong. She may have crushed the bones in both of my hands. I may never be able to jerk off again. I'm afraid you're going to have to do it for me."

I smile. "It would be my pleasure, but your tongue better still work."

He winks as he flicks his tongue suggestively at me.

Reagan moans. "If you saw the state of my vagina right now, you'd reevaluate that."

I giggle as I make my way to her, and Collin moves to Skylar.

We help them through their increasing contractions for the next thirty minutes. At some point, I hear commotion in the hallway. We both turn to the doorway to see Carter and Lance come barreling in like the giant men they are.

Collin breathes, "Oh thank god."

Carter rushes to Reagan, grabs her face, and kisses the shit out of her. When he pulls away, he has tears in his eyes. He gently kisses her hand. "I'm so happy I made it."

She has tears in her eyes as well. "Me too. I love you."

"I love you too."

I give him a few instructions regarding her contractions and back labor.

Collin starts to do the same for Lance, but he holds up his hand and smiles calmly. "I know. We've been through this a few times before." He crawls into bed with Skylar and pulls her close to him, kissing her face and head over and over. He seems to know the spot on her belly that needs to be rubbed and moves his hand to it. He whispers in her ear, and she smiles. You can see her relax into his body.

There's so much love in this room. It used to overwhelm me. For some reason, it doesn't right now.

I make eye contact with Collin and motion my head to the door. "Let's give them some privacy."

He nods in agreement.

We head out into the waiting room. Collin sits in one of the chairs and I start to sit in the chair next to him, but he pulls me onto his lap. He squeezes me close and buries his face in my neck.

He inhales me. "I can't be without you anymore. Move in with me. I don't want to spend another night without you."

"No."

He looks up with sad eyes. "What? Why?"

I rub his scruffy face with my fingertips. "My place is bigger. You move in with me."

"Okay. I don't care where we live, as long as we're together."

"Better yet, let's get a new place and make all new memories."

He smiles. "I like that idea. We'll take my bed frame though. I've invested a lot of hard work in that thing."

I laugh. "We should patent it and sell it to other freaks."

He lifts an eyebrow. "That's not a bad idea."

I meet my forehead with his. "I missed you."

He softly kisses my lips. "I missed you too."

We kiss again, but this time it turns deeper. Our mouths open. Our tongues meet. God, I missed his taste.

We hear a lot of commotion heading in our direction. We break our kiss, and both look up as my whole big, crazy family makes their way into the waiting area.

Darian looks at me. "Any news?"

I shake my head. "Carter and Lance just got here. Reagan is far along. She should go any minute. Skylar a little after. Both will be soon though."

My father looks at me sitting in Collin's lap with disgust. He starts to roll up his sleeves. "Fitz, I won't tell you this again. Keep your hands off my daughter. Get your pervert ass up so I can kick it again."

I stand and place my hand on his chest. "Dad, cut it out. Don't even think about touching him again. I love him. We're going to be together. Get over it. I'm not a child."

He jerks his body toward Collin's, but that's the last thing I remember before everything goes dark.

CHAPTER TWENTY-SIX

JADE

I peel my eyes open. My lids are so heavy. I feel like I swallowed a bag of cotton.

I look around. I'm in a hospital bed attached to a bunch of beeping machines. I see my father sitting in a chair. Melissa is in the chair next to him running her fingers up and down his arm in a soothing manner.

I turn my head to the other side of the room. I see Collin and my mother sitting together holding hands. Both of their heads are down. She's rubbing his back. She seems to be consoling him. It occurs to me at that moment that they're only a few years apart.

I croak out, "Collin?"

All their heads jerk up. All have clearly been crying.

They stand and make their way to me. Mom takes one hand while Dad sits next to her. Collin crawls into bed with me. He slides his arm under me and pulls me to his chest. It's like Lance was with Skylar. It's incredibly intimate and comforting.

I look around. "What's happening?"

Collin says, "You've been asleep for a year."

In a deep voice, Dad warns, "Collin."

Mom shakes her head. "We don't know. You passed out in the hallway about ninety minutes ago. Thank god Collin caught you, or you could have injured yourself. He called me to get here. He and your father have been yelling and screaming at the staff since I got here. They won't tell us anything. They said you'd wake up in a bit and they'd only talk to you directly since you're not a minor and not married."

I realize Melissa left. She returns a moment later with a woman who's wearing a lab coat. I assume she's my doctor.

The woman smiles. "There she is. I'm Dr. Cantor. You gave everyone quite a scare. Your father and boyfriend have been making everyone crazy. They're quite a team."

I let out a laugh. "A team?"

Dad rolls his eyes.

Dr. Cantor continues, "How are you feeling?"

"Like I'm hungover, but I'm not. Thirsty as fuck."

I can feel Collin laughing. He reaches for a cup and helps me get in a few sips of water.

I look at the doctor. "What's going on? What's wrong with me?"

She looks around at all the people. "I need to speak with you. Perhaps we should do it alone."

"Whatever it is, you can say it in front of them."

She nods as she flips through a file.

"Please. Tell me what's wrong with me? Just spit it out."

My mind is running through every terrible thing that could be wrong with me.

She gives me a small smile. "Nothing that won't go away in about nine months."

What. The. Fuck.

Dad stands and looks at Collin. "I'm going to fucking kill you."

I look up at Dad. "Why Collin? It's not definitely his. There are at least five or six guys it could be."

Mom, Dad, Melissa, and the doctor's faces all drop, but I can feel Collin laughing again. I guess he's the only one that understands my humor.

The rest realize it at some point. Melissa grabs Dad's arm and drags him toward the door. "Come on. Let's give them some privacy. Let's check on everyone upstairs."

I look at her. "Did the babies arrive yet?"

She shrugs. "We don't know. We've been down here with you since you passed out. We'll go find out and let you know." She grabs Dad again. "Let's go, crazy man."

Mom kisses my head. "I'll leave you two to talk with Dr. Cantor alone. I'll be right outside if you need me."

"Thanks, Mom."

She closes the door leaving me, Collin, and Dr. Cantor. I look up at her. "How far along am I?"

"It's very early. Just a few weeks in. I'm not sure an over-the-counter pregnancy test would have even detected it yet. Only a blood test. We can do an ultrasound to give you an exact due date, but you're better off waiting another month for that, there won't be much to see. Your blood pressure was very low, which is likely why you fainted. Have you been a little sleep-deprived the past few nights?"

"Yes." I can feel Collin squeeze me.

"You need to get more sleep. Please also make sure you're eating and drinking a lot. I'll have the nurse leave you with some information and prenatal vitamins. Good luck and congratulations."

"Thank you."

The doctor unhooks the machines monitoring my body and then leaves, closing the door behind her. I turn in the bed, so Collin and I are face to face. He has a huge shit-eating grin on his face. "Why are you so damn happy right now?"

"Because now you're stuck with me forever."

"That's what you want? Forever?"

"Hell yes." He rubs my face. "I love you. You're my forever. I've never been more sure of anything in my life. I'll probably start calling you my baby mama though."

I let out a breath. "I don't know how this happened."

"Well, when a penis goes in a vagina..."

I smack his chest. "I'm being serious. I'm on the pill. We always use condoms."

"Hmm, not always."

I look at him in question.

He shamefully mumbles, "The bar in Mexico."

My eyes widen in realization. "Oh my god. Our fucking baby was conceived on a swing in a bar in Mexico surrounded by fifty other people. And I had a butt plug in my ass."

He starts laughing.

I just shake my head. "It's not funny. I can't believe you're so happy about this."

"I'm ecstatic." He rubs a damn erection against me. "We don't have to use condoms for nine months. Totally worth you getting pregnant."

"I can't believe you're hard right now." I motion down my hospital gown-clad body. "This does it for you?"

"You're naked under the hospital gown. I may have

helped to undress you. I may have taken a peek at your body. I may have fondled you when you were passed out."

"You're a pervert."

He nods. "Totally. I think you dig it though."

I can't help but smile. "I do dig it."

He takes my hand and kisses it. He then rubs my ring finger. "Will you marry me?"

I shake my head. "We're not getting married just because we're having a baby."

"How about because we love each other, and we want to spend our lives together?"

"Can we shelve this until after the baby comes? We talked about moving in together. Let's see how that goes. What if you're an annoying roommate? And I may be too fucked up to ever get married. I swore I never would."

"You're not fucked up. You're perfectly imperfect, just like me. How are you feeling about the baby?"

"I'm in shock. I don't think it's registered. I'm not upset, just surprised."

There's a knock at the door. I look up and see that it's my mother. I wave her in.

She sits down next to me. "How are you feeling?"

"I'm fine. I'm not as excited as Howdy Doody over here, but I'm okay with it. I'll guess I'll be a young mom like you were."

"Except you have money, a job, a place to live, a supportive partner, and a crap ton of family around to help you."

I smile at the realization of everything she said. I do have all of that. My situation is nothing like hers. I have a huge support system and plenty of money.

Collin looks at my mother. "She won't marry me. Will you help me talk her into it?"

Mom lets out a laugh. "Jade does what Jade wants to do. Neither of us will ever talk her into anything. She's been like that since birth when she decided to flip seconds before delivery. I should have known then how she'd be."

He sighs. "I suppose. My family might kick me out of the family business for having a baby out of wedlock. I think I want to be a stay-at-home dad anyway. You can be my sugar mama."

"I thought I was your baby mama."

He smiles. "You'll be both."

I slowly sit up. "I need to get dressed. I want to check on Reagan and Skylar."

Collin sits up with me. "I'll supervise and observe you getting dressed. Maybe watch you get into the shower."

Mom stands. "That's my cue to leave. I'll wait for you outside the door."

I stand and stretch and then start walking toward the bathroom. I turn my head back and motion for him to join me. "Come on. I need a shower bra."

He smiles as he follows me in.

CHAPTER TWENTY-SEVEN

COLLIN

After a very good celebratory shower, we head back up to the maternity ward. None of Jade's family is in the waiting room, so we head down to their original room. It gets louder as we approach. We look at each other and smile knowing the whole big crew is in there, which means the babies have arrived.

As soon as we turn into the room, Darian runs to Jade and embraces her. "Are you okay? We were so worried about you. Your dad said you were fine but wouldn't say anything more."

Jade sighs. "I'm fine. Collin knocked me up." She points to the babies in Reagan and Skylar's arms. "I'm going to have one of those monsters soon."

I clear my throat. "*We. We're* going to have one of those perfect babies soon." I smile at Reagan and Skylar. "I did say when we got here that I have very potent sperm."

They both roll their eyes at me.

Darian hugs Jade. "How exciting. Congratulations." She turns to Declan with a big smile. "Congrats, Grandpa."

Declan scowls at her. I wink at him. "Should I start calling you Dad?"

"Fitz, if I were you, I'd sleep with one eye open."

"Love you too, Dad." I blow him a kiss.

Jade smiles at me. "This is going to be fun."

I nod. "Totally."

Jade rubs her hands together. "So, what did we have?"

Skylar kisses her baby's forehead. "This beautiful girl is Rylee." Like her siblings, she has a full head of blonde hair and a cute little nose.

We look at Reagan next. Carter picks up their baby and brings him over to me. He places him in my arms. His hair is light brown like Carter's, and he barely has any of it. "Collin, meet your godson. George Collin Daulton."

My hands tremble as I take him in my arms. "Me? You're naming him after me?"

"Is your name George?"

"No, that's your grandfather's name. I meant the middle name."

Carter smiles. "Yep. We named him after the two most important men in my life."

I can't help but tear at that.

At the same time, both Jade and I say, "George is an old man's name." We both laugh.

It hits me. We had the same thought. We finished each other's sentence. For some reason, that makes me happy.

I whisper to the baby, "Don't go by George. You'll definitely want to go by Collin. It will help you with the ladies."

CHAPTER TWENTY-EIGHT

COLLIN

Jade and I are headed to Lucy's T-ball game today. My whole family is coming. We're having a picnic afterward. With Jade's support and urging, I'm planning to tell them that I'm leaving the family business. We're also going to tell them that we're having a baby and not getting married. It's going to be a mess. I'm anticipating bloodshed, but I need to be strong and finally have some hard conversations. Jade has given me the fortitude I desperately needed.

We cheer for little Lucy throughout her game. She's so cute in her little uniform, with the pants practically falling off her. Ashleigh is sitting on the other side of Jade. I hear her telling Jade about her upcoming job interviews at schools. I love that Jade helped her in this process. Jade's strength and conviction are so attractive to me.

We all gather at the picnic table in the park afterward. I brought a cooler of beer. Jade brought

Snoop Dogg wine for the ladies, though she obviously won't be drinking. Lydia and Ashleigh are already a glass in, and Jade is making Snoop talk on the bottle. I don't understand the fascination with it.

I grab Jade's hand. She squeezes my hand knowing what's coming. She mouths, "I love you."

I nod before turning my attention to my family. "Everyone, can I have your attention? Jade and I have some news to share."

Everyone looks our way and I smile. I rub her flat belly. "We're having a baby in about seven months."

Ashleigh and Lydia scream in excitement, running to hug both of us. The rest of my family looks confused. My father asks, "When is da wedding?"

"Well, we're not getting married yet. We've only just moved in together. We're going to see how that goes. If we're so inclined, after the baby comes, we'll consider getting married then."

My father goes to smack the back of my head, but Jade snaps her head and gives him a death stare. He stops himself before making contact. Braden and I look at each other in complete and total shock. Is my father afraid of Jade? My father has never been afraid of a single human being in his entire life. He's so tough, I spent half my life thinking he was in the Irish Mafia. He's not scared of union workers or big construction guys. It's Jade McGinley that scares him? My blonde-haired, blue-eyed baby mama? I can't help the big smile on my face.

Jade says, "Before anyone does something foolish, like blaming Collin, know that waiting to get married was my decision. I'm young, and we've only just started living together. I need to make sure I like him before I commit to a lifetime. Frankly, I'm still on the fence."

Mac shakes his head. "Shit, if she lives with his messy ass, she'll never want to marry him." He smiles. He's trying to lighten the mood. I appreciate it.

"I'm not messy."

My mother scoffs. "Collin, you're a slob. You were always the worst of all my boys."

Jade raises one eyebrow. "I didn't know this about you. Perhaps I should reconsider the whole thing." She winks at me.

"I'm not a slob...anymore. I swear."

Mac holds out his hand. "Congratulations." I shake it. "Welcome to fatherhood."

"Thanks, Mac." Braden, and Shane all shake my hand as well. After a bit of hesitation, my father does as well.

That went better than expected. One dramatic revelation down, one more to go.

"While we're here, I have something else to say."

Shane jokes, "Did you get another girl pregnant, too?"

I narrow my eyes at him. "No. I've decided to go out on my own in construction. I'm leaving Fitz and Sons. I didn't arrive at this decision lightly. You guys are going in a different direction than I'd like, so I'm going to go at it alone and build the things I enjoy building."

My father sits down in obvious distress. "But dis is my legacy. Leaving dis company to my sons means everything to me."

I sit down next to him. "I know, Da, but it's not what I want. It doesn't make me happy. It's great that all of you enjoy building the houses we build. I think I'm just a more artistic person than you guys. I enjoy the creative aspect. I like building unique homes that I dream up in my head."

"How are ya managing it all? Da money."

"I've partnered with Carter and Reagan. They're financing it. The Wander property was supposed to be our first, but I wasn't ready to fully break from you then. But I am now. I'm ready. I'm trying to do what makes me happy, not what's easiest. I didn't come to this decision lightly. There was a lot of thought and planning involved. I have several projects in the pipeline, and I'm ready to hit the ground running."

He thinks for a few moments. "I'm both sad and happy. Sad to see ya go, but happy dat you're taking a risk and pursuing a dream. I'm proud of ya for dat." He sticks out his hand and I shake it. "I wish ya well, son. You'll always have a place here with us."

"Thank you."

I look up at my brothers. Mac shrugs. "I only have to split the pie three ways now instead of four. Works for me."

I give him the finger and he laughs.

My father turns back to my brothers. "Make sure ya support him. If he needs machinery or manpower, ya give it to him."

They all nod in agreement.

For the first time in a long time, we have a stress-free meal. I realize that I was holding onto so much animosity and unhappiness for a long time. I guess I'm finally in a good place.

I'm a roll today, so there's one more thing I want to say. I place my half-eaten burger down on my plate as I take a big breath. I look around, but my eyes land on Mac. "I have one last thing to say. I know I joke around a lot, and I know I made some immature decisions in my youth, but I'm not going to stand anymore for being this family's whipping boy. I work hard, just like the rest of you. I'm good at what I do, just like the rest of you. I'm a responsible adult, just like the rest of you. I'm about to become a father, a family man, just like most of you. I don't want you belittling me anymore, especially once my child comes. Jokes made in fun are fine. Nasty comments that aren't intended to be funny are not fine."

Jade has a huge smile as she squeezes my leg under the table. Ashleigh and Braden have big smiles too.

My father and Mac both nod in agreement.

After we eat, Jade and I walk back to my car. She grabs my hand. "I'm so proud of you. How are you feeling?"

"Happy. Ecstatic. Free. Like the weight of the world was lifted off my shoulders."

We stop at the car. She runs her hands up my chest. "Good enough for a pizza delivery? Extra anchovies?"

I grab her ass and squeeze it hard. "Can the delivery be on whatever playground I choose?"

She gives me that mischievous smile that I love so much. "You're on, Big Daddy."

EPILOGUE

TWO YEARS LATER

JADE

"I'm going to spank you into this headboard."

I turn my head back and look at my hot, sweaty man. "I don't have a problem with that though I don't think I need a bump on my head today, our wedding day. But whatever floats your boat."

His hips are slapping hard against my ass. I'm glad he's doing me like this. I need it hard and rough to get through today and he knows it. He always gives me what I need. He usually knows before I do.

When we're done, he unties my wrists, and we collapse onto the bed, both a bit out of breath. I lay on his chest.

Well, not his bare chest. "I hate that you're wearing a shirt. Your body is half the appeal to me."

"It's not my wit?"

"No."

"My charm?"

"Definitely not."

He's been covering himself for two weeks. He said it's an old Irish tradition. I've looked into it, and that's total bullshit. There's no such tradition.

"I told you. It's a tradition. An ancient one. One that you probably wouldn't find on something like Google, but a tradition nonetheless."

"Because you're such a traditional guy? I'm pretty sure fucking the bride five hours before the ceremony is against most traditions. Spanking her definitely is."

He laughs. "I suppose you're right." He slides me off him and sits up. "Okay, I'll take my shirt off. I was going to wait until tonight, after we're married, but you can see it now. It's healed."

"See what? What's healed?"

He removes his shirt. My eyes immediately catch the changed art on his left arm. The Claddagh ring has changed. It's way bigger and is somehow flipped upside down, showing that he's now forever taken. They've managed to change the top crown into my name.

I run my fingertips over it. "Oh my god. How did you do this?"

"I didn't want you to see it, so I did it all at once. That meant a shit ton of pain, but surprising you was worth it." He smiles. "Now it shows that my heart belongs to you, and only you. It's my wedding gift to you."

"I love it so much. You're going to be mortified when I leave you in a few years because you're too old to satisfy me."

He tickles me and I giggle. "I'll never be too old to satisfy you."

"All I got you was a new tub of lube and a flogger with

our monogram... because nothing says commitment like a monogrammed flogger."

He laughs and kisses my nose. "I love it. Please pack it for the honeymoon."

We're going on a full European tour for our honeymoon. Neither of us have ever been to Europe. We're so excited about it. We're seeing eight different cities in fourteen days. It's a dream come true for me. Melissa planned the whole thing.

My phone alarm goes off.

Collin scrunches his nose. "Ugh. Does that mean you have to leave to get dressed?"

"I do, I'm already late, but the alarm is for Dr. Pearl. She said she wanted to wish us well before the ceremony. Stay naked. Let's mess with her."

I set up my laptop. At precisely the agreed upon time, it rings with the video call. I turn it on. Though mostly covered, she can clearly see that we're in bed and naked.

She shakes her head. "Are you doing a wedding morning instead of a wedding night?"

Collin smiles. "We decided to do both. We aim to be thorough."

I look more closely at her. "Dr. Pearl, you're not in a cardigan. I've never seen you without one. Are you in a dress? A sexy dress?" It's lowcut and form-fitting. She has a nice body. Who knew?

"I'm not on the clock right now, Jade. This is a personal call just to wish you two well. I hope you have a magical day. I'm incredibly happy for you."

"Thank you."

"Mr. Pearl would like to wish you well. Would you like to meet him?"

"Hell yes."

A younger, highly attractive man appears on the screen. He can't be more than a few years older than Collin. I think both mine and Collin's chins drop.

The man smiles. "Hello, Jade. Chastity speaks so highly of you. Congratulations."

I'm speechless.

He shouts, "Can you hear me?"

I slightly regain my senses. "Yes, I'm sorry. Thank you."

Dr. Pearl appears on the screen again. I look at her. "That's Mr. Pearl? What in the ever-loving hell is going on? I was expecting Bob Barker, not Bradley Cooper."

She gives a small, sly smile. "You may like older men, Jade, but I like them a little younger." She winks and then waves at the camera. "Bye-bye. Have a great day." The video feed ends.

Collin and I turn to each other in complete and total shock. I eventually manage, "Her fucking name is Chastity Pearl?"

I SHOWER and make my way to the bridal room. Everyone is already there. I walk in and Mom breathes a sigh of relief. "There you are. We were worried that you weren't coming."

Cassandra looks me up and down. "No, Amanda, pay closer attention. She doesn't look like someone with cold feet. She looks like someone who has been freshly fucked."

I can only innocently shrug and smile.

Mom shakes her head. "That's what you were doing on your wedding day?"

"I'm pretty sure fucking is a wedding day tradition."

She scowls at me. "The tradition is *after* the ceremony, Jade. Not before."

"I'm not really a traditional girl."

I look around. "Where's Tyson?"

"Sweetie, I told you that the sitter would be with him while he naps. We don't want him cranky for the wedding."

"Oh, right."

Tyson McGinley Fitz busted into this world seventeen months ago and immediately stole my heart. I never considered myself maternal, and I worried about it throughout my entire pregnancy. But as soon as I saw my blond-haired, blue-eyed angel, all doubts went away. He's my everything. Our everything. Collin is the most hands-on, loving, energetic, and fun father you could ever imagine. He adores Tyson, and Tyson equally adores him.

Collin begged me to marry him throughout the entire pregnancy. I wasn't ready then, but a few months ago, I took Collin to the house we're building for ourselves, that we designed together, and I proposed. It was followed by a rather intense round of machinery sex. It's a good thing he's in construction so there will always be machines around.

Speaking of construction, after that day in the park, Collin officially broke free from his family business. C Squared quickly became one of the most respected construction companies in Philadelphia, specializing in custom, innovative homes and small offices. Braden left the family business and now works for Collin.

Collin's relationship with his family also changed after that day in the park. His father very much respects the new company that Collin has built. He proudly shows photos of Collin's projects to anyone who will listen.

Even Mac has stopped belittling Collin. I don't know whether it's because he respects him or he's afraid of me, but either way, he doesn't mess with my man anymore.

Given that Ashleigh and I have become so close, we end up spending more time with them than anyone in his family.

I kept my bridal party simple. It's only family, except Reagan. Between the bridesmaids and junior bridesmaids, it's still big. Reagan is officiating our ceremony. Apparently, she became ordained for Cassandra and Trevor's wedding.

It's a beautiful mid-summer day. We're getting married on the beach by Harley and Brody's shore house. I was at Skylar's wedding here a little over five years ago and loved it. I know that Harley and Reagan got married here too, but that was before I knew them. I like that it's become a bit of a family tradition. I wanted to be a part of it.

I get my hair and makeup done, and then get dressed. I'm nervously waiting with my father. I'm not nervous about being married to Collin, it's just the idea of marriage that frightens me at times. But I love Collin and I know he loves me.

I'm in a sleek, sultry, form-fitting, strapless, short white dress with an overlay that gives it depth. Thanks to Melissa, it's a designer label, but I personally don't care. I didn't want a traditional dress because, well, I'm not a traditional person. I'm confident that Collin won't mind the way I look at all. In fact, I know my fiancé won't be able to keep his hands off me all night. I inwardly smile at the thought.

The ceremony begins. I can't help but peek around the dividers to watch Tyson walk down the aisle as the ring bearer. He's in the same khaki pants and white linen shirt as Collin. He's so damn cute. Though he's a devil like both of his parents. I suppose we should have anticipated that.

He gets to Collin. They do a special handshake and Tyson hands him the ring. Aunt Darian then grabs Tyson and places him on her lap.

Dad takes my arm in his. "Are you ready?"

I nod. "Let's get this shit show on the road."

"I'm more than happy to take you and bail on this whole thing if you want."

"Not today, Dad. Let it go. I love him and he loves me."

"If he hurts you, I'll end him."

"I have no doubt you would, but he won't. You and I both know that." I pull him along. "Let's go."

We appear from behind the divider. Collin and I make eye contact. He's so handsome. He gives me a huge grin and I instantly feel at peace with what we're about to do.

We walk down the aisle, but when it's time for Dad to hand me off the Collin, he won't let go of my arm.

I whisper, "Dad, let me go."

"No."

I turn and look at Melissa with pleading eyes. She just shakes her head and smiles.

Collin takes a step and physically removes Dad's arm from mine. With force. "I've got her, Dad. Don't worry." He gives my dad a huge smile.

Dad definitely does not return the smile. I think I may even hear a little growl.

Reagan clears her throat. "Good afternoon, everyone. We're gathered here today to join Jade Tremaine McGinley and Collin Nolan Fitz as they *tie* the knot."

Tyson yells, "Mommy!" as he jumps off Aunt Darian's lap and comes running toward us. Before he crashes into me, Collin scoops him up and places him on his hip.

I smile. "I'm happier having both of my boys up here."

Collin nods in agreement, and Reagan continues with the ceremony. After a few routine items, she gets to the vows.

"Jade, repeat after me. I, Jade Tremaine McGinley."

"I, Jade Tremaine McGinley."

"Vow to be forever *tied* to Collin Nolan Fitz."

I narrow my eyes at her, and she gives me her mischievous smile. "Vow to be forever tied to Collin Nolan Fitz."

"I will honor him and spend time with him, never allowing myself to get too *chained* up with work and other distractions."

I see Collin trying to hold in his laughter. "I will honor him and spend time with him, never allowing myself to get too chained up with work, and other distractions."

"I will allow Collin to be his silly, funny self, never *shackling* that big personality of his."

I guess we're really doing it like this. I suppose I'll join in. "I will allow Collin to be his silly, funny self, never *shackling* that big personality of his."

"I will honor and obey the *binds* of matrimony."

"I will honor and obey the *binds* of matrimony."

She turns to Collin. "Repeat after me. "I, Collin Nolan Fitz."

"I, Collin Nolan Fitz."

"Agree to *loop* my life with Jade Tremaine McGinley's."

Collin lets out a small laugh. "Agree to *loop* my life with Jade Tremaine McGinley's."

"I will never *clamp* her wild side."

"I will never *clamp* her wild side."

"I will never *tether* down her humor and wit."

"I will never *tether* down her humor and wit."

"I agree to honor and obey her by *threading* my life with hers."

"I agree to honor and obey her by *threading* my life with hers."

"By the power vested in me, I declare that you are

permanently *cuffed* to one another as husband and wife. You may kiss the bride."

With our son nestled between us, Collin kisses me for the first time as his wife. I never thought this day would come. I wasn't the type who dreamed about it as a little girl. Just the opposite. But the security and happiness I feel in Collin and Tyson's love is real...

and it's everything.

THE END

ACKNOWLEDGMENTS

To Jade and Collin: I've never had more fun writing about two people than you two nuts. I already miss you, which means an extended prologue will happen one day. I'm not ready to let you go.

To the Queen, TL Swan: This amazing journey would never have begun if not for you and your selfless decision to help hundreds of women. You are a shining example of the girl power quotes I place in each dedication. Those are for you, girlfriend. This crazy and unexpected new path in my life has brought me so much happiness. I owe it all to you. Please know that I try every single day to pay it forward.

To Lakshmi and Thorunn: Thank you to both of you for pushing me on this book. Writing my first Scott-free book was scary AF, and your daily encouragement meant everything. I love when you two fight. I love that you're always available for bitch duty. I love that you two have become bookish besties. I love and appreciate how much you support me.

To Jade Dollston, Carolina Jax, and L.A. Ferro: You are my bookish besties. Our daily texts are my lifeline. I love the support we have for each other. I adore and trust both of you wholeheartedly. **Jade**: I dedicated the damn book to you. Do you really need more? **Carolina**: I adore you and your support. Your taste in football teams still sucks. **L.A.**: I hate when people younger than me are smarter than me, but I accept that in you. You are so incredibly selfless in our book world, and I'm thankful to call you my friend.

To Brittany Mckeel: Thank you for being the best ball-kicker around (J knows what I'm talking about). Your support for me and all indie authors is unmatched and so very much appreciated.

To My OG Beta Readers Stacey and Fun Sherry: Thank you for being there for me since day one. You've been my sounding boards and biggest, and hottest, cheerleaders every single step of the way.

To My Badass ARC and Street Teams: You bitches are the best. I appreciate every single ounce of support you throw my way. Your constant words of encouragement keep me writing. Our daily street team group messages always make me laugh. I love that you not only support me, but you support each other. You call often inspire different parts of my books. **Victoria**: Fruit Roll-Ups. 'Nuff Said.

To Chrisandra and K.B. Designs: **Chrisandra**: Thank you for making me feel illiterate. That's what makes you such a great editor. **Kristin**: Thank you for helping this artistically challenged woman. You have breathed life into all of my books. I'm so proud of them thanks to you.

To My Family: I truly feel bad for you. An immature mother and wife can't be easy. To my daughters, thank you for tolerating me (ish). Thank you for telling everyone you know that your mom writes sex books. I appreciate that by the time you were each six, you were more mature than me. To my handsome husband, thank you for your blind support. You never question my sanity, which can't be easy. But let's face it, you do reap the benefits of the fact that I write sex scenes all day long.

ABOUT THE AUTHOR

AK Landow lives in the USA with her husband, three daughters, one dog, and one cat (who was chosen because his name is Trevor). She enjoys reading, now writing, drinking copious amounts of vodka, and laughing. She's thrilled to have this new avenue to channel her perverted sense of humor. She is also of the belief that Beth Dutton is the greatest fictional character ever created.

AKLandowAuthor.com

ALSO BY AK LANDOW

City of Sisterly Love Series

Knight: Book 1 Darian and Jackson

Dr. Harley: Book 2 Harley and Brody

Cass: Book 3 Cassandra and Trevor

Daulton: Book 4 Reagan and Carter

About Last Knight: Book 5 Melissa and Declan

Love Always, Scott: Prequel Novella Darian and Scott

Quiet Knight: Novella Jess and Hayden

Belles of Broad Street Series

Conflicting Ventures: Book 1 Skylar and Lance

Indecent Ventures: Book 2 Jade and Collin

Unexpected Ventures: Book 3 Beth and Dominic

Enchanted Ventures: Book 4 Amanda and Beckett

Signed Books: www.aklandowauthor.com/books

EXCITING NEWS

Did you enjoy meeting Collin's cousin Cam and his wife, Shiloh. You can read about their exciting journey in **Deadly Protector** by my bookish bestie, Jade Dollston. The second-chance romance is available on Amazon and it's amazing!